TAKE THE MONEY AND RUN

TAKE THE MONEY AND RUN

LAURENCE PAYNE

PUBLISHED FOR THE CRIME CLUB BY
DOUBLEDAY & COMPANY, INC.
GARDEN CITY, NEW YORK
1984

For
JUDITH

friend,
wife
and
fellow conspirator

All the characters in this book
are fictitious, and any resemblance
to actual persons, living or dead,
is purely coincidental.

Library of Congress Cataloging in Publication Data

Payne, Laurence.
Take the money and run.

I. Title.
PR6066.A93T3   1984   823'.914
ISBN 0-385-19607-5
Library of Congress Catalog Card Number 84–8112
Copyright © 1982 by Laurence Payne
All rights reserved
Printed in the United States of America
First edition in the United States of America

1

I was being followed. Of that I was certain. I had sensed it ten minutes before and had ignored it. I wasn't, after all, going anywhere important, so I wouldn't be leading whoever it was to a safe house or a secret rendezvous. For one thing, I didn't know any safe houses; and for another, I had no knowledge of any rendezvous, secret or otherwise. Actually I was going to my office. If anyone wanted to know where that was, he had only to leaf through the Yellow Pages.

After a while I began to regard his persistence as a personal affront, so I slipped into the old routine and almost immediately began to regret it. He made circles around me. I went through most of what I had been taught, but it proved ludicrously inadequate. I didn't try all that hard, of course. I didn't, for instance, board a train bound for Glasgow, lock myself in the lavatory, cut a hole in the window, throw myself out on to the track and double back the way I had come via the Northern Line, changing trains twice just as the doors were closing. But even if I had he would still have been there, stuck to me like a barnacle on a ship's bottom.

I decided to duck into the Cathedral. You can't actually "duck" into St. Paul's, but Christopher Wren had designed the edifice with me in mind. "If you can't lose 'em, seek sanctuary," was what he always said.

Halfway up the front steps, I stopped, turned abruptly, and almost dislodged an elderly harridan wearing a man's cloth cap and carrying an enormous cat basket, which, judging by the strident yowling from within, was full of enormous cat. The woman sidestepped adroitly and, with a few well-chosen though un-Christian words flung over her shoulder, continued her climb to the hallowed precincts. I wondered idly why anyone would be taking a cat to church. Mice? A blessing, perhaps? Blood sacrifice?

I stood looking down towards Ludgate Hill. No one was rooted in sudden preoccupation with the morning newspaper; no one pulled his hat over his eyes or wrapped the lower half of his face in his coat collar before making off, frowning thoughtfully, in the opposite direction.

In view of the fact that it was a damp and unwelcoming Monday morning in November, however, there were a surprising number of people about, ploughing their way grimly through the morning chores, all apparently agog with indifference to their surroundings and to who might be standing around studying their habits. Whoever he was, he was good.

I climbed steadily onward and upwards into the echoing basilica. Removing my hat in deference to a God I was not sure I believed in, I wandered into the yawning mouth of the black-and-white-chequered nave, turning right to view the chapel of St. Michael and St. George and keeping a weather eye on the west entrance, through which I had just passed. For several minutes, I observed arches and piers and Corinthian pilasters, waiting hopefully for my tail to put in an appearance. But unless he was one of a brown-gabardined gaggle of schoolgirls who clattered in shepherded by a jolly-looking, bespectacled mistress, he was nowhere to be seen. I strolled down the south aisle, listening to the echo of breathless girlish gigglings and whisperings and the dragging of feet. I had lost him. I eyed the great, soaring dome with dutiful respect and made my way past the font and out through the south transept.

It was now raining.

As I settled my hat and stood at the curb with a dozen others to cross the busy thoroughfare the hair on the back of my neck once again began to bristle. He was there again. Since I could swear he had not followed me into the church, he could only have anticipated my reappearance. I ground my teeth with frustration.

A gap in the traffic appeared and the crowd surged forward, carrying me with it. I changed tactics, stepped back on to the pavement and moved up towards Cannon Street. No one altered course. No one followed. As far as I could see, that is.

To hell with it. I jaywalked across Cannon Street, tacked down Friday Street, into Queen Victoria Street and up into Godliman Street, where my office was.

Mitch was there before me of course, and when I arrived, panting and spent after the usual morning confrontation with seventy-eight stairs, she looked me over with a predictably cool smile, took my hat and wished me a languid good morning.

"If there's anything good about it, Mitch darling," I growled, "I've missed it." I preceded her through the outer office and into mine. "It's cold, it's miserable, it's blowing a gale and now it's pissing with rain."

I walked purposefully over to the window, which was streaming with condensation, and scrubbed at it with my gloved hands. When I flung up the sash and leaned out into the elements, Mitch must have concluded I was about to do away with myself, for she abandoned her up-market pose and clutched desperately at my arm. "Mark," she wailed. "No, wait. . . ."

Narrowing my eyes against the pelting rain, I peered down into the street.

"What is it?" Unnerved by her uncharacteristic show of concern, Mitch was now sounding cross. "What are you looking for? Who's down there?"

"Someone's been following me." I returned to her and slammed down the window.

"Who?"

"The Invisible Man." I slumped into my chair. "He's bloody good, whoever he is. Never caught a glimpse of him."

"How do you know he was there if you didn't see him?"

I stared up at her. Twenty-seven years old, five feet eight inches in her stockinged feet and slender as a pipe cleaner, she loomed over me like the Leaning Tower of Pisa. "I can always tell when someone's watching me."

"For an ex-actor," she remarked drily, "that's a devastating thought."

The rain slashed at the window. "Just look at that, will you?" I moaned.

"Are you going to sit there all morning in your wet mack?"

I regarded her steadily. "And are you going to be difficult all bloody morning?" I asked mildly. "Because if you are I shall go straight back home again."

I climbed out of my damp raincoat and she took it and hung it on the hook in her office, under my hat. I watched her swanning about for a moment or two, then asked if there was any coffee on the go.

During the morning, I brooded intermittently over my unknown shadow, childishly petulant at my inability to shake him off. Who the hell was he? Only a professional could be that good. And that worried me.

I dealt with a couple of letters which Mitch had opened and left on my desk. One enclosed a cheque from a mildly satisfied client, the other my October Access account debiting me for the various excesses I had indulged in during that month. I was left with a profit of twenty-three pence. It was the sort of financial scoop which rendered me breathless. I turned aggressively to *The Times* crossword puzzle, a pastime which, whilst purporting to improve the mind, usually does little to improve the temper.

I don't know what Mitch was doing next door; guarding the telephone, I suppose. Her chair creaked occasionally, and once I heard her bony knees crack; but apart from that the only sound was the pelt and roar of the rain gusting against the window.

Wet Monday mornings in Britain are apt to engender treasonable sentiments. It would be difficult to believe that even the staunchest of patriots has not at some time been tempted to withdraw the plug from this rain-sodden, island home of ours and leave it to founder, quietly and gently, with all hands. With dignity of course and no fuss, the Prime Minister at the salute on the woolsack, the Grimethorpe Colliery Band doing its best with *Nearer My God to Thee*, and the rest of us ignoring the vulgar shouts and general rejoicing from across the Irish Sea with the upper-class contempt for which we have deservedly become famous throughout the world.

If you can overcome a wet November Monday morning in England, then you'll be a man, my son.

I groaned aloud.

Mitch's head put in an appearance around the door. "What?"

"I groaned," I told her.

She eased herself into the doorway. "Shall I go and have what is laughingly known as my lunch?"

I shrugged. "You owe it to yourself."

Watching her rustling into the narrow confines of a transparent plastic bag and exchanging her high heels for a pair of bright yellow Wellingtons, I wondered, not for the first time, why she bothered. All that dressing up and hopping about on one foot for the sake of an unsweetened lemon juice and a couple of dry rusks seemed a trifle excessive. She read my thoughts. "The exercise is good for me," she told me, and tying a green plastic triangle over her neat blonde head, she was gone, thudding down the stairs in her sensible rubber boots like the skipper of a fishing fleet.

I returned to my ponderings, feet on desk, hands in pockets, with the crossword puzzle staring up at me offensively.

The sound of heavy footsteps with the inevitable accompaniment of grunts and short-winded moans labouring up the stairs roused me from my torpor. There are not many who can manage seventy-eight stairs without a murmur or two, and the present contestant was not one of them. If anything, he was a trifle more vocal than most, and when he ground to a halt on the landing below, I found myself hoping that he might be bound for Messrs. Probing-Hartwig, Schmidt and Harris, next door, to borrow some money from the World Finance Corporation. (A likely story.)

He wasn't.

He ploughed on like an icebreaker and, the assault on the final staircase accomplished, came to a creaking standstill outside my outer door.

Mitch had left the intervening door open, and through it I saw a pink face, hissing and heaving miserably, peer bulbously at the frosted glass. The door said, among other things, *Please Enter*, but several minutes elapsed before the invitation was taken up. When it was, *erupt* was the word I would have used for his mode of arrival.

He stood panting on the doormat, large and circular, wearing the smallest hat I had ever seen on anybody. Indeed, my first impression of him was almost exclusively bound up with that soggy piece of green tweed perched idiotically on a quite enormous head. The rest of him was wrapped up in a tentlike Gannex, which dripped steadily on to my lino.

I was so appalled at the visitation that I left my feet rudely where they were on the desk and moved not a muscle other than those necessary to restrain my jaw from sagging. He remained fairly static too. We looked at each other for some considerable time, and when eventually he managed to tear his eyes away from mine, he transferred them unenthusiastically to his immediate surroundings.

Anyone could see that he was not impressed. Neither was I, if it came to that. The only thing I had ever liked about the place was the view, and that was fast losing its charm. St. Paul's was all right, but the junk they had stuck up all around it took a lot of getting used to. At the moment, however, nobody could see anything of it. The rain was like an opaque sheet of wet polythene.

My rotund visitor narrowed his eyes at the glass panel of the door. "You Savage?" he demanded.

I wanted to say, "Only when I'm aroused," but refrained and admitted to my name instead, inviting him to come in and pull up a chair and put his feet up, removing my own from the desk in the meantime for good manners' sake. The gesture had no obvious effect upon him. However, he closed the door and lumbered through the outer office and into mine, the floorboards groaning beneath his elephantine tread. When eventually he subsided into the elderly visitors' chair—the visitors' elderly chair—its ancient springs set up an internal twanging reminiscent of important modern music at the Round House.

"You've got quite a climb going on out there," he observed, reaching down into his chest for some more wind.

"Seventy-eight steps."

"What's the 'M' for?" he asked abruptly, noisily unbuttoning his Gannex. I looked baffled. "On the door. M. Savage, it says, Private Investigator. What's the 'M' for?"

"Mark."

He paused in the midst of his feverish rustlings. "Sounds like an actor."

"What does?"

"Mark Savage. Actor's name."

"Never heard of him," I said. He stared at me with blank little eyes, then shook his head and went back to his gropings among the pockets of the hideous check tweed jacket now revealed beneath the open rainwear. A forlorn-looking packet of cigarettes and a box of matches came to light.

"You've got a reputation, did you know that?" He selected a bent cigarette from the pack, set fire to it and flicked the match nonchalantly over his shoulder. I eyed him sourly as he enveloped himself and me in a cloud of blue smoke. "Classy," he went on, talking about my reputation, with the cigarette now stuck firmly into the corner of his mouth, and waving the smoke away with a small, fat-fingered hand. "Your reputation, surprisingly classy, considering . . ." his hand now flapped at our surroundings.

He was welcome to his opinion.

The rain sounded as if it were trying to get in. I was so miserable that I could have screamed. Mentally I did. Take that bloody stupid hat off, I wanted to yell at him—and wasn't at all surprised when he did. He screwed it up in a small ball and wrung it out over my floor. I glowered at his great, round head, which, divested of its meagre covering, displayed a few stray tufts of tow-coloured hair sprouting at unlikely angles on an otherwise bald top.

"Good weather for ducks, eh?" he said without registering my discontent. He unrolled the hat, flattened it on his knee and began kneading it, like a pastrycook working on a Swiss roll. "Do a job for me, Mr. Savage?" His little eyes, reddish brown and bright beneath lowered brows, squinnied at me over the desk. I lifted my shoulders warily. "Nothing illegal," he added. "Deliver a package, that's all. Small package."

"Like a bomb, for instance?"

He wheezed merrily, wobbling his head. Then he took the cigarette from his mouth and peered at its tip intently, as if he had stumbled upon the answer to something. He looked like a fat garden gnome, but not nearly so friendly.

"Where?" I asked. "And when?"

"Welsh Wales." He stuck the cigarette back into his mouth. "And as soon as possible."

"Where in Welsh Wales?"

"Castellcraig."

"Never heard of it."

"No?" He screwed up one of his eyes against the rising smoke and, shoving a fist firmly into the crown of his hat, moulded the damp cloth carefully around it: when he had finished with it, it would fit him like a glove. "Well, maybe not, but it's there just the same. Has been for some little time. It has a castle, a war memorial and a branch of the International Stores." He ground out his cigarette on the Ovaltine-tin lid Mitch had provided for that purpose.

"How about a cup of tea?" I suggested in an effort to cheer myself up.

"The name's George Morton, by the way," he said, as if indicating the name of the brand of tea he preferred.

"Tea, Mr. Morton?"

He made a face and placed the remoulded hat carefully on a corner of the desk. "How about a spot of the hard stuff?" he countered. "Cement our relationship, perhaps, yes?"

"I don't," I said.

Again he flailed about beneath his raincoat, this time producing a small silver flask. When I started up to find a glass I knew didn't exist, he waved me back to my chair and reached for my plastic Snoopy tea mug on the desk.

"This clean?" He sniffed at it. I bent over and removed it from his grasp. "Snoopy doesn't drink either," I told him.

He made no comment and raised the flask to his lips; it was obviously the very hard stuff, for it made his eyes water.

He asked, "Will you do it?"

"What's wrong with Her Majesty's mail?"

He told me there was nothing wrong with her mail other than the fact that he had no wish to use it for this particular parcel.

"Fragile, is it?"

"Not particularly."

"Valuable?"

He pulled down the corners of his mouth and rolled his head from side to side. "I wouldn't care to lose it."

"How about a special messenger?"

He stared at me levelly for a moment. "Don't you want the job, Mr. Savage?"

"Why a private investigator?"

"Why not?"

"To deliver a parcel?"

He hesitated for a split second. "I would also like you to keep your eyes open."

"For what?"

He pursed his wet lips. "There might be something up."

"Ah." I gave him my sardonic smile. "Nitty-gritty time."

"Not at all." He was blandness itself and took another short swig from the flask and added with considerable caution, "Not necessarily."

I climbed to my feet and wandered over to the window to stare at the invisible view. "Mr. Morton, what sort of 'something' might be up?"

He was so long in replying that I began to wonder whether I had asked the question or only thought it. I turned to look at him. He was sitting hunched forward, with his heavy jowls well down over his chest, frowning belligerently at the wastepaper basket beneath my desk. When he looked up, his tiny eyes, almost lost in folds of flesh, were slightly hooded—cunning, I thought; shrewd, calculating and cunning. He looked like a great fat bird of prey too heavy to get off the ground, lurking in ambush until some other creature, more mobile and less wily, took the initiative and went in to make the kill. Only then would he show himself and take possession of the bloody prize.

"I don't know," was all he said. "I really don't know."

"What's in the package?"

"You don't have to know that."

"I think I do."

"In that case . . ." He heaved himself forward and reached for his hat.

"All right, all right. . . ." I felt irritated with myself. If I wanted the job I would obviously have to agree to his terms. And I wanted it. Not because I couldn't afford to turn it down but because I was so bloody fed up with sitting about doing nothing. "Well, so long as it's nothing nasty," I mumbled ungraciously. "I need your assurance that I shan't be carrying dope or top secrets filched from some benighted government department."

"You have it." My contemptuous grunt made him look up sharply. "Mr. Savage, I was assured that you were reliable, confidential and thoroughly honest, the last of course within the context of your own necessarily peculiar brand of private-eye ethics. On the strength of that recommendation I am asking you to perform a simple service which, in the process, may be found to acquire certain . . . overtones. I am willing to pay you twice—no, three times your customary fee, plus expenses, if you will just do the job cleanly and efficiently with a minimum of publicity and a maximum absence of damn silly questions. Now, was there something else?"

I glowered at him for a moment, but it was only while I learned to live with the fact that I was a materialistic slob.

"Two questions." He closed his eyes in resignation. "Who recommended me?"

"Ex-Detective Inspector Sam Birkett."

"Sam Birkett? You know Sam?"

"It would seem so."

"Does he still live in Wimbledon?"

"That's where he was when I last spoke to him."

He suddenly heaved himself to his feet and began prowling about: the room seemed to grow smaller as he did so. He finished up behind the desk, where I should have been. "You have one more question."

"Yes. These overtones or whatever . . . how about them?"

He exhaled a long breath like a deflating balloon, sank into my chair, and drew open the top right-hand drawer of the desk. He peered curiously into it, closed it again and did the same with the left-hand drawer. This time he evidently found what he was looking for.

"Left-handed, are you?" he observed, taking out the gun and placing it gingerly on the desk in front of him. He regarded it in silence for a long moment, his lower lip sticking out aggressively. "Got a licence for this?"

"It's a toy replica."

He stared at me soberly for a moment, then picked up the weapon and peered morosely down the solid barrel. When he looked up again, his eyes were sad.

I said, "It's just for frightening people."

He snorted. "Wouldn't frighten Pussy out of a paper bag."

Suddenly he reached into his Gannex pocket and drew out a dull blue

Walther PPK automatic. I shied a little, but he placed it carefully on the desk alongside the toy Colt and swung the butt towards me with a flick of his finger. "Take it."

On the wood-trimmed butt of the gun I could see the winged eagle and swastika of the Third Reich. I could hear the tick of the watch on his wrist. He was watching me, a slightly mocking expression in his eyes. "Not up to it, Mr. Savage?"

I stared back at him. "I don't like guns."

He shrugged. "Join the club. I don't either. But a man with a gun carries more weight than six without one."

"So they say."

"True or false?" I glared at him. He smiled for the first time. "I'm not suggesting you use it. It's insurance. Take it. Put it in your pocket. Lose it if you will, but don't say I didn't warn you."

From an inside pocket he produced a bulging wallet, from which he extracted a small slip of paper; he laid this beside the gun. "The address to which you are to deliver the package." Next he counted out twenty 5-pound notes. "One hundred pounds for immediate expenses. When the job is completed you will forward your bill in the usual manner. I will triple the amount and let you have a cheque by return. Be fair with me, Mr. Savage. You will find an accommodation address on the reverse side of that paper."

"And the package?"

From his other voluminous side pocket he withdrew a flat parcel about the size of a carton of two hundred cigarettes; it was wrapped in thick manilla paper, tied with white string, the knots of which had been sealed with red wax. I picked it up and weighed it in my hand. Not very heavy. About the weight of two hundred cigarettes.

I took up the slip of paper and read aloud: " 'Wanhope, Castellcraig, Dyfed, South Wales.' Wanhope? Is that a house or a man?"

"A house."

I balanced the package on the palm of my hand while he watched it with narrowed and careful eyes. "Do I give this to a house or a man?"

"To a man." He was being very patient.

"Does he have a name?"

He sighed resignedly, his eyes swivelling towards the window where the rain sluiced down the glass with regular and relentless monotony. "How about Mackintosh?" he enquired in a low voice. "That would seem to be appropriate. Why don't we just call him Mr. Mackintosh?"

"Which means he doesn't actually answer to that name?"

Once more he smiled. "In one, Mr. Savage; you have it in one."

I was becoming angry again. "And if he doesn't happen to be at home and

I don't know what the hell to call him, then what do I do? How do I find him
if I don't know who to ask for?"

He said calmly, "Not to worry, Mr. Savage. He'll find you."

Something sinister reached out and touched me. I felt like ramming his
hundred pounds down his throat, but instead watched him as he rose ponderously to his feet, reached for his hat and moved awkwardly around the desk in
my direction. I was surprised to discover that he was almost as tall as I; from a
distance, he had seemed shorter. He was close to me, the taint of garlic on his
breath. "There's a pub called the Dragon, the only one in Castellcraig with
accommodation. I suggest you put up there for the night. Can you manage it
tonight, do you think?"

I shrugged. "I suppose so, if it's that urgent."

He creaked over to the door. "It's urgent, quite urgent." He turned. "I
shall expect to hear from you in the not too distant future," he said, and
plastering his hat over that monstrous head, he departed.

I stood for a moment listening to the retreating clatter of his feet, then
swore with deep and therapeutic satisfaction.

The maniacs were abroad on the motorway. Their tacit declaration of war
upon all who ventured out of a sliproad was in full swing as I all but failed to
join the M4 at Chiswick. Only a fancy piece of pedal work, an elaborate skid
and a yearlong wrestle with a recalcitrant wheel saved me from disappearing
beneath the multiple molars of a juggernaut.

There are few places on this island where you can rely on the possibility of
an unrehearsed confrontation with your Maker, and the motorways are most
of them. Normally—and I snatch the phrase at random—I wouldn't be seen
dead on any of them, but on this particular occasion I was in a hurry and still
do not know why. I suppose I just wanted the job over and done with. Having
ascertained that British Rail had no truck whatsoever with anything called
Castellcraig, I had withdrawn my little old Triumph from her hangar, filled
her with petrol worth a guinea an ounce and headed west.

The afternoon turned out to be even less attractive than the morning.
True, the rain had let up a little, but the dirty grey pall had thickened and
closed in; by three o'clock we were all driving on headlights.

Hunched over the wheel, mesmerized by the metronomic flicking of the
wipers, I had plenty of time to speculate over the contents of the parcel
tucked away in the overnight bag on the seat beside me, to regret the ominous presence of the loaded Walther automatic in the glove compartment
and to reflect on the obese and obscure George Morton, who claimed so
glibly to be on speaking terms with an eminent and respected ex-member of
the CID. I even found a moment to ponder over the identity of the mysterious Mr. Mackintosh, conjured so adroitly from the wet morning air.

And yet, apart from an allergy to Morton, I could find little reason for my uneasiness. The job was straightforward enough. I had to take a package from A and deliver it to B. Nothing would seem to be simpler. Except that B was someone called Mackintosh who wasn't a Mackintosh at all. But even that was not a lot to get uptight about; after all, my name wasn't really Mark Savage.

Had I been more familiar with the business of private investigation, I might have persuaded myself that such jobs were ten a penny and should be undertaken on the general principle of take-the-money-and-run, but having been at it for little over a year, I was still pretty much of a novice. I had done my fair share of snooping for suspicious wives and jealous husbands; I had successfully traced some peculiar insurance documents for an elderly person in Tring and engaged in a couple of rounds with a would-be blackmailer who broke down and wept when faced with public exposure and a lengthy prison sentence.

To jolly things along, I had even taken myself off to the local joke shop and purchased a realistic-looking replica of a Colt .45 automatic to keep in the drawer of my desk, where, as one is led to understand from the movies and television, one should lay down a small arm or two as a deterrent to burglars and assassins. There it had remained, gathering dust, until George Morton had disturbed it that morning.

I leaned across the car and snapped open the glove compartment. My gloved hand closed gingerly about the Walther's broad butt. As I drew the weapon from the surrounding blackness, the flash of passing headlights drew a reciprocal glow of dull blue metal from the barrel. The weight was familiar to my palm, nestling within it with an almost customary comfort. But against the hiss of my tyres on the streaming road and the regular beat of screen wipers, the very stillness of its contained power made my skin crawl. My finger touched the trigger guard and retreated. I shoved the thing back into the dark compartment and slammed it shut. I wondered why I had brought it with me, and having done so why I hadn't unloaded it. After all, in my overnight bag, wrapped in a towel beneath the mysterious parcel, lay my Colt .45, safe and make-believe—like my former life as an actor. . . .

Lights and signals, batteries of road signs and a general slowing down interrupted my soul searchings and proclaimed the imminence of the Severn Bridge. I wound down the window and was promptly slapped in the face by a wall of water as someone alongside sloshed through a puddle and deposited most of it in my car. I wound the window up again and attempted to sponge myself down with a handkerchief.

Damn George Morton. Fat, sinister George Morton with the huge round head, the small bloated fingers and that nonsensical apology for a hat. All of that, and more, gathered together, had been distilled into a Machiavellian essence of guile, treachery and all things wily, which peered nakedly through the little, red-brown, foxy eyes, hooded and sly in their comfortable folds of pink flesh.

By the time I was edging up to the toll booth on the bridge, the prospect of my mission had become noticeably less attractive. I contemplated an unlawful U-turn to hightail it back to London, but the thought of the money helped me to resist.

I have never much cared for the Severn Bridge and had the feeling at the very moment of my arrival midway between England and Wales that the Meccano-like structure would not survive the savagery of the elements as they unleashed themselves on it. The entire edifice swayed and clanked alarmingly. Even my little Triumph, well accustomed to the vicissitudes of the open road, gave a hysterical toot as I grabbed frantically at her wheel and persuaded her to remain on the straight and narrow.

It was a Welsh wind, of course, screaming in from the northwest, wild and rampant as the Cadwallon dragon, determined to keep the English on their side of the fence. And quite right, too, but why take it out on me? I would be in and out like a dose of salts, no loitering on sensitive Welsh toes for me, gone before they could say honorificabilitudinitatibus or whatever that outlandish Welsh equivalent is which ends with gogogoch. . . .

With the approach of darkness, my thoughts too began to close down on me, shutting me in and edging me drearily back once again into the past. The yellow thrust of the headlights probed through the blackness of the bad times to the strangely halcyon days of my career as a stuntman in the movies, where the harder I fell the richer I became. Working hard at being a success, I began to look for something more rewarding than stuntsmanship and took the unorthodox step of a stint in the theatre to find out whether I could combine acting with stunting. It was a rewarding stint in every way, for it was not long before I discovered, not without a certain amount of dismay, that my sort of face and physique was what everyone in the film industry seemed to be looking for. Invariably I found myself in the right place at the right time, with directors and producers happily vying for my services. In a comparatively short time I became known as the only leading English actor who insisted upon doing all his own stunts. "Douglas Fairbanks Senior Strikes Again," one Sunday tabloid gratifyingly declared. Good publicity but an expensive gamble on the producers' part: a broken ankle or a back injury could have put them out of business.

In fact, it wasn't I who insisted on doing my own stunts but an extraordinarily energetic and progressive director/producer by the name of Andrew Elliot, who wheedled me away from the theatre with the aid of a heartwarming contract from Premier Film Producers. A perfectionist, he insisted upon my understanding at first hand everything I was called upon to do in the particular film under consideration. *Practical* understanding. Half my waking hours were spent in being trained by masters, the other half before the camera putting that specialised knowledge on to celluloid.

They dressed me in black and sent me swinging precariously over rooftops to perpetrate impossible robberies; they put me in racing leathers, flying gear, wet suits and space suits—on one occasion into a full suit of armour with a battle-axe I could barely lift. They taught me to surf and bring a chopper down on a sixpence. I familiarised myself with motorcycles, with and without sidecars, horses ranging from mettlesome thoroughbreds to sturdy, crutch-splitting Percherons, and in one particular biblical epic I raced a four-horse Roman chariot around an arena larger than Wembley Stadium. On another film I drove a Churchill tank, a continental juggernaut, a forklift and a 93 bus, the last down the Putney High Street during the rush hour. When they had finished with me, I could pick a lock, crack a safe, shin up the outside of the tallest building and scale a medium-sized cliff. Firearms became second nature to me, from the smallest .410 Derringer through a wide range of revolvers, automatics, duelling pistols and rifles, to double-barrelled shot guns, stens, machine guns of all shapes and sizes, even bazookas and flame-throwers; I hurled hand grenades, coped with mines, land and marine, mortars and booby traps, studied plastic explosives and their fuses. I blew up a bridge, sabotaged a train and hijacked an airliner. I was the living, walking, talking personification of Action Man, the envy of U.N.C.L.E. and the scourge of S.A.S.—when suddenly, early one bright May morning, I fell off a horse and landed face downward on a nearby rock to discover some time later that I had broken my collarbone, a leg and an arm, fractured my pelvis and all but dispensed with my left eye . . .

Newport and Cardiff came and went, Port Talbot, glowering on the port bow, spurted its reeling gouts of flame into the murky sky; towering thunder-heads, red-tinged and wind-torn, rolled out over an invisible sea; beneath them, sprawled and ugly, writhed the ferment of steelworks; an apocalyptic landscape which played havoc with my unnerved imagination. I was glad when the afterglow faded and the night closed in again, vast and black and empty . . .

I had a wife at that time—an actress named Sonia—and it was remarkable how quickly she managed to go off me after my dramatic and highly pub-licised mishap. Never particularly companionable, we had already pottered along for the best part of two years, growing steadily away from each other as the realisation dawned upon us that sheer physical lust was no substitute for love and not, after all, the sturdiest rock upon which to found a permanent conjugal relationship; it was, in fact, this very rock upon which our particular dreamboat eventually foundered. So that, when I became incapable, if only temporarily, Sonia found it expedient to depart on a provincial tour of a play aptly entitled *Whither Away?*

This desertion, coupled with the trauma created by the accident and the resultant months in hospital, much of the time under heavy sedation, caused my life to lose a fair modicum of its charm, and my thriving career went abruptly up the spout.

Pain seemed always to be with me and was kept at bay only by regular shots of morphine and its derivatives, supplied first by the medical profession and later by an understanding friend who had access to such things and who shall remain nameless. I needed Mandrax to put me to sleep and amphetamines to wake me up, eventually discovering, without much surprise, that I could dispense with neither. Nor did I wish to. I was well and truly hooked.

As if that weren't enough, I also contracted a special liking for alcohol. I was quite a mess one way and another, and continued to plough my way steadily downwards to the point where even my best friends—and there were precious few of them left—would have been obliged, if asked, to admit that I was a junkie.

I wandered around like a dispossessed soul in dark glasses and refused to talk civilly to anyone. The press, of course, loved the whole thing and it was always open season for me and my doings; they looked upon me as something that had escaped from a rather exotic menagerie. I was continually being rude and impossible to determined reporters and insensitive photographers, two of whose cameras I destroyed in the process and had to pay for. But I was also jollied along, mercifully, by a few well-meaning individuals heedful of my survival and eventual repatriation into the land of responsible citizens. . . .

It was seven o'clock before I branched north at Carmarthen. I was cold and hungry and my eyes, staring down the bright beams of the headlights, felt as if they had been driven across the Sahara in a sandstorm. To make matters worse, the rain came down vengefully again in conjunction with an unrelenting wind and flattened the wipers against the screen until they were virtually useless. I set my helm for a place called Conwil Elvet at a risible fifteen miles an hour.

George Morton now became the target for blasphemies the like of which would have surprised even him. He was cursed and damned well and truly, up the airy mountain and down the rushy glen, with no reservations. I was bitterly regretful of having done business with him, but what was done could not now be undone. I felt like a kamikaze pilot at the point of no return wishing he hadn't come. And like him, I was committed: I could see no way of welshing on my agreement now, no matter how unattractive it had become.

I snorted quietly to myself. "Welshing" . . . not the most felicitous choice of word. I mentally withdrew it and sought vainly for a more circumspect replacement on the wrong side of this wild and alien border.

2

The headlights picked up a dog sprawled on the wet road. Dead or asleep, the middle of the road was no place for him. I drew up, thankful for the respite, clambered stiffly out of the car and, feeling a lot more dead than he was, shambled over to take a look.

He was a biggish, shaggy creature with more than a dash of Welsh shepherd to him. A thin trickle of blood oozed from a wound on his temple, where presumably a car had struck him. It must have been a glancing blow, for I could see no indication of further injuries. I squatted in the middle of the dark and lonely road, wishing there was something I could do other than drag him into a hedge and leave him for the crows to pick at. I could certainly tell someone at the next village and hope that they would turn out and collect him and give him a good, Christian burial.

A twig snapped. I raised my head. The rain had ceased, but the darkness pressed stealthily against my little oasis of light. Trees creaked and branches scraped and stirred like the rustle of folding bats' wings. My shadow crawled sinuously out of the light into darkness. I could see nothing else.

I cursed softly and, taking the dog by the shoulders, dragged him as gently as I could into the gloomy verge of the road. He was still warm; it could have happened only a short while before my arrival. Miserably I patted the damp coat and turned to the car. At that moment, out of the darkness there came a thin banshee shriek. I froze. It hung for a second or two against the muttering background of the night and then was gone. I clutched desperately at what remained of my fraying nerves until it occurred to me, with an awesome rush of relief, that the sound had come from the dog, behind me. I recovered and trotted back like a schoolboy, a surge of real happiness overwhelming me.

His eyes were open and blinking up at me, his feathery tail rustling tentatively in the wet bracken.

"Well, hello," I greeted him, kneeling in the mud beside him. "You've come back. We all thought you were a dead dog." I sat back on my heels and wondered what I was going to do about him. "Have to take you in somewhere. Can't leave you here, can I?"

No, he said with his eyes, you bloody can't.

"Can you walk?"

He understood every word and made a couple of vain attempts to right himself. There appeared to be something very wrong with his offside back leg. "Come on, then, let's have you." I gathered him up in my arms. He was a great lump of a dog. "One of us," I confided, "is asking for a hernia." I stumbled to the car, propped him awkwardly on a knee whilst I heaved the overnight bag on to the back seat, then dumped him into the passenger seat, where he sighed loudly and fixed me with a resigned gaze. I got in beside him and slammed the door. "I'm taking you to Castellcraig, if that's all right with you." As I sorted out the gears, he settled himself in and began a cautious exploration of his forepaws with his tongue.

Scarcely a quarter of a mile further on, a sign juddered out of the night announcing that we were about to enter Castellcraig. The clock on the dashboard said it was nearly nine. I hadn't booked overnight accommodation. For some insane reason I had thought to arrive, deliver the package and turn round and drive back before the Welsh got me. But there seemed to be more to Wales than Cardiff and the Mumbles.

I nosed cautiously through the dark little town. There was an occasional street lamp, but they didn't amount to much. No one was about. The only sign of life was a white cat streaking like a meteor through the headlights.

"Pussy cat," I said, and my companion roused himself to growl dutifully. "There's a pub around here somewhere, isn't there?" I asked him. Beyond planting a soggy paw on my knee he didn't commit himself. "The Dragon," I told him. He gave a short whine.

A church loomed ahead, built, it seemed, in the middle of the road. The dog whined again. "That's a church, not a pub," I argued. But he was not to be deterred, pushing my knee with his paw. And then I saw it, just to one side, a dark sign creaking in the wind—shades of the Admiral Benbow—and a lamp glowing dimly in a porched recess.

I tucked the car half on the pavement at the side of the narrow road and prepared to investigate. I told the dog to stay where he was, but he had no intention of budging anyway.

The place was warm and smelled of pink paraffin; it was also very dimly lit and I fell down two steps just inside the front door, the racket arousing a lilting Welsh enquiry from an upper floor, presumably ascertaining whether anyone had been injured. An amply built elderly woman with a square head and dangling earrings followed hard upon the heels of the enquiry, panting a little as she came to rest.

"I fell down the steps," I informed her.

She nodded without sympathy. "There's a notice outside the door warning of them but doubtless you didn't see it. English are you, yes?"

"British, yes." I had no intention of leaning on her, but the slightly loaded question aroused a touch of the old ire in me. Owen Glendower had long since been laid to rest. "I was wondering whether you could put me up for the night."

"Just the one night?"

"Just the one."

"Luggage?" Her eyes had narrowed with suspicion.

"In the car outside. I've just driven up from London."

"I expect that will be all right, then. Just the one night. Perhaps you would like to sign the book, then."

She led the way to a small desk in a gloomy recess and put a ballpoint pen into my hand.

"Ah," I said, remembering suddenly. "I have a dog in the car. I picked him up on the road a way back. He'd been knocked down by a car, I think, stunned a little, you know?"

"Dog?" She made use of every note in the chromatic scale.

"A dog, yes. Presumably left for dead. So I thought I would give him a lift in. Otherwise some careless—someone else would have run him over and finished him off."

"No dogs."

With pen poised above the visitors' book, I paused and looked at her. I bared my teeth. "You misunderstand me. He is not my dog. I brought him in because he's hurt and needs attention. Also on the chance of finding out who he belongs to. Someone around here must know him. You'd probably recognise him yourself. Perhaps you'd care to take a look at him?"

She drew back a little as if in sudden fear and cut me short with an irritable jangle of her earrings. "No dogs on the premises." And when her mouth closed, her lips were thin and pursed.

"What seems to be the trouble?"

The stairs creaked a little as the newcomer with the oil-smooth voice paused halfway down. I could see only the lower half of him; tight black jeans, a slender, blue-veined hand grasping the banister, the knuckles white against sallow skin.

"No trouble—" I began.

The woman interrupted: "The gentleman has a dog. I told him no dogs."

I moved to the foot of the stairs. "I have already explained that the dog is not mine. He was lying in the road, hurt. All I want is to deliver him to whomever he belongs, or failing that, get a vet or someone to take a look at him, make sure he's all right. That's all. No trouble. No bother. I'll foot the bill for the vet."

The rest of him was shrouded in darkness, only the shadowy loom of a body and the metallic glitter of eyes. I had the feeling that he was about to tell me to get the hell out of it, but when he spoke again it was in Welsh and to the woman. Now, Welsh, surprisingly, is not one of my accomplishments, but I did catch the untranslatable word *television* bowling along somewhere among the mêlée of sounds. When he'd had his say, the woman gave a shrug and took her square head off down a passage, in a huff.

The man on the stairs moved down slowly into the light. I found myself staring, even retreating a step as he approached.

It was his flowing hair and beard which first riveted my attention—together, that is, with one or two of his other more salient features. But the hair, a deep rich brown, straight and silky, fell to beyond his shoulders, spreading like an inverted fan to frame a narrow, angular face and thereby exaggerating a natural pallor. The beard and moustache were equally fine. The lips were full without being sensual, the cheekbones high and pronounced, and above the finely drawn brows the forehead was broad and smooth, giving an impression of unusual intelligence. And then there were the eyes: deep-set, dark and alert with a wide, fanatical look about them. A black shirt was tucked into the leather-belted jeans, and about his neck he wore an ankh suspended from a silver chain. I placed him in his middle twenties.

"Her baby brother was bitten by a mad dog," he informed me quietly. I had no idea whether he was being serious; it was like being told that someone had been dropped on his head when a child. I slipped my face into neutral and awaited further intelligence. "He died of rabies." My face registered sympathetic dismay. "The dog, I mean." I gave up. "The baby brother lived to be sixty-nine and eventually died of cirrhosis of the liver." He smiled suddenly. "I'm being fatuous, I'm sorry. But my aunt still retains a healthy terror of dogs. If she says no dogs, it's no dogs I'm afraid. It's her place and she makes the rules. Which is a pity, because I rather like dogs."

At that moment an ear-shattering cacophony erupted in the street outside: the frantic barking and snarling of a dog interposed with a man's voice, surprised and panic-stricken, rising angrily to a sharp cry of pain—and through it all the insistent blaring of a motor horn. My motor horn.

Precipitously I made for the door, falling up the two steps and thudding my head hard on the nearby wall. And as if that weren't enough, as I stumbled into the street, stunned and swearing, I was sent flying by a body which cannoned into me and flung me breathless back into the arms of the square-headed lady's nephew pressing hard on my heels. Clasped amorously to each other, we listened to the pounding footsteps as they made off in the general direction of England.

We disentangled ourselves and lurched over to the car. Its door hung open, and the dog, having heaved himself over on to the driver's seat, was standing, one paw firmly on the horn button, snarling alarmingly.

"For God's sake," I protested, removing his foot with difficulty from the horn button. "You'll wake the whole bloody neighbourhood."

The charged silence which fell at the cessation of the motor horn seemed to impress us all; it certainly quietened the dog, who immediately stopped his racket and fell to licking and nuzzling my hand as I comforted him. "What the hell was all that about?"

My foot struck something in the road. It was my overnight bag. The young man stooped to pick it up. "Yours?" I nodded, taking it from him. "Someone doing a spot of car-lifting, by the look of it."

I gave the dog a cautious pat on the head. "Well done, old mate, I hope you had a good go at him."

"Looks as if did." The young man reached across me and picked something from the seat of the car, peering at it closely under the dim interior light. "A bit of someone's coat sleeve—a wrist strap off a raincoat, I'd say."

A spot of liquid glinted on the seat. I put the tip of my finger on it. "Blood, too," I told him with a certain amount of satisfaction. "Whoever it was has now got a bad hand. With any luck he will develop rabies like your uncle—no, sorry, your uncle didn't die of rabies, did he?"

"Cirrhosis of the liver." He smiled, straightening up. "We'd better get everything inside. Including the dog. Auntie will just have to lump it. And I'd lock the car if I were you. If he's still around he might decide to have another go." He frowned. "That sort of thing doesn't happen in this part of the world, busting into cars. I'll take your bag while you cope with the dog. He knows you and I'd sooner not lose a hand just now."

As I handed him the bag I remembered the gun lodged in the glove compartment. "You go on. I'll manage the rest."

I reached for the gun, which was still there, thank God, and slid it into my raincoat pocket, where it hung like a millstone. I turned a critical eye on the invalid. "I suppose it's no good my asking if you can walk; if you could you would be halfway to Cardiff by this time, after your friend. Come on, then, off we go again."

I heaved him up into my arms, locked the car and weaved an unsteady course back to the hotel, where the young man was in attendance at the open door warning me, unnecessarily, of the two steps I had already discovered.

The moment he caught sight of the dog in the light he recognised him. "He belongs to Julie Remington, at the other end of town. Bruno's his name." He indicated a cushioned oak settle by the wall. "Shove him down there while I raise her on the phone. She'll be worrying. She doesn't usually let him out on his own, certainly not at this time of night."

"You'd better tell her to bring a vet."

"She is a vet."

I looked up in surprise. "Well, bully for her. Then, you'd better tell her to bring along her little bag of tools. I think he's got a busted leg."

I slumped down on the settle beside the dog and watched the young man as he moved towards a wall telephone. "Tell me something. . . ." He paused. "We haven't met before, have we?"

"Not that I know of, have we? My name is Michael Davies if that means anything to you, which I doubt. To my certain knowledge there are at least two other Michael Davieses around here and there are bound to be others. We Welsh are an unoriginal lot so far as names are concerned. Most of us are called Davies or Thomas or Evans or the like."

"It's not the name. You just look familiar, that's all."

He grinned suddenly, showing a perfect set of teeth. "El Greco perhaps?"

"Pardon?"

"There was a man staying here during the summer—an artist—said I was the spit and image of an El Greco Christ. Wanted me to sit for him. I told him that since El Greco had already done it, there didn't seem much point in someone else doing it. He didn't care much for that."

I stared impolitely. That was it. Christ. That was exactly who he looked like. No wonder I thought I had met him before. I grinned sheepishly. "I think you've hit the nail on the head." I added an apology. "I don't know whether I should say sorry or not. Is it a compliment to tell someone that he looks like Jesus Christ? It can't be bad, I suppose. But you never know nowadays."

He reached, smiling, for the telephone. "I'll take it as a compliment." He gave a number to the operator and placed a hand over the mouthpiece. "So long as you don't call me Jesus."

Then he was mumbling away to someone in Welsh. I clambered out of my raincoat, conscious of the weight of the gun in the pocket. I laid it carefully on the settle beside the dog, who was drowsing peacefully now that he was at least halfway home and dry, blinking up at me now and again through contented half-closed eyes and beating his tail spasmodically against the cushions. I took a closer look at the wound on his head. It looked clean enough and had certainly stopped bleeding. "So where's your collar, then, you old fool?" I whispered. "Name and address and all that. No dog should be without one. You should know that at your age."

On the wall over the settle, a small framed map drew my attention. I crossed my eyes to look at it. Drawn quite crudely in coloured inks, it was a homemade plan of the little town and its immediate surroundings, a grubby mark where countless fingers had rested indicating the Dragon.

The telephone pinged. "She's on her way," said Michael Davies. "Very put out. It's blaming her dad she is. She and her dad don't always see eye to eye. Now, then." He came and stood over me. "How about me giving you a drink on the house? That's the least I can do after such a bumpy welcome. Let's go into the warm. I have a hidey-hole on the other side of the bar if you'd like to follow me."

"What about Bruno?"

"Oh, he'll be all right."

And since the dog didn't seem eager to move, I snatched up my coat and fell in behind Davies, following him through a low doorway beneath the stairs. "Mind the step down," he warned too late, as I cannoned into the far wall of a narrow, dimly lit passage. He must have thought I was a walking disaster. "You all right?" he called back. I mumbled something in the affirmative and continued on down the passage behind him, becoming aware as I did so of a growing murmur of voices. He shoved open a door and we were in the bar, the voices now deafening and the air so polluted with tobacco smoke that my eyes watered.

"Step up," he called, too late again. He should have known. He received my full weight between his shoulderblades.

Several heads turned in our direction. Shadowed faces loomed in the dim light, mouths half open. The volume of sound lessened noticeably as one by one the occupants of the room became aware of our presence; smiles faded from the faces and the laughter died; heads craned, eyes peered. The silence, except for the shufflings of feet, was total. I half expected to hear the cry: I spy strangers! Indeed I would have welcomed it. I nodded companionably to one or two of them but there was no acknowledgment. My guide, busily elbowing his way through the close press of sweating bodies, seemed to be unaware of the hostile atmosphere which surrounded us. I caught sight of the bartender, a large, florid man in a blue fisherman's jersey, hand frozen to a pump handle; his eyes met mine, bulging and thyroidal in the uncertain light, and below them the mouth gaped wide and wet and unpleasant: a gargoyle one might expect to find in a fairground haunted house. As Davies reached his objective, a door at the further end of the bar, a single voice was raised in the silence, an insolent, singsong voice. What it said I had no way of knowing, for it spoke in Welsh, but its portent was fairly obvious, for it was greeted by several disagreeable sniggers from the back of the room, and someone whistled low and lecherously.

Once I was through the door, Davies slammed it violently behind me. He was trembling, his face chalky white, eyes black with fury. "Bastards," he snarled. "Dirty, filthy, shitty bastards."

Lurching across the room, he hunched himself over a table bearing drinks, his hands clutching at its edge so that the bottles and glasses on it rattled and tinkled.

I stood at the doorway, shaken by what had just occurred but unable to comment. On an ornate mantelshelf a large black marble clock ticked loudly; one of its hands was missing, the other pointed to eleven. I looked about me. The room was square and compact, its only source of light a warmly shaded, elegant wrought-iron standard lamp. The furniture and carpeting were surprisingly tasteful, the only nod to hotel convention being a couple of dumpy, chintz-covered armchairs crouched before the fireplace, where the embers of a dying fire still glowed. The wall on my right was lined from floor to ceiling with books and records, whilst its opposite number was taken up almost entirely with full-length curtains of dark velvet which matched the carpet and possibly concealed French windows. To the left of the door where I stood was an expensive hi-fi system, tuner, amplifier, cassette deck and record player, all neatly stacked one above the other, whilst a reel-to-reel tapedeck, surrounded by a formidable array of boxed and annotated tapes, rested on a small table in the corner. Prominently displayed on the table was a silver-framed portrait of a blond young man of about the same age as my host.

Davies stirred at last, his breathing now under control, his flare of manic fury past. "I do apologise," he said in a low voice, his back still toward me. "What will you drink? Scotch, gin, beer . . . ?"

I said tonic water would do me nicely, apologised for my inadequacy with regard to strong drink and moved a step into the room. Busy now with the drinks, he glanced over his shoulder. "Put your coat down, sit somewhere. Julie won't be long and we may as well make ourselves comfortable for a couple of minutes."

I spread my heavily weighted raincoat carefully over the back of one of the chairs and lowered myself into the cushions, watching him as he broke the seal on a fresh bottle of Johnny Walker. As I did so I became aware of a presence behind me. I turned my head. The wall to the left of the door was dominated by an outsize drawing in red chalk of Hector Berlioz, shock-headed and mesmeric, eyes blazing like a wild cat's, the pale taut face draconian in resolution.

"That's rather fine," I remarked as he handed me my drink.

He eyed the portrait with some satisfaction. "Yes, I think so too."

"One of Ayrton's, isn't it?"

"That's right." He sounded surprised that I knew the artist. "Berlioz was an obsession with him. Do you like Berlioz?" He threw me a look which was almost a challenge. "Or aren't you into that sort of music?"

I smiled. "I'm into music, yes, and what I know of him I like very much. It always surprises me how early he is."

"Oh yes, he was long before his time." He raised his glass more to the portrait than to me. "Cheerio." There was a moment of silence before he said compulsively, "I think he's one of the greats. Knew what he wanted, never compromised—not in his work, anyway." I sensed he was riding a hobbyhorse. "Mind you, I think he was a bit barmy, but what genius isn't? He was a revolutionary, single-minded, fanatical and couldn't abide idiots." He gave a sudden short bark of laughter. "Do you know the story about him and Cherubini after the first Paris performance of Beethoven's Fifth? They met in the foyer. Berlioz couldn't stand Cherubini, thought he was old hat, and Cherubini, not surprisingly, wasn't all that enamoured of him either. Hector was bubbling over with enthusiasm. 'Well, what did you think of it?' he asked the old boy. Cherubini obviously hadn't understood a bloody note of it—he just shrugged and said, 'Promising, promising.' And Berlioz was so incensed that he whipped out a penknife and attacked him, had to be hauled off before he did any permanent damage."

I laughed. "I've never heard that one."

"Sums up old Hector perfectly, don't you think? I understand that attitude. I think I know what he went through, what he was after." His eyes seemed suddenly to reflect the blaze of those in the portrait. As I buried my nose in my glass I wondered uneasily what his own particular obsession was. The slightest suggestion of imbalance disturbs me.

"Another?" He had removed my glass from my grasp and was at the table uncorking his Johnny Walker before I could answer. "Sure you won't have a proper drink?" I shook my head. "You up here on holiday?"

"Dear God, no, not at this time of year, nor in this weather. No, I'm on a flying business trip. Didn't expect to be staying the night as a matter of fact, but the journey took longer than I expected. Many people staying here?"

"In the hotel?" He returned my replenished glass. "Not a soul. Not a single solitary soul. Except you, of course. We don't really cater for many, even at the best of times. This isn't a holiday resort. Tourists settle for Cardigan, a few miles away. Mind you, we have got an old Norman castle; they come to look at that occasionally, what there is left of it."

"I was studying your map on the wall out there. You don't happen to know a place called Wanhope not far from here, do you?"

I could have sworn he stiffened slightly. "Wanhope?" he repeated, his eyes flickering for a split second in the direction of the silver-framed portrait. "What is it, a village or a house?"

"A house. That's all I know. And I'm supposed to find a bloke who goes by the name of Mackintosh, but I'm fairly certain you'll never have heard of him."

He shook his head. "Strangers descend on us from time to time of course, buy up derelict houses and cottages, convert them, knock them about a bit and then let them out to summer visitors, or keep them as retreats for themselves. Could be one of them, perhaps. Ask Julie Remington when she comes. She'll know if anyone does; as a vet she gets around more than most of us."

He slumped into the chair opposite, stretching out his long legs towards the fire, at rest for the first time since we had met. He looked quizzically over his glass for a moment. "I don't even know who you are, do you realise that?"

When I gave him my name he frowned slightly. "You seem familiar somehow. As I did to you. You haven't been up here before, have you?"

I shook my head and steered him away from the subject. "Do you and your aunt run this place on your own?"

"With a couple of part-timers, yes. There's a full-time barman, whom you probably saw out there in the snake pit." The narrow face tightened with hatred. He obviously felt much the same as I did about the barman. He stared soberly at the amber liquid in his glass. "It would be lovely to get away from here."

"No chance?"

His eyes met mine almost wearily. "You need bread to go charging off on your own, and I'm more than a little short of bread at this moment. I'm not complaining; well, not much anyway, but this place—" He broke off and shook his head helplessly. "It's high time I moved on." His eyes moved again to the silver frame.

The sound of a car pulling up brought him to his feet with an alacrity which suggested relief at the interruption. "That'll be Julie." Moving quickly to the curtains, he flung them apart and unbolted the windows. "Let's go this way, rather than run that loathsome gauntlet again."

Following him through the windows I found myself in cold, blustering darkness. He refastened the windows. "Up here," he directed. We were in a narrow lane which ran alongside the hotel and linked up with the main road a few yards further up.

An elderly Morris Traveller had drawn up behind my own vehicle, and as we rounded the corner its lights were doused and a small figure clambered out of the driver's seat.

"Julie?" called Davies.

"Mike." She reached back into the car for a large bag and as we came up slammed the door. "Hi," she said. "So where's that animal of mine?"

"Let's go inside, out of the cold," he replied, taking the bag from her. She hadn't noticed me bumbling along in the rear and only became aware of me when she all but shut my face in the door. "I'm terribly sorry." She was abject in her apologies. "You all right?"

"I'll live," I assured her. "Not to worry."

She squinted at me in the dim light. "You're the one who found him, I bet." I nodded. She slipped off an enormous glove and gave me her hand. "I'm Julie Remington and I'm grateful to you, really grateful. He might easily have been killed. Most people would have just left him there."

Her hand was small and ice-cold. Michael Davies mentioned my name. Her elderly, tightly belted riding mackintosh was several sizes too large for her, perversely making her appear even smaller than she was—the top of her head barely levelled with my shoulder. There was something almost oriental about her; smooth, straight blue-black hair, oval face and dark, upward-tilting eyes, intelligent, sexually aware eyes that undressed me adroitly as they swept me once from head to foot.

In the background, Bruno was making whinnying noises and thumping his tail on the back of the settle. "Goodness, what a fuss," she said, turning away and kneeling beside him. "Now, let's see what you've been doing to yourself, you silly old mutt. Mike, be a pal and get me some warm water, will you?"

I moved in beside her, watching the deft, sensitive fingers probing and manipulating the damaged leg. A half-suppressed yelp was followed by an apologetic wagging of the tail. "Sorry, old lad, but you've got a busted leg and we've got to do something about it."

From her bag she produced a folded towel containing a hypodermic and a couple of glass ampoules. The dog eyed the preparations with sidelong suspicion. "I'm not going to hurt you," she promised.

"Is his head all right?" I asked.

Busy with cotton wool and disinfectant, she nodded shortly. "Superficial cut, that's all. Looks okay." Filing the neck off one of the ampoules, she drew the colourless liquid into the syringe and administered the injection, dabbing the tiny puncture with cotton wool. "There," she whispered, scratching the dog comfortingly behind the ear. "All over. You have a nice sleep, and when you wake up you will learn to hate me." She produced some bandages and laid out a couple of medieval-looking splints. She said, "I really can't thank you enough for coming to his rescue. He's such a dear thing, I'd be lost without him. I hope there's something I can do to show my gratitude, like—er—" She made a wry face which turned to an impish grin. "Like the very tiniest contribution to your favourite charity."

"You can tell me where Wanhope is."

Michael Davies returned at that moment with a bowl of warm water and placed it on the floor beside her.

"Wanhope?" The girl's brow puckered.

"It's a house or a cottage somewhere in the vicinity," I explained.

Folding a piece of lint and soaking it in the water, she bathed the dog's head gently, a thoughtful expression on her face. "Wanhope . . . Wanhope . . . It does ring a vague sort of bell. I remember thinking what a desolate name it was for a house." She leaned in towards her patient. "You asleep? Bruno . . . ?" She smiled up at us. "He's away. It's all systems go."

The setting of the leg was a lesson in quiet precision. The gentle hands moved caressingly for a moment or two up and down the injured leg, checked for a moment, became very still and tightened suddenly; with the merest of clicks the bone slid into place. "There," she said. "Now the splints and bandages and away we go. I'll put it in plaster when I get home." She smiled up at me. "Perhaps you'd care to autograph his plaster; he'd be very proud of that." Her eyes held mine a little too long for it to have been a chance remark.

While she occupied herself with the splints, she went back to brooding about Wanhope. "Wish I could remember . . ." She stopped suddenly. "I *have* remembered. I know where it is. It's off Bourne Road, over the bridge. Up by Will Evans' farm. You know it, Mike, you must do. It's where there was that fire—past the Evans' farm and on up towards the beacon. It's high up there on the left, a couple of cottages knocked into one, whitewashed. It's invisible from the road, but there's a board with the name on it and a steep drive up to it."

"Is it far?" I asked. Mike was saying nothing.

She shrugged. "Couple of miles as the crow flies." I glanced at my watch. "I hope you're not thinking of going up there tonight. You'll never find it in this weather. You'll get lost."

I was more than ready to listen to her advice. The thought of venturing again into that Stygian blackness, which seemed to have a feel all of its own, made my hair curl.

"If I don't do it tonight it'll have to be first thing in the morning." I looked at Davies. "Any chance of something to eat? I feel as if I haven't eaten for days."

His face lengthened. "Nothing substantial, I'm afraid. I could knock you up a sandwich, fry you an egg perhaps, something like that."

Julie Remington's case closed with a loud, decisive snap. "I have the perfect answer. I will give you something to eat." She raised a hand as I was about to interrupt her. "When Mike rang up I was about to indulge myself in an enormous beef casserole. I shoved it back into the oven and it's sitting there now, ready and waiting. If you've been driving all day you want something nourishing. Fried eggs are no bloody good, nor yet a sandwich." She restrapped herself into her voluminous rainwear. "How about it? Settled?"

"Well . . ."

"Legitimate payment for saving my dog's life. And I'll take you and bring you back so you don't lose yourself. You just can't refuse." She gave me a ravishing smile. "Now, can you?"

"I wouldn't dare," I grinned.

"Good. Then, as soon as you're ready we'll get along."

"I'd better move in first, hadn't I?"

Davies nodded. "Should have done that before." He unhooked a key from a rack. "Number One. What else for our only visitor? The room with the view." He brought out my overnight bag. "Didn't you have a raincoat?"

"O Lord yes, I left it in your room."

"I'll get it." He put down the bag and made for the door beneath the stairs, hesitated, exchanged a glance with me and retraced his steps. "On second thought I'll go the other way."

I remembered the gun in the pocket. There was no way he could ignore its weight, and if I judged his character aright he would waste no time ascertaining the cause of it. "Let me go," I said, starting forward, but he waved me aside and plunged out into the darkness.

"Anything wrong?" asked the girl, noticing my uneasiness.

"I hate putting people out."

"Who are you putting out? For me it is a pleasure, for him it's his job."

"He mentioned you had a father."

"Oh, Dad'll be in bed by this time. Early to bed and early to rise . . . he's one of those." She drew down the corners of her mouth. "We shall be quite alone," she intoned solemnly, but with a humorous glint in her eye.

Before I could answer, Davies clattered back breathlessly. "One raincoat." He held it for me, and as I turned to slip it on I caught his eye and he smiled slyly. He knew about the gun. "I'll show you your room, give you a front-door key and then you can stay out as long as you like."

The room on the first floor was shivery and occupied by an enormous brass bedstead, a wash-stand bearing a large china bowl with a matching jug to stand in it, a wardrobe and very little else. He put my bag on a low rack at the foot of the bed and handed me the key, promising to install an electric fire to take the chill off the room.

Downstairs he parted with a large front-door key and took the girl's bag while she humped the slumbering Bruno into her arms and, preceding us out to the Morris, deposited him on the back seat, covering him with a blanket and making him generally comfortable.

Holding the door for her, Michael Davies exchanged a couple of *sotto voce* words with her as she got in. I clambered in beside her. The engine sprang into life, we waved to the shadowy Davies, and she let out the clutch. She smiled at me, her face glowing in the reflected spill of the headlights. "À *chez* Remington." She smiled.

3

When we exchanged the somewhat formal atmosphere of the Remington dining room for the soporific warmth and comfort of what she called the "back room," I had the feeling that question time was just around the corner. The realisation had no qualms for me, for by that time I was prepared to lay out my life for her, reveal my darkest secrets, make public my most intimate thoughts. The armchair to which she directed me was one of those designed to take possession of one's entire being. In conjunction with a blazing fire, soft lights, good coffee and—for her—an outsize brandy, it prepared the stage for an unprecedented surrender of my innermost soul.

The meal had been homely and perfect, the large, ovenproof casserole being brought to the table, its contents, beef and carrots and onions and heaven knows what else, ladled piping hot on to warm plates and served with potatoes baked in their jackets. Excellent cheese and crackers completed the repast.

While we ate, the small talk—initiated mainly, I am bound to say, by Julie Remington—was quite remarkable for its triviality and could only have been a deliberate ploy on her part: weather, food, local flora and fauna and the inadvisability of drying up head colds with capsules filled with tiny multi-coloured pills being just a few of the earth-shattering topics touched upon. Under normal circumstances I would have been carried from the room in hysterics, but the circumstances in that sombre and upright dining room were far from normal. For Julie was there, opposite me, small but by no means demure, exquisite as a Japanese doll, with the strength of a strangler in her delicate hands and a voice as warm and sultry as a midsummer night. She was sheer magic and utter logic, fire and earth, Venus in a loose-fitting yellow polo-neck, grubby blue jeans and a pair of lamb's-wool bootees which made her feet look like those of a lady hobbit. The speed with which I fell in love with her did not confound me in the slightest. It amazed me but did not confound me. It might have confounded Mitch, 250 miles away in merry old England, but not me.

And now, imprisoned in that tender trap of a chair, I viewed her lissome form again, curled like a cat in the corner of the sofa. Screaming gusts of wind hammered the rain against the window and rattled down the chimney, driving flurries of blue smoke curling about the room. The fire blazed like a village smithy.

She was smiling at me over the rim of her brandy glass. "For the first time you are at rest."

"Everything's so warm and peaceful, how could I be otherwise? Thank you for looking after me."

"Thank you for looking after my dog."

"Love me love my dog."

The firelight flickered warmly in her eyes.

She was smiling again, though not, this time, at me.

"Why are you smiling?"

"I was wondering why I haven't asked you a lot of daft questions."

"And why haven't you?"

She looked into her glass. "You've had enough of that in your time, unless I'm much mistaken. Or maybe I just haven't an inquisitive nature. In any case, I know quite a few of the answers already."

"About what?"

"About you." She hesitated. "For instance, Mark Savage is not the name I associate with your face. A few years ago you were a well-known film star; you had an accident, a bad accident, and—went off the rails. The newspapers had a field day. After that you seemed to disappear off the face of the earth. People worried about you. Some even thought you were dead. I think I did. You'd probably be surprised at our concern." Another silence; then she murmured, "And now here you are—Mark Savage—with me."

We sat looking at each other for a while; then I smiled. "I knew about the concern. A lot of people wrote offering help. I was very touched. I also had thirteen proposals of marriage."

She hooted with sudden laughter. "I don't believe it."

"Would I lie to you?"

"Aw shucks!" She made a mock rueful face. "If only I had written."

"If only you had," I said quietly. The remark produced a momentary hiatus. I went on almost defiantly. "If a footballer or a boxer, a jockey, has a bad accident he's out of the game, isn't he—for good—no matter how young he is?" She was watching me intently. I shrugged. "I had a few good innings." It was a long cool look of appraisal. "It's never easy to start again from nowhere."

"And now you carry a gun."

That quiet statement took me completely unawares. "Who says so?"

"Mike Davies."

I dropped my eyes for a second, then met hers again. "So I carry a gun.

What of it?" I still managed to retain a thin edge of defiance. "As a matter of fact I carry two guns. One is a toy and is in my bag at the hotel and belongs to me. The other is here in the pocket of my raincoat, is by no means a toy and does not belong to me."

"So why?"

It was her first question and, fighting the temptation to shy away from it, I took a deep breath. "I'm a private investigator." If her expression changed at all I missed it. "I ferret out other people's indiscretions, turn up questionable alliances, expose clandestine assignations. Pay me for it and I'll snoop into your closest friend's private affairs—into yours if the price is right."

"With a gun?"

"Not usually, no. This time, for reasons best known to my current employer, yes, with a gun. It came with the contract."

She stirred uneasily and gave me a pallid smile. "You're on the defensive. What's wrong with being a private investigator? You don't have to run yourself down. It's a job, don't knock it."

Uncoiling herself she reached a long arm for the Courvoisier. "Sure you won't have some?"

I shook my head. "Wine, yes, occasionally. Spirits never."

She replenished her own glass.

"Why," she asked, "a private eye?"

It was a long time before I answered her. I said hesitantly, "I've only really talked to one person about my problems—apart from a regiment of psychiatrists, that is." I listened for a moment to the wind slashing the rain on to the windows. "You said something just now about my going off the rails. It was worse than that. I went off my head. If it hadn't been for one person, I wouldn't have survived. Why she bothered, how she managed, I'll never know, but she did. I met her first at the hospital. She was a voluntary worker —a 'friend' I think she called herself. When I was discharged she disappeared. Then I began to make those headlines you mentioned. I was on the bottle. I was into drugs. I tried to go back to work but didn't seem to be able to do it any more. My nerve had gone; couldn't even remember the bloody lines. In the end of course none of them would touch me with a barge pole. My wife had . . . bowed out fairly ungraciously some time before; eventually we were divorced. So there was no one, not a soul. It didn't worry me. I was long past all that.

"And then, suddenly, Mitch was back—Mary Mitchell, my 'friend,' breaking the door down, shouting and swearing at me, pleading and cajoling. She knocked me down and picked me up and gradually, over a long long time, she contrived to put me together again. She practically moved in. She did move in at one point. She slammed me into a clinic, sat with me and fought with me while I dried out and screamed my way through the worst period of my life, bar none! The Great Withdrawal. I wouldn't wish that on my worst enemy . . ."

I stopped and stared into the fire, sweating at the memories of those appalling weeks. Julie sat motionless and said nothing.

"Poor old Mitch," I went on. "She got very little out of it. Just the satisfaction, I suppose, of seeing me upright again on my own two feet. It took months. It seemed for ever. After that came the question of what I was going to do with this brand new life she had given me. I didn't *know* anything. I had no talents other than those I had exploited on the screen. Then it occurred to us that some of those talents—some of the more reprehensible ones, that is—like picking locks, shinning up and down drainpipes and my general au fait with guns and knives and battle-axes, some of these talents surely could be made use of. We cooked up a plan. With what little money I had left after my excesses I rented a couple of rundown office rooms in the City and we set up shop. Mitch came along as my assistant, Tinker to my Sexton Blake. She does all the donkeywork, foot-slogging and paper stuff, while I get on with the magnifying-glass bit."

"And changed your name to Savage."

"Yes. Because that's how I felt at the time." I lifted my shoulders. "That's it. Yours truly in a nutshell."

"And this particular job?"

"Ah." I made a face. "Yes, well, this particular job is something else. On the face of it, it would seem to be simplicity itself, so simple in fact that it smells, and I wish to God I knew why."

I told her about George Morton and his great fat head and his little piggy eyes and the way he threw spent matches over his shoulder and wrung out his hat over my floor. When I had finished, she took a swig at her brandy, swirled the liquid languidly around her glass and said, "So all you have to do is deliver this package to Wanhope?"

"Right."

"To a Mr. Mackintosh who doesn't exist."

"Right."

"Simple enough."

"Very."

"So why the gun?"

"Overtones, he called them."

"And you have no idea what's in this package?"

"Looks like two hundred cigarettes."

She watched the fire for so long I began to think she had nodded off with her eyes open. "It's very fishy, isn't it?" she said at last.

"I think so."

"If I were you I'd get it over first thing in the morning."

"I intend to."

"Then you can beetle back home and collect the money."

I hesitated. "Yes?" I said with the slightest of rising inflections.

Our eyes met and held. "Yes," she repeated softly and drained her glass.

I glanced at my watch. "Christ, it's nearly one o'clock. I must let you get your beauty sleep."

As if in derision, the rain and the wind roared down the chimney with a great boisterous shout. The fire hissed and a huge cloud of smoke rolled out into the room; Julie Remington sprang to her feet and flapped belligerently at the smoke with a newspaper.

I also got to my feet. "It's been a lovely evening," I said when the excitement had died down.

She nodded a couple of times. "New friends are rare in these parts." She glanced at me. "I don't suppose we shall see each other again."

Kneeling abruptly, she snatched up a small brush and busied herself sweeping the wood ash and debris clear of the open hearth; she took a log from a pile at the side of the fireplace and laid it carefully on the fire, where the flames caught at it greedily, crackling and spitting sparks into the room. One landed on the knee of her jeans, where it glowed brightly for a second until she slapped down at it hard with an open palm as if she were swatting an insect. The hand remained where it was, small and taut.

I knelt beside her. "Julie . . ."

She nodded quickly as if to check me. "Yes, I know. . . ."

We remained where we were for some time, wrenching away at our thoughts and staring into the fire. "It could be the brandy," she whispered at last.

"I haven't had any brandy," I reminded her gently, and after another lengthy silence added, "I don't think I want to beetle back home tomorrow."

She looked at me. "You must, mustn't you?"

"There's nothing special about tomorrow."

"Mark, listen. . . ." She took my hand in hers. "I worry about the gun in your pocket. And I worry about Mary Mitchell. Most of all I worry about her."

"I just work with Mitch," I said gruffly. "And the gun isn't mine."

"It's in *your* pocket." She looked at me long and seriously. "I'll see you tomorrow, then," she whispered. "If you're still here." Her lips touched my cheek fleetingly, then suddenly she rose to her feet. "Now I must look in on Bruno, and then I'll drive you home."

"I'll find my way. You can't turn out on a night like this."

"Mr. Savage, I'm a vet. Mares and cows don't wait on the weather. Come on and don't make a noise or you'll wake Dad."

Obediently I fell in behind her. "I don't believe you've got a dad. I think you made him up."

She snorted like a schoolgirl. "Nobody could make up my dad, not even the Brothers Grimm."

In the compact and scrupulously scrubbed surgery room where a few hours before I had watched her putting Bruno's leg into plaster with such neat and speedy expertise, the dog lay in an enormous wicker basket covered with a brown and red striped blanket. He raised his head as we entered, blinking in the sudden light. Julie squatted down beside him and drew back the blanket. "How are you, then, old boy, eh?"

I wandered about the surgery, peering inquisitively into this and that and generally exercising my privileges as a private eye. Her headed notepaper read, J. Remington, MRCVS, in black boldface, whilst framed on the wall hung an impressive-looking document explaining that she was a splendid veterinary surgeon and was hereby etc., etc. . . .

"I see you got your degree in Bristol. Why Bristol? Do you come from there?"

She glanced up from her patient. "One, all the best vets come from Bristol, and two, no I come from the Midlands. I was born in Solihull and went to school at King Edward's, in Birmingham, where a certain Mr. J. R. R. Tolkien was educated, he of *Lord of the Rings* fame."

"I knew you were a hobbit. You've got hobbit's feet."

She squinted down at her bootees and grinned. "Ah yes, two small furry feet." She tucked the blanket carefully about the dog. "There, he'll be all right for a bit. I've given him a sedative, which should see him through the night." She scratched the dog gently on the nose. "Now, you be a good dog and don't go eating your plaster, understand?" She got to her feet with a loud arthritic groan. "Right, off we go, then. Say good night to Bruno."

"Good night, Bruno," I said; he blinked blearily at me and lowered his ears in salutation. In the passage I helped her into her ancient riding mack.

"Oh yes," I murmured, standing back to get the full effect as she strapped herself into it, tugging the belt tightly around her slender midriff. "Very fashionable."

"You're being rude about my mack."

"Makes you look about twelve."

"I got it in the Oxfam shop. Forty pence. Not bad, was it?" and when I smirked she added, "You don't go stumping around animals and muddy farms in your best chapel clothes, you know." She made for the back door.

"Are you going out in your hobbit feet?" I asked mildly.

She swore softly and I eyed her with amusement as she threw off the slippers and rolled about on the lid of an old oak chest, grappling with a pair of muddy Wellingtons.

In the car, against a boisterous background of wind and rain, I brought up the subject of her genealogy. "If you were born in Solihull you're not officially Welsh."

"My father's Welsh, mother was English. Silhillian in fact. Now, there's a silly word: Silhillian. I was born in Solihull because that's where my mother happened to be at the time. She and Dad fought like Kilkenny cats and Mother kept going home to Mother, if you see what I mean. I was delivered during one of those rest periods. In the end they agreed to separate, so Mum went back to Solihull and Dad of course had to stay here to attend to his practice."

"He's a vet too?"

"Was, yes. It's in the genes. I read Veterinary Science at Bristol and graduated the same week that Dad had a stroke and Mother died of cancer. That was quite a week. So I came up here and took over the practice and have been here ever since, getting on for three years now." She drove in silence for a while. Then she said, "Dad doesn't do much these days."

"Is he still laid up?"

"Physically he's recovered, but it's taken its toll. He's become more . . . remote; more difficult, I suppose. But he's still a lovely man."

We were passing over a hump-back bridge when she leaned across me and pointed upward. "That's the turning for Wanhope, up there. You'll find it all right in the daylight. Ask Mike Davies; he'll direct you."

I stared out along the beams of the headlights. "Mike Davies—does he really look like Jesus Christ or does he just make up like that?"

She chuckled. "Both, probably."

"It's disconcerting, meeting him for the first time on a dark stairway."

"We've all got used to him."

"The customers in the bar haven't."

"They don't understand him."

"Never likely to, either. He's frustrated, that's his trouble. Wants to get away from here."

"He's frustrated in more ways than that."

"You mean he'd prefer my knickers to yours."

She laughed aloud. "That's a terrible way of putting it."

"Succinct, though. Perhaps I should take him in hand."

"I'll smash your face in if you do." She drew up with a scream of brakes. I looked at her, startled.

"What's up?"

"We're here."

"I thought you were going to tell me to get out and walk."

She switched off her engine and groped for my hand. I leaned in towards her. "Julie, I'm not fooling around, you know that, don't you?"

"Yes, I know that." She squeezed my hand. "I'll seek you out tomorrow some time. I've several calls to make in the morning, so I'll look in about two if that's okay with you. If you're not here, I'll know you've had second thoughts and gone steaming back to the Big Smoke and Mary Mitchell."

"I'll be here." I kissed her gently on the lips. She responded quite coolly for a second or two and then slowly placed her arms about my neck. When we came up for air I held her close to me. "Your mack," I informed her softly, "smells like a secondhand tyre dump."

"Ah," she whispered in much the same tone. "What a lovely thing to say to a girl. Now you really *can* get out and walk." She leaned across me rewardingly and opened the door. "Off you go."

I watched her wrestle with a three-point turn, avoiding the wing of my little old Triumph only by chance, and then she was gone, waving and blowing a kiss at me. I stood in the pouring rain until the glow of the rear lamps had disappeared.

I climbed wearily to my room. Davies had been as good as his word. The two-barred electric fire radiated only minimal warmth, but there was a hot-water bottle in the bed.

When I opened my bag, my senses prickled. Someone had been through it. The sealed package was still there unfortunately. I stared at it. It appeared not to have been tampered with. I shook it, listened to it, even smelt it, and then tucked it away again. To hell with it.

Later I stood before the mirror over the washstand and stared critically at myself, trying to put myself into her shoes and seeing myself as she must see me. I shuddered, and climbed, depressed, into the outsize bed, knowing full well that I wouldn't sleep a wink.

I slept superbly, dreamlessly, and like the proverbial log.

4

My first thoughts on waking next morning were of Julie Remington, and these kept me occupied for some time, luring me along primrose paths of speculation of which my mother, for one, would never have approved.

The bedsprings complained loudly when I finally decided to relieve them of my weight. I groped my way in the half-darkness to the window, where I drew back the curtains to acquaint myself with the state of the weather. I needn't have bothered: the windows were of frosted glass, which seemed odd for a room with a view. Then, peering a little closer and scrubbing at the wet panes with my hand, I discovered that they weren't frosted at all: it was simply the Welsh weather outside trying to get in. A grey-white mist obliterated everything. I stared miserably at the opaque cloud of nothingness and shivered. I then took a look at the water jug; it contained an impressively well-proportioned spider, happily, for my peace of mind, dead, and that was all.

Climbing into my raincoat, which was still cold and clammy and without which I seemed destined to go nowhere, I found myself wishing I'd had the forethought to pack a bath-robe, but the likelihood of an overnight stay had been so remote that even a razor, toothbrush and pyjama bottoms had seemed an unnecessary encumbrance. I found a bathroom where even the paraffin heater burned with a blue flame and the water was ice-cold. Sprinkling some of it over my face, I dried off on what was obviously a communal towel and stumbled back to Room One and into my rumpled clothes. I stuck that bloody gun into the waistband of my trousers, rather than leave it lying around whilst I was at breakfast. I pulled my jersey down over the butt, fastened the lower button of my jacket and went to have a look at myself in the mirror: I looked like a man with a gun tucked down his trousers.

Downstairs I banged with uncalled-for vigour at a bell on the reception desk and raised a small, birdlike woman with a pink cloche hat secured to her head by a green woollen scarf tied in a vast knot beneath her chin.

"Breakfast?" I enquired in the stentorian tones one usually reserves for foreigners. She nodded wordlessly and beckoned me to follow her down the passage where the square-headed proprietress had disappeared the previous evening.

The dining room, dark and unwelcoming, was heated with yet another paraffin stove, which flickered and popped alarmingly. With self-preservation in mind, I chose the table furthest away from it and, on turning to enquire what the menu had to offer, found myself alone; my guide had vanished as if she had never been. A moment later, however, Michael Davies, in tight blue jeans and a bulky Iceland sweater, turned up in the doorway.

I greeted him cautiously and was informed there were coffee, eggs and bacon and toast, all of which suited my needs admirably. As he turned away I noticed that his hair was gathered up behind in a ponytail and tied with what looked like a bootlace.

"Any possibility of my staying on for another night or so? I rather thought I'd like to look around a bit while I'm here. Norman castle and all that."

"Yes . . . sure . . . why not?" He didn't seem at all sure. "The room's there . . ." and certainly couldn't think of a reason why not.

"Oh, and incidentally"—I waylaid him in the doorway—"someone went through my things last night while I was out. Would you have any idea who it might have been?"

His face darkened a little. "You're quite sure?" I watched him calmly until his eyes shifted away. "No, I'm afraid I have no idea who—" He broke off, his frown deepening. He had an idea, all right, but he was not about to part with it.

"It doesn't matter," I said carelessly. "I have nothing of value. I just thought you should know."

"Of course." And after a brief moment of hesitation and a muttered promise to look into it, he departed, leaving me with the certainty that it was not he who was responsible for the snooping. Who, then? Auntie? Not the type: intolerant, narrow, almost certainly inquisitive—but not inquisitive enough; too pious, too chapel. Who else? Two of the staff, he had said last night, were part-timers, which presumably meant that they slept off the premises; one of them was obviously the Pink Cloche Hat; I would absolve her from going through an open door, let alone through someone else's luggage. There remained the man in the fisherman's jersey, the gargoyle barman, permanent staff.

Michael Davies returned with coffee, cutlery and accoutrements, laid the table with fastidious care and, studiously avoiding my eye, left without further communication. And then came Pink Cloche Hat—the hat now superseded by an extremely unlikely auburn wig complete with tortoiseshell hairslide—bringing a plateful of eggs and bacon, which, along with toast and marmalade and lashings of good hot coffee, went some way to restore my drooping spirits.

I was on my final cup of coffee when Davies came to enquire whether I needed anything more, and then, the debris of my breakfast balanced on an undersized tray, continued to hover over me uncertainly; I asked about the weather and if the mist would be likely to lift and if so, when.

"Are you still thinking of going to—?"

"Wanhope, yes, if you'd be kind enough to put me on the way."

I got up, and together we made our way to the entrance hall via the kitchen, where he deposited the tray.

Indicating the homemade wall map, he laid a well-manicured fingernail on the grubby spot called the Dragon. "This is where we are. Your car is pointing in the right direction. Carry on to the end of the road, bear right until you come to a hump-back bridge—here; over it and turn immediate right— here—and it's up there on the left somewhere, a couple of miles, according to Julie. She says it's signed; I don't remember. In fact I don't remember the place at all." Something about the way he said that made me turn my head to look at him, but the moment had passed and he was peering through the glass panel of the door at where the street should have been. "I'd leave things for a bit if I were you, until it lifts. You could easily get lost and it'll be very unpleasant up there; you're halfway up a mountain."

I was already on the stairs when he said suddenly, "I'm sorry about that other business. I think I can guess who it may have been." His eyes flickered warily up the stairs over my shoulder and his voice lowered a fraction. "I'll have a word."

"Not on my account, please." I shook my head. "He's bigger than both of us."

He was startled and came closer, looking up at me. "The barman?" he asked softly. I nodded. "What makes you think that?"

"Who else is there? What's his name?"

"Williams. Emrys Williams."

I came down a couple of steps. "You don't seem to like him. Couldn't you get rid of him?"

His eyes held mine for a second, and there was a glint in them, almost, I thought, of hope; then they flicked away again. "It's not my responsibility," he mumbled, and turned to go. "Drive carefully," he added over his shoulder.

Back in my room I returned the gun to my raincoat and slid the sealed pack of cigarettes, or whatever it was, into the other pocket.

Visibility outside was practically nil, no more than a couple of yards at best. Hunched in the ice-cold, stationary car and peering through the streaming windscreen, I debated whether, since my decision to stay overnight had dispensed with urgency, it might be more sensible to follow Davies' advice and, for the time being at least, abandon Wanhope to the weather. The alternative was to hang about the pub with nothing to do until two o'clock, when Julie had promised to look in.

I switched on the headlights, which made even more nonsense of the visibility, gunned the cold engine into life and with elaborate caution edged out into the road.

Not surprisingly, there was little traffic about, most of what there was being confined to essential services. Oncoming vehicles, their strategy similar to mine—adhering to the white centre line—presented me with a nerve-wracking series of head-on near collisions. Once, a great throbbing bus, reful-gent in an aureole of lighted windows, loomed up alongside and all but leant on me; from it a schoolgirl, a potential Brünnhilde if ever I saw one, with blonde plaits, crossed her eyes at me and stuck out a long, coated tongue. I stuck mine out too, hoping that it looked a mite more hygienic than hers.

It took me the best part of half an hour to reach the hump-backed bridge. Trusting implicitly in my directions, I edged the wheel over and cautiously aimed the car at a solid wall of mist, which revealed, as I approached, the opening I'd been promised. The turning proved to be so acute that I was almost facing the direction from which I had come, and the road, hardly more than a lane, began to climb steeply at what must surely have been akin to one in six. With no run at it, the little Triumph laboured painfully, grinding forward at a snail's pace in her lowest gear, with no extra power to call on. I gritted my teeth and willed her to keep going. At the very moment that the speedometer registered no appreciable progress, the road levelled a little, not much, but sufficient to ensure continued forward motion. Here there was no white centre line. The road writhed alarmingly. On the left, as far as I could make out, was a solid wall of rock, where the road had been hacked out of the hillside, and on the right a low hedge and then nothing but blank grey mist, piled and packed into the valley, which deepened beside me as I climbed.

My eyes streamed with tears as they strained to focus on anything more substantial than that eternal void of mist. Any irritation I had felt at embarking upon this exercise shifted now to a seething anger of self-reproach, and that anger stealthily became fear, and the fear panic, sudden and inexplicable.

I slammed down my foot and pulled hard on the hand brake. I switched off the engine and sat in a still, cold sweat. Without my having realised it, the road must have widened considerably, for all around me, on every side, there was nothing, nothing but a white wall of mist. Emptiness. I could have been poised on the edge of the world. If I left the car I would step into space.

Pulling myself together, I opened the door, and with only the slightest of hesitations, got out of the car, treading on solid ground I could hardly see. The silence was awesome. With one hand, for comfort, on the overheated bonnet, I moved around the car and then, like a blind man, made for the invisible inside verge of the road. It was no more than six paces away and reared up before me, a dark overhanging cliff of stone. I was in a lay-by cut to allow passage for vehicles abreast. With my back to the wall and glad of its rough support, I stood for a moment thankfully aware of the loosening of my unreasoned panic. The only excuse I offered myself was that I was in Wales, a country more alien to the English than the average Englishman would care to admit. Both in the raging of the elements and in the muffled secrecy of fog, the shades of Merlin and Glendower seemed to hover ominously close to the Celtic earth.

I decided to abandon the car in the lay-by and continue on foot; Merlin or no Merlin, having come so far and at such cost to my jangled nerves, it would be imbecilic to give up now. From where I stood I could hear the faint tick-tick of the Triumph's cooling engine; rejoining her, I was in the act of opening the door when the beat of huge and powerful wings swept down on me with a roar. As I threw up an arm to protect my head, black wings swooped over me; the mist swirled; I felt the icy blast of the bird's passage, saw the momentary spread of deadly talons and heard the plaintive echo of its scream as it soared upwards and was gone.

I leant on my little Triumph and, for several lengthy moments, chattered to her as if she were a human being; anything to prevent myself from jumping over the edge of something. Little comfort was to be found in the knowledge that the buzzard, if that's what it had been, was probably every bit as shaken as I was. He was obviously having trouble with visibility too; no self-respecting buzzard could, surely, mistake me for a rabbit. Or maybe it wasn't a buzzard at all; maybe it was Merlin. . . .

Clambering into the car, I started up and drove her carefully close against the overhanging cliff, where I switched off, got out, locked up and gave her an encouraging pat on the bonnet. "Don't go away," I said. "I'll be back." I hope, I added to myself, casting a wary eye at the sky.

Progress was easier on foot. Davies had said a couple of miles or thereabouts: I must have covered more than half of it in the car. I peered at my watch: ten past eleven. I trudged on, wishing I'd brought a warm overcoat instead of a raincoat and meditating on just how much of a wild-goose chase I was engaged in. What would I do, for instance, if there was no one at home at Wanhope and the house was locked up?

I continued more slowly. Was I being set up? And if so, for what? What had been going on behind those piggy little Morton eyes? And why the gun? My hand closed around the butt, my index finger caressing the trigger. "Overtones," he had said. Overtones aided and abetted by a gun meant dangerous overtones.

The back of my neck prickled. I became aware that my heart was beating faster—whether because of my uneasiness or as a result of my relentless pounding up the side of a Welsh mountain, I had no time to consider, because just then it stopped altogether. In sheer fright.

A shadowy figure had loomed up out of the mist.

I grew roots.

The figure was quite motionless, the head cocked to one side as if listening. For a moment, I could have sworn that he had seen me, until I realised that his back was towards me. Swiftly I sidestepped behind a small promontory in the overhang. The figure made no move.

There was no cogent reason why I should be skulking by the roadside practising invisibility: it was, after all, a public right-of-way; whoever it was could be taking his daily constitutional, should he be idiotic enough to be so inclined, and stopping to listen to the cry of a passing buzzard. But I could hear him breathing, low, irregular rasps of sound, as if he'd been hurrying. Then he swung round and started in my direction. I cowered against the bank. My heart had started up again and was making a terrible noise under my shirt.

He was thick-set and bulky, with short legs and massive upper works but was surprisingly lithe and silent in his movements. Mercifully he stuck to the far side of the road, so that a good seven or eight feet of mist separated us. Directly opposite me he paused again to look back, his head bent, listening. I frowned to myself; there was something familiar about that bull neck and head.

Moving on again, he almost at once began to fade into the mist—not only laterally but downwards, as if sinking into the earth. The last part of him to go was his head, which vanished from my sight at road level. I stared at the spot for some time, half expecting him to rise again, like Lazarus from the dead.

When nothing happened, I shuttled quietly across the road to investigate his unorthodox disappearance; a break in the bordering hedge that opened on to a downward path was the explanation; he had simply turned off the road and plunged down the hillside.

I was half tempted to follow him, for I had remembered where I had seen those broad shoulders before: in the bar of the Dragon. Emrys Williams, the gargoyle barman.

It was a worrying discovery. Brooding over its implications, I became aware that I was holding the gun in my hand, safety-catch off, ready to shoot. That, too, was worrying, the more so because I had no recollection of having drawn the thing. Uneasily I thrust it into my pocket and forged ahead, onwards and upwards.

I was consoling myself with the thought that, had Williams continued on down the road, he would almost certainly have noticed the car tucked into the lay-by and gathered that I was somewhere in the neighbourhood, when it occurred to me that it was after all probably I myself who had started the game running: he was here solely because of me; he needed no oracle to know that I was bound for Wanhope; by this time the whole of Castellcraig must know it. If Williams' intention had been a private appointment with me, I could only heave a sigh of relief that he had decided not to wait; he was nobody's idea of a blind date.

I pulled up. A falling away of the bank to my left resolved itself into the entrance to a narrow driveway. A gate post carrying a couple of rusted hinges and no gate bore a plain white-painted board with the word Wanhope scrawled upon it in thick black letters.

From where I stood, there was nothing to recommend the place. Across the driveway and blocking it almost completely, the blackened branch of a tree had fallen. I looked up. A huge elm soared ominously into the cold mist, its upper branches lost to sight; there was no breath of wind, but the tree creaked and chattered, grunting to itself. An old saying elbowed its way up from my subconscious: Ellum hateth man and waiteth.

I clambered over the fallen branch and struck upwards into the drive. The going was steep, steeper than any part of the road; my little Triumph would have had to go up backwards. Ten yards of it, then a left-hand hairpin levelling out as the building loomed pallidly into sight. Regaining my breath, I stared at it curiously. But for two tiny gabled dormer windows, it could have been a bungalow; long, low, it boasted a couple of large windows on either side of a narrow porch. The pallor of the walls suggested a coating of Snowcem or whitewash.

I felt suddenly idiotic standing there in a thick Welsh mist, wrapped up in my damp raincoat with a gun in one pocket and a sealed packet of something in the other, preparing to beat on the door of an obviously empty house and ask the nobody who eventually wouldn't open the door if a man who didn't exist would mind accepting a package which did.

I delivered myself of the rudest word I know. Loudly. And felt no relief.

So I pounded on the door with a large iron knocker which was clearly a collector's piece and would hardly have been out of place on the front door of the Tower of London. The echoes I aroused were splendid and lightened my burden considerably. Not expecting an answer, I didn't wait for one but gravitated instead towards a window, scrubbing the smeared glass with a gloved hand and fixing my eye to it in the hope of seeing something worthwhile. Nothing. I cupped my hands and peered again. Not much more. Immediately below the window was a table bearing a vase of what could only be dusty plastic roses and a collection of hideous knickknacks. Beyond that, I could make out nothing but indistinct lumps of furniture and dim reflections in the glass of a framed picture on the wall opposite.

Turning away, I wandered inquisitively around the building—at least I tried to wander around it, but discovered that the rear wall was part of the actual hillside and there was no throughway; the house had been built to adjoin the rock face. Looking up, I could just make out the overhang of the cliff several feet above the roof. Not, I thought, particularly safe should the hillside ever decide to shift.

A solid side door, securely locked and bolted, led, presumably, judging by two empty refuse bins and an untidy heap of coal and logs, to the kitchen quarters. A narrow window of frosted glass prevented a sight of them.

Retracing my steps and rounding the corner of the house, I realised that the mist was at last beginning to thin, just enough to shed somewhat more light on the proceedings. And not before time, I thought, sourly glancing around me and wondering what was now to be done.

The building was perched high above and facing the road, which was invisible from where I stood; the lofty elm at the entrance to the drive soared skywards immediately opposite the front door; between the house and the tree lay the gravelled drive and a narrow stretch of neglected lawn with grass a foot high and bounded by a low wall of red brick.

High overhead, I could hear the distant thunder of a plane, and somewhere a bird was twittering.

All at once I was alert. In the house, something had fallen.

I swung around and stood frozen with horror.

Splayed hard against the window was a hand, wet with blood, sliding slowly down the glass and dragging an ugly smear behind it; a face, distorted, pressed suddenly against the pane, the lips stretched wide, screaming soundlessly, blood bubbling in the gaping cavity, spewing out over the chin and dribbling on to the glass; eyes, beseeching, ablaze with terror. . . .

I raced to the door and flung myself against it. It didn't budge. I drew the Walther from my pocket and fired point-blank at the lock, blowing it away; the door burst inwards and I followed, deafened by the explosion. As I stood in the doorway, gun in hand, the dying man, clutching convulsively at the tabletop with scrabbling fingernails, attempted to drag himself to his feet, twisting his head towards me, a horrifying bubbling chuckle coming from his distorted lips, the eyes rolling upwards until only the whites remained.

He was dead before I could reach him.

As the table, clenched firmly in the lifeless hands, toppled in slow motion on to the fallen body, a great gout of blood spurting from the mouth splattered to the floor and over my shoes; the glass vase shattered, plastic roses exploding from it; the nasty ornaments pattered around the corpse like hailstones, one of them, an outsize china wasp, tasteless in bright yellows and browns, lodging in one of the staring eyes. A brass bowl rolled drearily to and fro for a second or two and then was still.

I have no idea how long I stood, shocked and incapable of motion; it could not have been more than a couple of minutes; it felt like an hour. In the wake of that sudden and horrific eruption of sound the silence closed in swiftly, tight and muffling, like a velvet-gloved hand clamped about the nose and mouth.

At last I stirred and in a stupor stooped to remove that hideous ornament from the dead man's face; violently I flung it into a corner, where it smashed to pieces, a tiny splinter ricocheting to strike my cheek and draw blood—the sting of a china wasp.

I looked at the still figure pinned to the floor by the weighty table. He was a man of indeterminate age, the right side of forty perhaps, though the lank, thinning hair and deeply lined face could have added a further ten years. The eyes stared blankly, the lower arcs of the upturned pupils only just visible as they seemed, uncannily, to probe the inner recesses of his own head. With sudden distaste I snatched at an antimacassar on the nearby chair and half threw it, half spread it over the pallid face; even as I turned away, the blood had begun to seep through the material.

Cautiously, and with the gun firmly in my grasp, I searched the house thoroughly; not a cupboard, wardrobe or wall niche was overlooked; from its moorings in the kitchen ceiling, I slid a folding ladder and climbed to the tiny attics lit by the two gabled windows; no place of concealment was ignored. I drew a blank. Apart from the dead man, I was alone.

The gargoyle head of Emrys Williams flashed on the screen of my mind's eye like a lantern slide and continued with irritating insistence to do so. If he were responsible, then his victim must have lain around dying somewhere for the best part of ten minutes; it was more than ten minutes since I had encountered Williams on the road.

Once again, I went through the house, and there it was, in the bathroom, a darker stain on a dark red bath mat. I bent down and laid a finger on it; the mat was soggy with blood. So he had lain here in the bathroom losing blood and presumably unable to move until he had heard me making a din at the front door and then, with a final burst of energy, reached the window to attract my attention. From bathroom to kitchen, across a passage, pausing, and finally into the room where his body now lay, I followed his progress, a glistening trail of blood leading the way.

I pulled myself up. The police. Ah yes, the police. I should call the police, shouldn't I? Every good citizen should contact the police upon encountering a dead body. With no enthusiasm, I prowled around looking for a telephone and was delighted to find none. At least I had tried. I was neither in the mood nor yet a position to exchange words with a policeman; the beady eyes, the pencil stub poised over the ubiquitous notebook and, worst of all, that perpetual pulse of suspicion beating away beneath the helmet. Not one word of my evidence would he believe; and who could blame him? I found it difficult to believe myself. To convince a distrustful policeman, it would need a lot of rewriting and some very good acting.

For some reason I couldn't immediately put my finger on, I needed to know just how the man died.

Heaving the table off him—nothing must be moved before the arrival of the police—I almost leapt out of my clothes when the corpse kicked me smartly on the shin. I didn't know all that much about dead bodies, never having had the need nor indeed the wherewithal to make a close study of them, but I presumed hopefully that it was some sort of reflex action, stiffening of the muscles or some such; whatever it was, I preferred not to dwell upon it—if he wanted to kick me it was perfectly all right with me.

Steeling myself against the welter of blood, the nauseous stench of which was beginning to turn my stomach, I knelt beside him. He had been stabbed; in the upper abdomen, as nearly as I could make out; a vicious upward thrust.

Surprisingly the murder weapon remained in the wound: as far as I could see it was an ordinary kitchen carving knife with a bone handle.

I had seen enough and was about to replace the table across the fallen body when the sleeve of the man's raincoat caught my eye; the wrist strap was missing, the shredded threads of the material suggesting that it had only recently been torn away. I groped around in my own pocket and brought to light the strap which Davies had found in the car the night before. I did not need a second glance to know that the telltale threads matched. With a finger, I gingerly raised the cuff of the man's coat; a grubby strip of bandage was twisted ineptly about the wrist where the teeth of the dog had drawn blood.

I felt suddenly drained, the implications of that dirty bandage overwhelming me. I squatted back on my heels. Even had I previously been able to cling to the idea that Emrys Williams' furtive movements in these parts were unrelated to my own, I now had proof that in some way this man's death was connected with my presence.

Who was he, and why had he been killed?

Reluctantly I bent over the body and slid my hand into his inside pocket; no wallet, but my fingers closed on a paper of some sort. I drew out an envelope; scrawly handwriting: Mr. George Mathews, Garrach Cottage, St. Dogmaels, South Wales.

I stuffed it into my pocket and awkwardly tipped the table back into position; the dead lips seemed to curl, the mouth gaped and slowly filled with blood as the full weight of the table rested against the body's chest. My stomach heaved. . . .

Only gradually did I become aware of the sounds on the roof. I dismissed them as the scrabblings and scratchings of pigeons or starlings rooting about among the tiles. But when there came a sudden thumping sound followed by a long slithering movement, I became thoroughly alerted and made hastily for the open front door.

Hugging the wall of the house, I doubled around to the side door, from where, I remembered, it was possible to command a clear view of the overhang. By the time I arrived, all was quiet again. I scrambled noisily over the heap of coal and up on to a flanking bank of earth into which had been driven a fence of sturdy wooden uprights, presumably to ward off possible landslides.

I could see nothing untoward. Several lengthy skylights of frosted glass were recessed into the roof; these and the surrounding tiling showed signs of earth and stones broken away from the hillside; some wildflowers had even taken root in the gutters and appeared to be flourishing. I glanced up at the sky; it was clearing at last, a few twisted wraiths of mist curling away upwards like flying spume. In the valley, the cloud persisted, close-packed like grey-white cotton wool.

A small avalanche of earth and pebbles pattered suddenly on to the roof, a short pause, then another, this time carrying with it a clump of earth, which landed with a thump on to the tiles and after a second slithered slowly away out of sight.

Someone was clambering about on the hillside. Clinging to the fencing, I leaned outwards in an effort to see something of the incline, but succeeded only in confirming what I already knew, that it was both steep and thickly overgrown with stunted trees and windswept bushes. There seemed to be no way of getting up there. Standing on tiptoe, I craned my neck to study the lie of the trees at the far end of the house. In the uniform closeness of the growth I thought I could perceive a darker patch, possibly indicating the entrance to a path.

I returned to the drive and scuttled over on to the lawn. I stared upwards. The hillside was steep, and thick with trees and undergrowth. Putting up a hand to shade my eyes from the overhead glare, I tried vainly to detect any sign of movement. How the hell did he get up there, whoever he was, and what was he doing, anyway?

Next moment, I knew exactly what he was doing.

I saw the flash and heard the shot, and felt myself momentarily jerked off balance as my coat was tugged violently away from me; with an unpleasant thud, the bullet buried itself in the thick trunk of the elm behind me. When the second shot came, I was already bent double, haring for the shelter of the house and listening to the splintering of brickwork as the bullet struck the low wall and whined away in a ricochet.

With my back safely to the house, I snatched a quick look at my raincoat: the bullet had passed beneath my upraised arm and provided the coat with two extra ventilation holes. The raising of my hand had been a happy inspiration. I might otherwise have sprung a ventilation hole in my upper arm.

With the house between myself and the gunman, I made my way to the far end of the building, where I could view the break in the trees with safety. I was right: a narrow path thrust upward through the crawling morass of dead vegetation. I stuck my head around the corner; the high fenced bank which had been erected at both ends of the house would shield me from any further sniping. I could in fact have strolled nonchalantly over to the path without danger. I didn't, though—I had done all this too often in films to ignore the possibility of a touch of drama. Bent double, I ran, zigzagging a little, Walther at the ready, and lived to be enormously grateful for my dramatic instincts, since a bullet zipped past my right ear and sent me plunging into the narrow path, where, regardless of briars and branches, I fought my frantic way several yards into the undergrowth before catching my foot among the roots and finishing up on my front with a mouthful of mud. As I came to rest, another bullet whined over my head, snapping angrily through the bare branches. The sniper had obviously been quick off the mark and changed his position, gaining higher ground and moving around to my right.

Sprawled there for some minutes spitting muck and puffing like a grampus, I found myself thinking, quite irrelevantly, about Andrew Elliot, my old director, who by this time would have been shouting, "Not too much of the bloody panting. You're in top form, remember; highly trained, never out of breath—never in too much of a hurry. . . ."

Silly bugger! Did he know what the real thing was like? Had he any conception of the urgency that live ammunition added to the situation, helping a chap on his way with a burst of speed he never even knew he had? You may not be fortunate enough to outrun a bullet, but it's always worth trying.

Come to think of it, up to then I hadn't had much of a notion either. Nobody, certainly to my knowledge, had ever before, with malice aforethought, discharged a real live firearm in my direction. It was a sobering experience, to say the least.

I rolled over on to my back and lifted my head with caution. The path was a couple of yards to my right and not much more than a break in the trees winding up and away into virtual darkness, but its intention was clear: if you wanted to reach the top of the hill, that was the way to do it. Through the closely woven entanglement of bracken, I could barely see the sky, which meant that with any luck my would-be assassin could not see a great deal of me, either. Slithering to my feet and moving parallel to the path, I began the tortuous ascent; in the space of a few minutes I was awash with sweat. I stumbled like a drunk, several times measuring my length in the mushy stinking compost of rotting leaves and obscene-looking fungi. Apart from my own animal gruntings I could hear nothing. Several times I paused to listen and get my bearings; the occasional glimpse of Wanhope's roof confirmed that I was climbing steadily and steeply; judging by what I could see ahead, I would continue to do so for some time.

I came abruptly to a natural clearing, no more than a narrow cleavage in the thick growth and, with less sense than caution, stood upright to take a couple of deep breaths; I was fortunate to get away with my scalp; the bullet howled past my left ear with no more than an inch to spare. I legged it across the clearing like a demented ostrich and once again hurled myself into the undergrowth. The bastard had known about that clearing and had been waiting, gun trained, for me to surface.

Away to the left and slightly above me, I heard the sudden sharp snap of a twig. I raised my head. Between the trees I caught the slightest sign of a movement, as if he had frozen into immobility as the twig snapped beneath his foot. I stared at the spot without blinking until my eyes watered. He was there, I was certain of it; something lighter in colour, more solid than its surroundings. Slowly I raised my gun, gripping the butt firmly in both hands; I squinted along the sights and gently squeezed the trigger. The explosion made my head ring. The Walther had more kick than I had expected and the shot went wide but it set the game running. The solid mass I had aimed at plunged away through the undergrowth.

Following up my advantage, I charged off after him, even more careless now that I had him on the run. It had never occurred to me that there might be more than one of them. There was.

He stood hunched and unlovely, immediately in my path.

I juddered to a standstill and we stood looking at each other for an endless moment. He was short and squat in a black oilskin and gum boots and was in charge of a face that should have gone back to the drawing board long since. He carried no weapon, but with a set of hands like those attached to the ends of his simian arms, who needed weapons? An untidy mass of greasy black hair hanging low all but extinguished his eyes, but not enough for me not to realise that they were just about the most unpleasant eyes I had ever had the misfortune to look upon. My gun was trained at a point midway between them. My ears told me that his companion, the one with the gun, was making good his escape whilst this goon and I were standing glaring at each other.

"Out of my way," I growled. I said it with a snarl. In a film it would have been a good line and would have had a devastating effect; in the present situation it carried no impact whatsoever. He just stood there swinging his arms and exposing a full muster of unsanitary teeth.

With slow deliberation, I lowered the muzzle of the Walther until it pointed unwaveringly at his crutch. "I'm not joking," I warned quietly. I tightened my trigger finger. The gaiety in his expression faded as his eyes flickered nervously in the direction of the finger's whitening knuckle. Perhaps I really did look as if I meant what I was saying: a sudden glint of fear was in his eyes. "Don't tangle with me, there's a good lad," I pressed on. "I've no quarrel with you"—except that you're such an ugly sod—"only with your friend up there. And he's gone and left you in the shit, hasn't he?"

At that moment, from somewhere above, a car engine burst into life; there came the grinding of gears, a roar as someone's foot stamped down on an accelerator; tyres screamed and the sound drew away with a wrench, fading quickly into silence.

The nasty eyes were back on mine and there we were again, facing each other like a couple of bookends. I was beginning to wonder just how long either of us would be able to keep it up without laughing when, all at once, he waggled his hands, looked warily at the gun, raised his massive shoulders and muttering something in Welsh, clearly extremely rude, took off precipitately down the hillside, crashing his way through the undergrowth like a wild boar. In a couple of seconds he had disappeared.

It had been an easy victory but had nothing to do with me. I patted the Walther on the muzzle and shoved it away in my pocket. I ploughed onwards and upwards. Somewhere in the vicinity was a road, or at least something sturdy enough to carry a car.

Within a couple of minutes I had reached it, a narrow tree-lined track, no tarmac but wider than a footpath. On the far side and facing me through the trees as I broke out of the scrub, the ground fell away to a breathtaking vista of rolling hills and white, mist-compacted valleys; the sky seen through a latticework of interwoven branches was pastel blue and after the murky passage of that hideous climb blazed with light. I remember thinking that with the trees in leaf the sky would be almost invisible.

The dirt road, churned up and black with recent tyre tracks, fell away sharply to the left, hugging the side of the ridge.

I looked down the way I had come. Wanhope snuggled comfortably in the shallow niche cut into the hillside; as the crow flew it was no more than five hundred yards distant—an easy shot with a rifle. The road beyond was lower, and invisible. He must have been shooting from about the position where I now stood, and taken off to lower ground when I moved.

For a couple of minutes, I prowled to and fro searching the verge of the track and presently found what I was looking for: a couple of spent rifle shells. I examined them: 7.92. Fired, at a guess, from something like a German Gewehr 43—a relic of the war perhaps. A formidable weapon in anybody's book of arguments. The use of such a weapon against me put me on the boil again. I might just have been willing to forgive a pistol or a revolver, or even a Lee-Enfield .303, but not a bloody great gas-operated semiautomatic Gewehr 43.

Peevishly I pocketed the shells and was on the point of retracing my steps to Wanhope when something else caught my eye, something green, caught, like Abraham's ram, in the thicket. Knee-deep I waded through the soggy bracken and retrieved it carefully between finger and thumb.

What is it Henry V says? "I was not angry . . . until this instant." The same went for me, too. If there is a white anger, I knew it then as I stared at the thing in my hand. I had last seen it perched on the bulbous head of George Morton; a misshapen, green tweed hat.

Distantly, perhaps across the valley, still lost in the mist, a car's engine muttered. A shadow wheeled slowly across the sun. I heard the plaintive mewing cry and squinted upwards. Almost motionless on a rising thermal of air, the great bird hung patiently in the pastel sky, its outthrust head moving slowly to and fro, quartering the territory with practical diligence.

5

The splintered remains of the china wasp crunched beneath my feet. The place looked and smelled like a slaughterhouse; blood seemed to be everywhere, smearing the window, glistening on the overturned table; dark splashes of it besmirched the walls, and it had flowed into the pitted and uneven surfaces of the stone floor, where it lay in quiet, glutinous pools. Who would have thought the old man to have so much blood in him? I looked down at my feet; my recent alarms and excursions on the hillside had cleansed my shoes but not my trousers; splashes of blood remained on them.

On the front doorstep, behind me, was an outward-pointing imprint of a blood-stained shoe. It could have been mine but wasn't; I had set my foot against it. The shoe which had made it was larger than mine.

Avoiding the signs of carnage, I wandered into the passage, through the kitchen and into the bathroom; the bath mat was as I had left it, a sticky mess. In the kitchen, however, a dresser drawer stood half open; I slid it out gingerly. A carving knife lay among other kitchen implements; a carving knife with a familiar bone handle. I lifted it out. It had been washed but not carefully; the thickest of policemen would have recognised those telltale stains. Brownish stains were also evident in the polished-steel sink. I frowned at the taps and wondered about fingerprints.

In the doorway of the main living room I surveyed the bloody shambles with hatred. Except for one thing, all was as I had left it. The one thing was the body. That had gone.

I was finding it quite impossible to marshal my thoughts. The events of the past hour had left me unresponsive. I was prowling about the place like a weary host after an oversuccessful party picking his way among the empty bottles and fallen glasses and wondering idly who had been responsible for this stain on the carpet and who for that, whether any of his guests has been left behind to surface on the morning after in the broom cupboard, and if those who had departed somewhat the worse for drink would arrive home safely . . . and who the bloody hell had removed that bloody dead body from the middle of the bloody room?

One thing was certain. I jerked up my head. This place was as unwholesome as a rat-infested sewer, and the sooner I got myself out of it the healthier I would be—and incidentally the longer I would live.

My worst fears concerning the obese and malignant George Morton had been realised, my dismal prognostications confirmed. The whole wretched operation stank to heaven. And it was not about to end there either. What now occupied my mind, to the exclusion of all else, was the immediate future —*my* immediate future. What had happened in this house now, inevitably, concerned me, whether I cared to admit it or not. There was no way in which I would be allowed to turn my back and walk away. None.

I left the house warily, pulling the door to; since I had blown away the lock, there was no way of securing it. With hands thrust aggressively in my raincoat pockets, the left gripping the cold hard comfort of the Walther, I tramped noisily down the drive, the tremor between my shoulder blades betraying the knowledge that my departure was not unnoticed. I had considered holing up in the house until after dark and then making good my escape; but whoever was watching me at this moment was more familiar with the terrain than I was, and stumbling about in the darkness would only have placed me at a greater disadvantage. This way, at least I should have the satisfaction of seeing the ground as it came up to hit me.

Rounding the hairpin drive, I flicked a furtive eye over the house and the ground beyond it; not a vestige of movement; the bland, pastel-blue sky; black, skeletal trees etched against it; nothing stirred. At the end of the driveway I stalked the sturdy trunk of the elm tree like a hunter closing on his prey; an army could lie in ambush behind it.

There was nothing, no one.

Negotiating the fallen branch was the worst moment; high-stepping over the obstacle like a chicken in a barnyard and coping with the tangle of knee-high twigs and lesser branches, I presented a perfect target and was in no position to take to my heels should the necessity have arisen. Again, nothing showed itself.

By the time I was on the road I had begun to perk up a little. Not a lot, for recent events had so shaken me that my normally sanguine spirits had plunged to an unprecedented low; confusion and fright, coupled with sheer rage, had crippled my reasoning faculties and reduced me to little more than a perambulating vegetable whose sole motivation was that most primitive of human instincts, survival—plus of course the urge to shake the dust of that hideous house from my shoes.

Now that Wanhope was behind me, I found myself looking forward to exchanging a friendly nod or two with an ordinary fellow human being going about his daily business with no threat in his eye or gun in his pocket; on the other hand of course the mere sight of me, looking like a participant in a horror movie, might easily send him screaming back to wherever he had come from.

I had caught a glimpse of myself in a mirror back there: my face and hands wore a fine tracery of scratches interspersed with occasional deeper gashes some of which still seeped blood, and my raincoat was a virtual write-off, its additional air holes the least of its problems. Being of that provocative dun colour considered by manufacturers to be the ultimate word in masculine rainwear, the fact that it had fought its way through thickets, rolled in leaf mould and thick black mud—to say nothing of standing idly by whilst a dying man had splattered it with his life's blood—all this had done little to improve its image. Even Julie Remington's Oxfam shop would need to be hard-pressed to offer it to a gullible public on the bargain-of-the-week rail. I removed it and carried it over an arm, the Walther in the pocket crashing now and again against my knee.

I still wondered about that gun. If it had been George Morton's intention to use me for target practice, it would seem, on the face of things, an unintelligent move on his part to supply me with a loaded gun so that I could, with any luck, return his fire. Face value, however, I was beginning to appreciate, was not something to be associated with George Morton.

The sun was high and bright and the day was turning into something quite pleasant. All the same, I was surprised to register as I lurched downhill that the mist in the valley on my left had not yet cleared and stretched away to further distant hills in a shimmering lake of white lather. I glanced at my watch. Twelve-forty. A plan was beginning to form in my mind. My reluctance to return to the Dragon before making myself more presentable persuaded me that a trip into Cardigan might have its advantages; I could clean myself up, get a shave, buy some new pants and a coat of some sort, and then ring up Julie and get her to drive over and meet me; with her help I might profitably broaden my knowledge of the local inhabitants and their peculiarities. She would, of course, preface all by telling me to go home before I got myself killed; admirable advice to which, twenty-four hours ago, I might have acceded. Other considerations had now taken precedence. First, there was Julie herself and what she and I intended to do about each other. Second, there was my fury and frustration over what I had endured during the morning. Being unprepared to limp back over the border with my tail between my legs, even should I be allowed to do so, I had conceived a determination to run George Morton to ground and impart a few well-chosen words in his ear, or, if there wasn't time for that, a well-directed bullet in his fat and misshapen head. As a prelude to which, I needed to talk to someone local, to sort out things and people in my mind. In spite of having established a bridgehead of sorts with Michael Davies, a further exchange of confidences with that latter-day imitation of Christ was not one of my priorities.

A car was coming down behind me quite fast—too fast, I remember thinking. Hugging the low hedge on my left, I scanned the bend in the road ahead to check the absence of oncoming traffic and, standing aside, turned back to wave the vehicle on. Only then did I realise that its precipitate course was set to include me. Hasty decisions are not usually in my line but I took one then. I stepped smartly back, fell foul of the hedge and executed a neat backward somersault into the void below; as I fell, I remembered hoping that it was neat, because if it wasn't, Andrew Elliot would make me do it again. The car missed me by literally a couple of inches, bombarding me with earth and pebbles. Agonisingly my shoulder struck a projection; I heard an unseemly belch as my lungs emptied themselves of air; I rolled, hung for a moment, and dropped again, my hands lashing out frantically to grasp anything which might happen to lie in their way; there was nothing and I continued to plunge downwards, engulfed by an ever-increasing avalanche of earth and stones. Blue sky and black earth reeled ridiculously, trees soared and flattened, a small screeching animal leapt from my path.

Solid ground came up and hit me with a crunching thud. I rolled again and my ribs seemed to cave in as they brought my crablike momentum abruptly to a halt. As consciousness left me, I could hear, above the sputtering falling of earth and pebbles, the grating snarl of an engine being thrust cruelly into reverse. . . .

Through the shifting murk of semiconsciousness, I became aware of slow and careful footsteps slithering among the treacherous shale. Panic gripped me. I tried to fight against the wild, insistent waves of pain which were engulfing me. Darkness closed in, and then the light again, red against tender eyelids. Silence. The blood pulsed in my ears. Someone was breathing nearby, harshly through an open mouth. I slitted open an eye. He was standing over me, less than a yard away. Rubber boots, brown corduroys, brass-buckled belt, donkey jacket . . . my eyes blurred. Now the breathing was nearer as he squatted, bending over me . . . my focus returned. Through the shifting haze, the two great bulging eyes of the gargoyle barman . . .

I was being carried, slung over a shoulder like a sack of potatoes, a powerful arm encircling me, merciless against my bruised ribs. Twigs and branches clawed at my back. I watched a pair of blood-stained hands swinging below me, realising slowly that they were my own . . . beneath them the measured careful strides of black rubber boots . . . the ground sliding stealthily away. . . .

I stared incuriously at a cracked, pink-washed ceiling. From a lampholder in the centre of it, a length of flex led my eye to a small table beside me on which stood a pink-shaded lamp, half a glass of water and a packet of Disprin.

I was in a narrow iron bed covered with a pink eiderdown. The room was also narrow, and also pink; as far as the eye could see, everything was pink; pink curtains, pink striped wallpaper; I couldn't see the floor covering, but I was willing to lay odds that it was pink. In a multichambered manor house this would be called the Pink Room. I was in no aristocratic country seat, however. Neat, clean and sparsely furnished, I judged the room to be rarely used—probably the spare bedroom. On the wall facing the end of the bed hung one of those framed and uncomfortable texts so dear to the hearts of our Victorian forebears. Amidst a flurry of pink roses sprouting on cruelly thorned stems, black Old English lettering warned: *Curse God and Die.* That was a new one on me; I thought it a little creepy. Turning my head, I encountered another, which stated simply: *In All Labour There Is Profit.* Untrue, I thought, turning my head again, but more warily, to ascertain whether the pain was a figment of my imagination. It was not. My head was pounding like an iron foundry at full blast.

I eyed the Disprin on the side table and wondered whether I had the fortitude to stretch an arm in their direction.

At that moment, the door to my right squeaked open a couple of inches and a bright eye was applied to the crack. I grunted, and the door opened wider to admit a soft-faced, smiling woman of about fifty with a bunch of pepper-and-salt hair tied up in an untidy bun just off-centre of her head; her sleeves were rolled above her elbows, and a damp-looking plastic apron displayed a brightly coloured picture of Paddington Bear eating a marmalade sandwich. She looked as if she might be in the middle of the week's washing, and was indeed drying her hands on a towel as she came in.

She nodded kindly at me. "Good, you are awake." She spoke with a delightful lilting Welsh accent. "How are you feeling, then? Or is it too soon to know?"

When I answered with a further grunt, I began to wonder whether I had lost the power of speech.

"There now, don't talk," she interrupted. "I just looked in to see if you was all right, see. Rest now. The doctor said for you to rest."

"Doctor?" I had broken the spell.

"You had a bad upset. We were worried lest you had damaged yourself badly, but you will be happy that all is well. Bruises and cuts but nothing serious, thank God. The doctor said you need to rest properly, so we took the liberty of putting you to bed; I hope you don't mind." She lowered her eyes. "The doctor undressed you; men are so modest, you see."

"How long have I been here?"

"Not so long. It's just gone two. I came to see whether you would like some soup. It will make you feel better."

"You're very kind."

She smiled. "Not at all, you are most welcome. Our name is Evans; I am Annie and my man is Will, Will Evans. Our farm is just below where you had your accident; Emrys found you and brought you to us—Emrys Williams, that is. He was afraid lest you had cracked your poor ribs, but they are quite in order—just bruised."

"I'm grateful."

"I will go now and fetch soup. Have some aspirin, do your head good."

She came round to the table and popped three Disprin into the glass of water, swirling the foaming pellets around as they dissolved. I concentrated with difficulty on her apron. *Life,* it said, *is like a Marmalade Sandwich. You only get out what you are prepared to put into it.* Quite right, too; much better than *Curse God and Die.*

Annie Evans was speaking. "Emrys thinks you were knocked over by a motor car."

"Over the edge, yes."

She clicked her tongue sympathetically and handed me the glass. "There, drink up like a good boy."

Disprin not being one of my favourite drinks I made a face as I swallowed it; she chuckled happily as she smoothed the pillows. "I never thought I would have a famous film star in my bed, and that's a fact. I recognised you, see? Moment I saw your poor face I knew. On holiday, are you?"

"Not really, no."

She seemed to sense that I was not eager for further confidences and, taking the glass, went back to the door. She smiled over her shoulder. "Perhaps you will sign my book for me before you go? That would be lovely."

"Mrs. Evans . . ." I eased myself higher on the pillow. ". . . er—are you on the telephone? I was supposed to be meeting someone this afternoon. Could I get a message through, perhaps?"

Her smile broadened. "Oh yes, Miss Julie Remington. She is coming here as soon as ever she has finished her rounds. A bonny girl," and she went off, nodding knowingly to herself.

I stared after her, wondering whether the whereabouts of the strawberry mark on my inner left thigh was by this time being noised abroad in the village.

Under the eiderdown I was stripped down to my Y fronts. Peering around the tiny room, I could see no sign of the rest of my clothing. There was no chance of a hasty getaway even had I felt capable of one. The fact that someone had called a doctor and had even thought of contacting Julie put my present hosts in the category of goodies. Did it follow that Emrys Williams was also of that persuasion? Or was he, with a face like his, up to some nefarious esotericism all his own? However, what's in a face? Quasimodo, we are led to believe, had a heart of gold beating away beneath his misshapen doublet.

So what had Emrys Williams been doing prowling around Wanhope at the very moment that someone was taking the life of Mr. G. Mathews? And whilst I was about it, where were Mr. G. Mathews' earthly remains, and who had removed them, and why?

This was a fortuitous moment for the reappearance of Annie Evans with a tin tray bearing a bowl of vegetable soup and a couple of chunks of stone-ground bread. She helped me into an upright position and dumped the tray firmly on my lap. "There, t'will do you good. Eat it up like a good boy, and then we'll see—"

A small man wearing a cloth cap and a grubby waistcoat over a collarless shirt put his head in the door. He clutched a smouldering pipe in his hand. "Oh," said Annie, clearly put out, "this is my husband, Will." Will nodded and politely removed his cap. "And put that old pipe away," she added in a loud aside. "It'll stink the place out."

His face was brown and weather-beaten, but only up to that point where the cap normally rested: above it the skin was pale pink, the line of demarcation quite vivid, as if he had forgotten to make up his forehead.

I mumbled my pleasure and thanks at finding myself in his home and hoped I would soon be able to remove myself. He shrugged, smiled, nodded, resumed his cap and left, his wife clucking indulgently after him. "Curiosity killed the cat, see? He has been dying to come in all morning. Eat your soup, *bach*, before it gets cold." At the door she said, "I'm drying your clothes and trying to scrub off some of the mud. They will need to go to the cleaners." She hesitated. "That's not a real pistol in your mack pocket, is it? I said to Will, no it's not a real one, he's an actor, see. But he said not to touch just in case."

My heart turned over, an awesome vision overwhelming me of Annie peering down the barrel of the Walther and tugging on the trigger to prove the thing was a toy. "He's right," I said shortly. "Not to touch, please."

Her simple kindness together with the wholesome soup did much to revive me. A soporific warmth began to creep over me; the voluptuous feather-stuffed eiderdown engulfed me and, surrendering to its comfort, I embarked woozily on a minor trip down memory lane.

I thought about the car. A Volvo, of that I was sure; the diagonal trim across the radiator was unmistakable. About its colour I was not so confident. My eye had caught and held it for no longer than it would take a camera shutter to transfer an image to film. My retina, less photographic and less reliable, was reasonably convinced that the colour had been a lightish grey or blue, fawn perhaps. No, not fawn. Blue, light blue. And there had been something else, something unusual. A badge, bright in the sun. Not the yellow of an AA badge nor yet the blue of the RAC; this had red in it somewhere; a symbol easily recognisable. What the hell was it? A cross of some sort. A Maltese cross, black on a red and white ground. That was it. Vividly my mind's eye recaptured it quite clearly now, hurtling towards me, a blue Volvo with a Maltese cross on its radiator where one might have expected an AA badge.

A scratching at the door heralded the reappearance of Annie Evans' motherly features. "Here she is, sir." She collected the tray and beat a discreet retreat before I could open my mouth. Julie, anxious and appealing, stood in the doorway.

I stretched a hand to her and she came in, closing the door, taking my hand and leaning down to kiss my cheek; she touched it with a gentle finger. "Your face is cut. You were knocked down by a car, they said. Is that right?"

"As right as makes no odds." She was sliding out of a black leather jacket. "What happened to that lascivious riding mack of yours?"

She folded the leather jacket over the foot of the bed. "You were so mean about it I left it in the car." She took in the room's décor with wide, incredulous eyes. "I'm glad to find you in the pink," she chuckled, and added in a stage whisper, "Did she also make you drink 'lavender-water tinged with pink'?"

I grinned and my jaw hurt. "Please try not to make me laugh. I have a headache and several bent ribs."

"May I see?" She assumed a vet's face.

"No, you may not. I'm stark naked under all this." She smiled broadly as I adroitly changed the subject: "Have you finished your duty calls?"

"All except this one." She settled herself at the end of the bed. "Are you going to tell me about it?"

"I don't want to involve you."

"You haven't anyone else."

"That's true."

"Did you find your Mr. Mackintosh?"

"I found someone; but he was dead before he hit the ground."

She listened in silence as I told her the story of the visit to Wanhope, finishing up with the car sequence, my descent into the abyss and the reawakening in Annie Evans' pink spare bedroom.

She sat as if sculptured, her denimed ankles demurely crossed, knees apart, a hand poised on each, her back upright against the foot of the iron bedstead. In all but the most improbable aspects she might have been a Yogi at meditation. I regarded her for some time in silence, then said, "Speak to me."

Her only reaction was to shift her eyes from wherever they had been back to mine. "They tried to kill you."

"Several times."

"Why?"

I shrugged the question away. "Do you know anyone called Mathews?"

"Not offhand, no."

I described the dead man as best I could, in the hope that she might be persuaded to recognise him, but she shook her head. "He's not local, I'm sure."

The man with the ape arms, up on the hillside, produced a more positive response. "There's a chap called Pithy who answers to that description. He lives on his own up beyond the beacon and is generally recognised, if one has to be brutal about it, as a sort of village idiot. Was he a bit potty, do you think?"

"More than a bit, I'd say. He certainly seemed—I don't know how to put it—'uninvolved' is as good a word as any, I suppose. Though I must say he looked pretty homicidal for a moment or two. He must have known damn well I wasn't going to shoot him down—I made beastly noises and did a bit of coarse acting, but even he couldn't have been fooled. He could have run me down like a bull elephant if he'd wanted to. But he just stood and glared at me and then dived over the edge."

She nodded. "Could be Pithy. Not the prettiest sight."

"I've seen prettier."

"And it was your George Morton shooting at you?"

"Unless someone else planted that hat, yes it was. And he's not *my* George Morton."

With some difficulty she unwound herself, slid off the bed, and went thoughtfully over to the window. Some way off, a dog was barking with irritating regularity.

"I believe," she said at last, "that Emrys Williams is on the side of the angels."

"You'd never think so to look at him."

"He can't help the way he looks." She came and stood over me. "It was he who told me you were here and what had happened. Why should he do that if he wasn't on our side? It was also Emrys who brought you in from the cold." She sat on the edge of the bed.

"It was also Emrys," I reminded her a trifle sourly, "whom I saw skulking about the road a few minutes after someone had been stabbed to death at Wanhope. And I suppose he just *happened* to be on the spot when I was elbowed off the public highway?"

Glumly we stared at the pink striped walls. "So what happens now?" she asked.

"I'm still thinking."

"Police?"

"No."

"They'll have to know some time."

"Why?"

"Someone's been killed."

"Prove it. Where's the *corpus delicti?* On the other hand, there's quite a lot of blood about and a fairly comprehensive selection of my fingerprints. I also shot the lock off the front door with a gun for which I have no licence. I don't think I'd come out of a police investigation too well."

"I thought private investigators were supposed to wear gloves."

"That's the criminal classes. Private investigators are supposed not to touch things."

"And you touched everything?"

"Absolutely everything. Do you know something?"

She nodded. "You haven't got a leg to stand on."

"Right."

"Now is the time," she said thoughtfully, "for you to beetle off back home."

"And pretend it never happened?" She gave a silent shrug. "Since eleven o'clock this morning or thereabouts I have narrowly escaped liquidation at least four times."

"Next time they might succeed."

"If they want to knock me off they can do it just as easily in London."

"Perhaps they only want to put the wind up you."

"They want to kill me and I want to know why. I haven't done anything to them. Don't you think I owe it to myself?"

"Not if you're going to get yourself . . . liquidated in the process."

I sighed. "You're being very difficult."

She nodded. "Good."

Silence. "I think I want to get up."

"You can't. You're naked."

"That could be remedied."

She moved to the door. "I shall ring for your clothes." She hesitated for a second, then turned and looked at me thoughtfully. "Since you are a captive audience, so to speak, and I'm not likely to have another such opportunity, I wouldn't mind saying a few words about last night." She leaned against the doorjamb and studied her Wellington boots with care. "I've been thinking . . ."

"And?"

"Two things: I've been thinking that life with you could be a lot of fun." She looked up and met my eyes. "But I'm not ready to pop into bed with you. Not yet. If that sounds prudish, or even presumptuous, I'm sorry, it's not intended to be either; it's meant as a compliment. Please don't misunderstand me; I'm not untouched by human hands; it's just that with you it would be nice if it were something better. . . . I just don't want to spoil anything. Also I do a job which means a lot to me. If a woman's capable of doing something worthwhile I think she should do it. Cooking meals and rearing children to the exclusion of all else is not for me. I know I'm jumping the gun and you haven't even mentioned any of these things, but I know what you're thinking. It's better to say it all now so we know what's what. Last night you caught me unawares and you know it, defences down and not a little tiddly. I don't mind; may it happen again and often, so long as we both stay on opposite sides of the bed—for the moment. I just don't want you to think I'm a tease. When we get to know each other . . ." The sentence hung around unfinished. "I don't think there's anything more to say except that I think you're a steaming hot dish and I'll go and get your clothes without another word."

She nodded, gave me a quirky smile and was gone.

There was, strangely, no feeling of disappointment. Indeed, the disappointment would have been there had she thrown herself on the bed. Sex for its own sake was a familiar companion, fun while it lasted, but downright burdensome when one was reclothed and inhaling the postcoital cigarette. For my part, remembering my marital experiences, the body—like patriotism —was not enough.

With the need to move approaching, I initiated a tentative exploration of my bruised body. I had survived the morning's excesses remarkably well. Everything hurt like hell, particularly the shoulder I had bounced off, but at least the collarbone was intact, a fact which astounded me. At school, in the hurly-burly of the rugger field, it was always going. All it ever needed was for a muddied oaf to pass that nasty, greasy ball into my keeping and I would be pinned to the earth by a rabble of sweating maniacs; then would come that familiar small snap, the agonising screech of pain followed by blind oblivion and then several joyous weeks off school, recuperating.

When I breathed deeply, my ribs poked at me painfully. Legs and feet seemed pretty sound, head ached and jaw hurt when I smiled.

So breathing and laughter were out.

Julie reentered with what appeared to be the discarded remnants of a jumble sale. "They've been on the boiler," she explained, "so they're bone dry and utterly intractable; you'll just have to avoid being seen in public places until they've softened up a little." She laid them across the bed, reading off each article like a quartermaster sergeant. "Trousers, one pair, private eye, for the use of, one shirt, one singlet, jumper, jacket and one ruined raincoat, filthy and riddled by bullets."

I stuck my finger through the bullet holes. "I'll charge him extra for those."

When I began unloading the pockets, Annie's pink eiderdown took on the appearance of the white-elephant stall at the aforementioned jumble sale. Pride of place went to the Walther, then came the sealed package, the tab from the murdered man's coat sleeve, the key to my hotel room, a blood-stained handkerchief, two spent rifle shells, the damp green-tweed travesty of a hat and lastly the letter purloined from the dead man's pocket. "Looks like the contents of Pandora's box," I said, staring morosely at the collection. I picked up the letter. "St. Dogmaels. Where's that?"

"Near the coast, a few miles away, near Cardigan." She took the envelope. "Mr. George Mathews. The dead man? The one you found?"

I held up the wrist tab. "This also belonged to him. That vicious dog of yours ripped it off his sleeve when he was burglarising my car last night."

"Burglarising?"

I shrugged. "If you can believe what they say on the telly. How is Bruno, by the way?"

"Stumping about on three legs and right as rain." She was still on about the envelope. "Garrach Cottage, St. Dogmaels, South Wales. Posted in London E1 last Friday." She peered inquisitively into the envelope. "There's a letter inside."

"That's what envelopes are for."

"Don't you think we ought to take a quick look?"

I wrested the envelope from her grasp. "That is a private letter."

I extracted the single sheet of matching paper.

I read aloud.

"Dear George,

"We thought you'd want to know that Doris got married. At last. On Tuesday. Registers office of course. We was going to invite you but Grandad said he thought you wouldn't want to come with your feet being what they are and it being such a long way and you not caring a lot for Doris anyway. We didn't have nowhere to put you up anyway. She married a bricklayer named Alfred Hitchcock—isn't that comical? He's thirty-three. So now she's Doris Hitchcock. If you want her address you can have it but I don't suspect you'll want to write. They've gone to Leigh on Sea for their honeymoon, next to Southend-on-Mud. Hope this finds you as it leaves us. No other news. Granddad's poorly again but that's no news is it? It's his head again.

"Sister Amy

"P.S. Fancy going to Southend for your honeymoon!!!!
"P.S.S. Why don't you send her a little something, though? She'd like that.
You don't have to spend much.
"P.S.S.S. Lots of love to I."

I replaced the letter in the envelope. "Writing sketchy, spelling original;
an ordinary run-of-the-mill family letter. Not a clue in sight."

"Except that we've got his address."

I nodded. "We've got his address. And the initial of his wife, or girlfriend,
or brother or whatever."

"Poor Grandad's head; hope it gets better." She took up the sealed packet
between finger and thumb and eyed it suspiciously, then, putting it to her
ear, she shook it gently.

"Careful," I said, "it might go off!" When she dropped it on the bed, I
retrieved it. "My curiosity is killing me."

"You're not going to open it?"

"Well, I'm not taking it back, that's for sure. At least it may tell us what's
going on. I want to know what is so important about it to merit someone
getting a knife in his guts and me getting shot at."

I broke the seals.

"Do be careful," she whispered, backing off a little. "It could be a bomb."

By that time I couldn't have cared whether it was a bomb or a can of
baked beans. I snapped the string and ripped off the wrapping. A familiar
blue and white carton stared up at me. We exchanged glances. Gingerly I
lifted the lid and stared blankly at the contents. I slowly upended the box.
Ten cellophaned packets containing presumably twenty cigarettes each cas-
caded on to the pink eiderdown.

6

Dressed and in my right mind, I stood at the window idly watching Will
Evans trundle a leisurely wheelbarrow across the cracked paving of his overgrown little yard; a thin wraith of blue smoke straggled from the pipe between his teeth. On her knees in a neat square of kitchen garden, Annie

grubbed in the brown earth with a trowel, a half-filled basket of something on the ground beside her. Her husband's shadow passed over her as she worked; neither acknowledged the other's presence; each was immersed, each secure in workaday familiarity.

The smallholding was ramshackle and haphazard, and its buildings, some badly in need of repair, encroaching messily on to the yard. Chickens strutted and pecked; a gaggle of geese, necks craned, looking neither to right nor left, waddled importantly about their business; behind a low wall were the fat backs of rooting pigs; on the stump of a felled tree a smiling black Labrador sat sentinel.

My eyes slid upwards to where the road clung to the hillside.

"Bodies only disappear in second-feature films," I muttered dispiritedly. " 'But there *was* a body, Inspector. I saw it with my own eyes.' 'I don't doubt it for a moment, sir. Fortunately for us, sir, dead bodies are not in the habit of getting up and walking away. However, should he happen to return I'm sure you will be the first to give the station another ring, sir.' "

"You should have been an actor," Julie approved from behind me.

I turned away from the window. "I should have remained an actor." I eyed the cigarettes on the bed. "Perhaps they're stuffed with heroin."

"Could be."

"That bed would be worth a fortune if they were." I picked up a cigarette and sniffed at it. "Smells like tobacco." I stuck it in my mouth. "Got a light?" She delved around in the pocket of her leather jacket and produced some matches.

"Careful it doesn't explode."

I lit the cigarette, holding it delicately between two fingers like a ten-year-old taking his first drag in the school lavatory. "It tastes like tobacco," I said, savouring the acrid smoke.

"Can I have a go?"

She took a genteel puff and coughed. "Horrid! Yuk! Old army socks."

"It *is* tobacco." I gave her a bleak look and a pink ashtray. "I've been put upon, haven't I? Set up. A fall guy. Aunt Sally. Those," I said, wagging a finger, "are cigarettes, ordinary, common-or-garden cigarettes."

"We've only tried one."

"You're welcome to the other hundred and ninety-nine. "I'm satisfied." I examined the carton, the packets, the foil and the wrappings for anything unusual; a mark, a sign, a cryptic note: Dear Mr. Savage, So who's a patsy then? I drew a blank.

"I saw a film on television," said Julie, "where the stamp on the envelope was worth a fortune and nobody could see it because it was staring them in the face."

"We haven't got a stamp."

"Sealing wax?"

I powdered the wax into the box. "Powdered sealing wax."

"Microdots?"

"You've seen too much television."

"So now what?"

I thought for a moment. "Well, the first thing I have to do is to collect my car, which is still sitting up there on the mountainside, I hope, and go and buy myself some new clothes. I can't go rollicking about the countryside looking like this."

"You're staying, then?"

"Until I've seen this through, yes. I'll ring Mitch to tell her I'm still alive. If I'm not, you can ring her."

"Where will you start? You've got nothing to go on."

I shrugged. "There's always Mathews' address; that's a start. And I wouldn't mind a quiet word with Emrys Williams."

She was silent for a moment and then said, "Suggestion?"

"What?"

"Come and stay at my place. More private than the Dragon, handier for the telephone, because you'll know it's only me listening. Also you won't have to pay anything and you can charge George Morton, Esquire, top hotel rates."

"What about Father?"

She waved her father aside. "He'll not mind. He might even welcome a new face. Apart from which, since I want to know more about you, what better place could I choose than under my own roof?" She took my hand. "How does that grab you?"

I sought out Annie Evans, who stood on her toes and gave me a wet kiss on the cheek and a book to sign: I scrawled my erstwhile name and a grateful message; she refused to consider payment for her hospitality. "You just drop in any time you like, my dear, that will be payment enough. You'll always be welcome."

Outside, Julie said, "If we pick up your car now we could be in Cardigan before the shops close."

"What for?"

"You wanted some new clothes, didn't you?"

We climbed into her Morris Traveller and drove off downhill until a sharp right turn shunted us upwards on to the road above which lay Wanhope; after a bit, the road widened, and there, pressed soulfully against the hillside, lurked the deserted Triumph, looking cold and desolate. I changed cars and wound down the window. "If they've read that second-feature film script I mentioned, they've drained the brake fluid, cut the cables and buggered the steering."

She grinned. "In that case I'd better go first so you can lean on me."

They evidently didn't attend the same films, for everything seemed to be in working order; she gave a bit of trouble starting, but then she always did and I would have been lost without those cautionary coughs and grunts which I had come to recognise and respect.

A turn in the narrow confines of the road was a hazardous, six-point undertaking, faultlessly executed by me, bungled twice by Julie, who was clearly more at home in a surgery than a car. When our noses were pointing downhill, she leaned out of her window. "We'll leave your car at my place and go into Cardigan in mine, all right?"

In less than ten minutes, I had parked the Triumph in a tumbledown barn at the rear of her home and was climbing into the Morris beside her. "I won't go in now," she said. "Bruno would only want to come with us and he's not really good at the shopping."

"I could go on my own. I'm quite capable, in an uncapable sort of way."

"I'd like to come," she said, backing recklessly out on to the road.

A red, bloated sun was bathing the landscape with flares of dull crimson and deeper shadow, etched around with blackened trees. In the valley slightly below us the river Teifi flowed, like blood.

" '. . . and my imaginations are as foul as Vulcan's stithy . . . ,' " I intoned softly.

She slid a pair of dark glasses on to her nose. "What?"

"Quoting, just quoting."

"From?"

"*Hamlet*. Who else?" I nodded at the windscreen. "Hellfire. Quite impressive. Like a smithy going at full blast. It could only be old Vulcan." I glanced at my watch.

"What time is it?" she asked.

"Three-thirty."

After a few minutes she said, "We could come back via St. Dogmaels if you like. Take a look at What's-his-name's place. It's only a little out of our way."

I shook my head emphatically. "No. They'll be shooting at you next. That I won't have."

"Oh, come on! Shooting in St. Dogmaels?"

"Don't mock," I remarked a trifle tartly. "We've had a fair sample of it this morning in the middle of nowhere."

She made a couple of impatient noises, and I thought at first that they were directed at me, but then I noticed she was peering crossly and intermittently into her rear mirror. "I hate people sitting up my exhaust pipe," she grumbled. "Why the hell doesn't he pass?" She wound down the window and made an impatient hand signal urging the driver on.

I glanced over my shoulder and went cold. "Oh, Christ!"

"What?"

"It's him. The one who ran me down. The Volvo. Can you see his radiator in the mirror or is he too close?"

She put her foot down gently. The car surged forward. "What am I looking for?"

"A Maltese cross. A badge."

A second later she said quietly. "One Maltese cross."

"He must have been with us ever since we left the farm. You can't outstrip him in this, can you? He'll have quite a burst of speed under that bonnet."

"I can try."

"What about turnings?"

"There's one coming up on the right. Goes to Llandygwydd. I know a farm up there. If we can get enough headway we could disappear for a bit. Try?"

"Try."

Without another word she slammed her foot down violently and the ancient Traveller streaked ahead like a front-runner. There was no sign of a turning, woodland to the right and to the left, the river now running parallel to the road, but she obviously knew what she was up to. I took a hasty look through the rear windows. The driver of the Volvo had been taken unawares by our sudden acceleration; a good hundred yards now separated us, but even as I looked, the distance began to close.

"Hold on to your hat," muttered Julie.

With an awesome scream of brakes, we took a sharp right turn at a speed I did not care to guess at, swung steeply into a heart-stopping skid during which the car, teetering drunkenly on two wheels, made a vain attempt to roll over, and then attempted to continue its turn through 180 degrees. Thrown off balance by the violence of the manoeuvre I pitched on to Julie's shoulder and received the point of her elbow full in my chest as she wrestled desperately with the steering. The vehicle eventually righted itself and was brought under control. Once again her foot went down and we plunged forward. Only then did she let out a great screech of excitement, like a drunken cowboy on a Saturday night. She had actually enjoyed it. I lay like a landed whale, gasping for breath.

She was staring into the mirror and let out another sudden whoop. "He's overshot."

"He'll be back," I panted, returning to an upright position. "Do we know where we're going?"

"Hang on."

The next few minutes were sheer Keystone Cops. We shot through a gate which just happened to be open, juddered over what felt dangerously like a ploughed field, through another gate, beneath an arch which was so low that I instinctively ducked. A squawking riot of chickens parted before us like the Red Sea before the Israelites, flapping and galloping for their lives; a surprised cow stood foursquare in front of us, her mouth agape, cud forgotten—we avoided her by millimetres, rather than inches. A narrow lane, a sudden braking, a bone-jolting excursion over a cattle grid, a smooth stretch of concrete and sudden darkness; then a gentle squealing of brakes, finally silence as she switched off the ignition. The blessed stillness ticked in time to the overheated engine.

Although I couldn't see her, I was aware of the lessening of tension in her body. She let out a great sigh.

"Now," she said after a lengthy moment, "what was it you were saying about Hamlet?"

I stared ahead of me into lightening darkness. "I take back everything I said about your driving."

"I don't remember you saying anything about my driving."

"Perhaps I just thought it."

There was no sound other than the usual racket of farm animals. "Whoever he was we've shaken him off. He'll never find us here."

"Where are we?"

"In somebody's farm."

"Won't somebody mind?"

"Not if we explain." She climbed stiffly out of the car and I followed. "They probably don't even know we're here."

"I would doubt that, considering the noise we were making."

"That was somebody else's farm, not this one."

Apart from us and the Morris, the barn contained a tractor and a brand-new Range Rover. "They're not short of a penny or two," I remarked, casting an approving eye over the smart vehicle.

"They're English, that's why." She smiled. "They also have a Merc and a Bentley Continental, to say nothing of several splendid thoroughbreds tracing directly back to the Byerley Turk." As we emerged from the building, she hesitated. "On second thoughts, you know, it might be best if you don't show yourself. Somebody might recognise you, although looking like that—" She was prevented from further criticism by a distant hail. "Too late. Never mind, do a bit of coarse acting. Be a serf or something and stay in the background."

She left me hovering in the barn doorway, where I adopted a hangdog expression and a hump. The origin of the hail was a tall, metallic-looking man in a deerstalker hat, Norfolk jacket and riding breeches. Gentleman farmer, I assessed, dressed for the part. The face was grey and wedge-shaped, well-trimmed steely moustache, straight grey eyebrows; I was too distant to make out the colour of his eyes but was willing to bet they were grey. The ascot he wore instead of a tie was of plain grey silk and had a hard sheen, like zinc. He carried a walking stick under his arm like a swagger cane.

"Hello, m'dear . . ." A voice calculated for distance; Regular Army . . . retired . . . colonel probably. "What can we do for you?"

They shook hands, and though I strained my ears I could make nothing of Julie's reply. *Her voice was ever soft, gentle and low, an excellent thing in a woman*—except when she was whooping like a cowboy. He was shaking his head. "She's fine, absolutely fine. The injection worked like a charm. No bother." He threw a curious glance in my direction over her shoulder. She was muttering on and backing off slightly. "Most kind of you," he brayed in answer. "Come and have a look at her if you like; she's just about to have her feed. No? Right, then. . . ." Now he was looking at me squarely and moved a couple of paces towards me. The question in his eyes could no longer be ignored.

"Oh, sorry, Colonel," said Julie, rising to the occasion and noticing me as if for the first time. "This is Mr. Chumley, Spillers' new representative for cattle feed in these parts. We think he might eventually be centred further north, don't we, Mr. Chumley, but in the meantime I'm showing him around a bit. This is Colonel St. John Hazlitt-Martin."

"Chumley. . . ." The colonel's nod was summary but all-inclusive. The eyes were steel grey of course and took in every detail of my slovenly appearance. Even the moustache seemed to curl. Had I been in his regiment I would have been on a charge. I humped my shoulder a bit more, all but touched my forelock but stuck out a hand instead, which I knew he wouldn't touch.

He turned back to Julie. "Well, if you don't want to come up and take a look at Kingsway I'll be off. Thanks for looking in, kind of you I'm sure. Good afternoon to you, m'dear. Funny sort of afternoon, what? All red." He looked at me briefly. "Mr. . . . er . . . er . . ." He turned on his military heel and strode off, head up, chest out, stomach in, left, right, left, right. . . .

"Chumley," I said to his departing breeches.

When he was out of earshot I turned on Julie, who was giggling insanely. *"Chumley?"*

"Spelt Chol-mond-eley, of course," she snorted. "You were a bit ham, I thought. Not up to your usual standard."

"I have to be given notice of a character called Chumley. I don't even know what a Chumley looks like. And isn't it a good thing he didn't want to know about the latest developments in cattle feed?"

She was climbing into the car. "Do you want to go on to Cardigan now? They could be still hanging around."

"Oh, hell, why not. I can't drag around looking like this for the rest of my life, being put upon by superior people like you and Colonel St. John Hazlitt-Whatsit. With a name like that he should have been an organist. Can we go by another road, just in case they've taken possession of the 484?"

"We can get on to a B road from here, the 4570. It'll serve. Come on, then."

In the ever-increasing gloom, she picked her way carefully among narrow lanes and byways and eventually unearthed the 4570, which looked like any other B road; she turned confidently into it and trod firmly on the accelerator.

She said, "One of his mares, Kingsway, had a touch of the colic some weeks back, so I pretended I was checking on her. I don't think he suspected anything, do you?"

"Only me. Can you imagine Spillers having me on their payroll?"

"Why an organist?"

"What?"

"You said he should have been an organist."

"Organists have a habit of collaring the double-barrel market. Reginald Goss Custard, for example, Christopher Bowers Broadbent, J. Dudley-Holroyd, George Thalben-Ball, to name but a few. Colonel St. John Hazlitt-Martin would seem to have the edge on them all. Can't you imagine him driving the Albert Hall organ down the M1? He's Croesus around here, isn't he?"

"He's well heeled, certainly."

"How did that come about? Not from the Army, I'll bet."

"Wives, I think. Merry widows and all that. Two, I believe, if you can trust local gossip. The present one's into horses in quite a big way—mares actually, brood mares—most of my dealings are with her. She's nice enough. Not happy, though."

There was no sign of any further pursuit, and by the time we dropped down into Cardigan it was quite dark and I felt as if I had just completed a round trip on the Trans-Siberian Railway. In fact we had been on the road for little more than an hour.

The shops were surprisingly good and, being of standard size, I found most of what I needed without effort. In addition to some Levi's, a denim shirt, socks, shoes and a black polo-neck sweater, I armed myself with a splendidly sexy black trench coat with epaulettes and D rings and huge pockets to accommodate most of the junk I invariably attract to myself. Julie oohed and aahed over it for so long that I offered to buy her a crisp new riding mackintosh to offset it, on condition that she lay the Oxfam number to rest; she would have none of that, however, uttering words which amounted to the fact that rather than find herself under obligation to me she would lie down in the street and die.

We found a uniquely civilised pub in the High Street where, instead of the usual unsocial racket of a jukebox, a discreet Brahms's Fourth was being siphoned through the system. Companionably we sat together, she over a large Scotch, I with a life-preserving pineapple juice.

When we had thawed out a little and my worries could no longer be ignored, I asked, "I suppose you didn't happen to notice how many people were in that Volvo?"

She shook her head. "I was too busy breaking the law." She frowned suddenly and crossly. "Who are they? What do they want?"

The question had to be rhetorical, but I answered it nevertheless, by putting a couple of thoughts together. "Wanhope's the key, I'm sure of that. If I had hung around up there for any length of time I bet I would have learned a lot more than was good for me."

"And ended up like George Mathews."

I nodded glumly. "Very messy." I hesitated, my glass to my lips. "Too messy perhaps." I placed the glass carefully on the table. "I wonder if there's anything in that? Apart from cleaving somebody's head with an axe I can't think of a messier way of disposing of anyone. Logically, that would argue a case for unpremeditated murder; it happened on the spur of the moment, the killer, unprepared, panicked and reached for the nearest weapon—which happened to be a carving knife. To get it in the stomach, Mathews would have to be coming towards him, or vice versa." I broke off and took some refreshment. "Having struck him down, the murderer bolts; the fact that he doesn't do the job properly suggests that he doesn't care whether the man is dead or not. Now, minutes later, I appear on the scene, break into the house, the victim dies at my feet and I'm left prowling around the hillside being shot at. From the moment I arrived to the moment I got back cannot have been much more than fifteen minutes, and yet during the short time I was away the body was removed. So, assuming, of course, that murderer and whoever was shooting at me are one and the same, Ape-Arms, What's-his-name—Pithy—was not the killer."

"If Pithy was in the sort of hurry you say he was, he could have done both. He dived straight down the hillside, you said, cutting off all the corners, while you went up to the top and wandered around looking for things. . . ."

I shook my head. "The removal of the body doesn't fit the nature of the crime. Potty he may be, but if he'd stuck someone in the guts with a knife, would he really go back for the body five minutes later? Would you? I wouldn't. Certainly not with people swarming around shooting at each other."

"So what are we saying?"

"That the *corpus delicti* was removed by someone else."

"A third party?"

I nodded. "The driver of the Volvo. Why not? After which he had a go at getting rid of me because of what I had seen."

"But if he wasn't the killer, would it matter to him what you had seen?"

"I think it would, yes, if that house is the key to something else. Let's face it, it's more than a little odd that I am paid a lot of money to deliver a box of perfectly ordinary cigarettes to someone who doesn't exist. Now, why?"

She thought for a second. "To attract attention?"

"Exactly. To *draw* attention to that house." I stared at her blankly. "Again why?"

She shrugged. "To panic someone perhaps?"

I went on staring at her and then nodded slowly. "To panic someone into doing something, into showing his hand. Supposing, just for a moment, something's going on up there in that house, something nasty, and supposing that a stranger—me, Muggins—turns up out of the blue and starts asking questions: 'I'm looking for a place named Wanhope? Where is it? Who lives there? How can I get there?' In a place the size of Castellcraig, everyone knows everything before it even happens, so we can take it for granted that 'whoever it may concern' is lined up under the goalposts waiting for Muggins to convert the try."

She grinned, shaking her head. "I think I'd sooner be a vet." Then the grin vanished as quickly as it had come. "And if at first they don't succeed . . . ?"

I shrugged. "Meet your old Aunt Sally," I said with a wry smile.

"How are you feeling?" she asked, flashing her lights at a jaywalking pedestrian as we groaned our way out of the pub car park and up a steep incline into the High Street.

"Frail," I told her.

The pedestrian raised two suggestive fingers. "That's very rude," said Julie.

I wound down the window. "It would be a pleasure," I informed him quietly as we passed, "to tear your pin head from your shoulders." He responded by hitting the car with his fists; looking back, I saw him sucking at his knuckles.

"He's hurt his hand."

"Ah," she said. "Poor chap."

She wrestled with Cardigan's complicated one-way system, discovered the castle, beetled slowly over a narrow bridge spanning what I presumed to be the Teifi, and then hung about for oncoming traffic to clear before turning right on to a steeply climbing hill.

"We didn't come this way."

"No."

"And we're on the wrong side of the river."

"Yes."

I met her eye. "We're going to St. Dogmaels, aren't we?"

She nodded.

"I said no."

"I thought we might have a word with 'I,' whoever he or she is."

" 'Hello, "I,'' we've just popped in to tell you your beloved George has been killed.' "

I allowed her to drive unmolested for some time. Then I said, "Wonder who actually owns Wanhope?"

I recalled the shrouded furniture and the frightful ornaments and the large double bed which looked as inviting as one of those old Queen Elizabeth was reputed to have slept in; I remembered the cupboards I had peered into, empty except for household linen; no clothes, no shoes, nor any personal knickknacks lying around, no obvious signs of habitation. Also, of course, there was that great tree trunk lying across the driveway.

"Could be a holiday cottage," I suggested.

"If it is, it'll be easy to find out about it. I'll make some discreet enquiries. Leave it to Julie. What else have you got to do?"

"Pick up my things from the pub. Call Mitch." I hesitated and added almost as an afterthought, "I wouldn't mind ringing old Sam Birkett either."

"Who's old Sam Birkett?"

"Ex-CID. Used to be a detective inspector. We're just pub acquaintances really, not much more. His wife was a fan of mine once apparently and I've read a couple of his books. He burst into print with some of his experiences. So it's a sort of mutual admiration society. George Morton says it was he who suggested me for this job. I would like to doubt that; he could just as easily have found me in the Yellow Pages. But he *did* know that Sam and I knew each other. If Sam says Morton is okay I'd be inclined to go along with him. But it'll have to be a pretty high commendation to forgive him shooting my mack full of holes."

"You don't know that he did."

"I don't know that he didn't."

A sign slid by in the headlights, heavily obscured with mud. "St. Dogmaels," she said.

"That didn't say St. Dogmaels."

"It did under all that muck. The Welsh-language people periodically take it into their heads to daub stuff over everything that looks remotely English. Can't really blame them; they've got a language, they want to use it."

"But they're not a foreign country."

"Aren't they?"

I remembered the overwhelming sense of alienation I'd felt driving across the Severn, the warring Welsh elements, the dark unfriendly hills and the lowering hostile faces in the bar of the Dragon.

She pulled up at a brightly lit grocery store. "Don't go away."

I watched her through the shopwindow as she purchased a loaf of bread and information from the lady assistant, who took to making semaphore signals in the direction of the ceiling.

Rejoining me, Julie handed me the loaf and let in the clutch. "Straight up," she said with a theatrical Welsh lilt. "Chapel on the right, a fork on the left, see? Up a slope and down a slope—you can't miss it."

Needless to say, we did. We found the chapel and missed the fork. We backpedalled for a bit, and a few minutes later drew up at Garrach Cottage. The place was plunged in darkness, with no welcome sign on the mat.

"Home from home," murmured Julie. With the road scarcely wider than the car, she backed the Traveller carefully into a shallow niche fashioned presumably for that very purpose.

I tugged at a metal bellpull set into the wall of the tiny gabled porch and came away with the knob in my hand. Sighing heavily, Julie leaned across me and placed a finger on the button of a previously invisible bell push. Her moment of triumph was short-lived, however, for there was no answering jingle of a bell from inside. "Out of order," I whispered, indicating a scrawled notice beneath the bell push. I thumped lustily on the door. Nothing stirred.

" ' "Is there anybody there?" said the traveller, knocking at the moonlit door.' "

"What are we going to say if there is?" Julie enquired plaintively.

" 'Good evening, I've come about your husband.' "

" 'I'm not married.' "

" 'Good evening, I've come about the man you're living with.' "

I broke off abruptly as, with a mind-singeing grating sound, the door swung open. The hair at the back of my neck began to bristle, and I was only slightly mollified to hear a whinnying intake of breath from Julie beside me. The darkness was so intense that I could see nothing. The door opened further, and as I stared into the void, straining my eyes and preparing to take to my heels, I became aware of a small spectral form taking shape on the doormat—like an emission of ectoplasm at a seance.

"Hello," said Julie conversationally, more at home with tiny ghosts than I was. "Who are you?" Who indeed?

"Da's out," said a very young voice.

My heart plummeted. He had a child.

"Is your mother in?" Julie persisted.

"She's dead."

The ensuing silence indicated Julie's thoughts as well as mine.

"Would you let us come in?" said Julie at last. "You'll catch cold standing there in your nightie." Staring intently at the little pale form, I could only envy my companion's superior night vision—according to my mother, only a diet of raw carrots would do it.

Julie pushed past me and entered the house. A small voice from the darkness said, "Can you please put the light on? I can't reach. It's up here."

And there was light. I stepped over the threshold.

The child could not have been more than eight years old and small for her age. Sleep was still in her eyes as she blinked at us in the sudden glare, cornflower-blue eyes reminding me incongruously of those of the softer creatures in Disney films. She wore an ankle-length nightdress of pale pink brushed nylon decorated with blue roses; honey-blonde hair hung over her shoulders in two sturdy plaits.

I closed the door quietly. She stared up at me inquisitively. "Hello."

"Hello. Are you all alone?"

She nodded. "Da's out."

Julie took her hand. "Could we talk somewhere?"

"The kitchen's warm," said the little girl and solemnly led the way down a passage to a door at which she waited for Julie to touch another switch. The child was right. The room, heated by an Aga stove, was very warm and evidently used as a living room: apart from table and chairs and the usual kitchen equipment, there were an armchair, a television set, some books and a pile of newspapers. On the table, pathetically evocative of the absent Da, lay a pipe and a round tobacco tin.

"What's your name?" Julie asked, sitting in the comfortable chair.

"Imogen Mathews. What's yours?"

"Julie Remington. He's Mark Savage."

The child looked at me with a frown. "Savages are black."

"Not always."

"They come from Africa."

"I come from London."

"Da's been to London." She heaved herself up on to one of the kitchen chairs. "I could give you some milk if you like. Would you like some milk? It's supposed to be good for you."

Julie said, "No, thank you. Do you and your Da live here all alone?"

The little girl nodded. "Yes."

"Doesn't anyone look after you when he's not here?"

"Mrs. Thomas-on-the-Hill comes in to make the beds and cook the dinner. She looks after Da. I look after myself."

Julie's helpless eyes met mine; I shrugged my shoulders and raised my eyebrows. The child was an orphan, but there was no way in which either Julie or I could break it to her.

I said, "We were hoping to have a word with your father. You don't know where he is, I suppose?"

"He went to work this morning. He didn't say he was going to be late."

"Where does he work?"

"Poppit."

"Pardon?"

"Poppit Sands," supplied Julie. "What does he do down there?"

"He drives a tractor. On Mr. Gooding's farm. Can I have a biscuit?"

"Yes, of course you may. Where are they?"

Together they collected a biscuit tin from a cupboard. "How about some lemonade to go with it?" asked Julie. Imogen nodded and whilst they settled down together I wandered off on a fact-finding expedition of my own.

The house was small and on the whole ill-furnished. Two of the three rooms upstairs were merely storerooms and contained a gallimaufrey of un-used furniture stacked untidily against the walls. Piles of books revealed a surprisingly catholic taste and ranged from paperback thrillers through book-club editions of Brontë and Dickens to Caesar's *Gallic Wars* in Latin and Sophocles' plays in Greek. There was also a dusting of mathematical text-books. And he drove a tractor for Mr. Gooding? But maybe they had be-longed to his deceased wife?

Imogen was in charge of the third room on that floor; it was small, neat and pretty and positively abustle with Pooh Bear and Paddington.

Downstairs again, I found myself in Mathews' bedroom-cum-workroom, at the front, the bed neatly made, the rest a masculine shambles and reeking of stale tobacco smoke. At a dilapidated table/desk I began fingering through his private life. Almost immediately, I came up with a photograph of Sister Amy, which pleased me. Homely-looking in an orange swimsuit, she was a bulging sort of woman hanging heavily on the withered arm of a patriarch who lacked teeth and waved a crooked walking stick encouragingly at the photographer. The picture, according to Amy's scrawl on the back, was enti-tled "Grandad and Me" and had been perpetrated at Poppit Sands. At this particular time there seemed to have been nothing wrong with Grandad's head, for a jaunty sailor's cap was perched upon it, its ribbon proclaiming him to be a crew member of one of HM's submarines—a declaration I was in-clined to doubt.

George Mathews had clearly found it next to impossible to throw anything away, storing it instead in the drawers of his desk presumably against a rainy day: nails and screws, bits of string, elastic bands, paper fasteners, foreign stamps and coins, sea shells and the tops from toothpaste tubes. I drew open another drawer and exposed a red armband with a black swastika on a white circle, the silver skull from a Nazi cap, an Iron Cross with ribbon, a Knight's Cross, several breast eagles and half a dozen pictures of Hitler culled from newspapers and magazines. A black notebook contained various memoranda concerning Adolf Hitler, written in what I assumed to be Mathews' handwriting: date of birth, death, attempted assassinations together with the names of those who had died to expiate them; appearances at rallies and parades complete with dates and the estimated number of those present. Quotations from speeches were also there, mostly in German.

I leaned back in his chair and stared bleakly at the book, flicking over the pages and wondering about little Imogen, whom I could hear in the kitchen chattering merrily with Julie.

I was depressed and tired. I'd had a busy day. Getting to my feet, I wandered uneasily through the sordid claustrophobia of that room, wondering how anyone could have called it home. Everything about it was unmemorable, not a picture, stick of furniture, curtain or ornament would I ever wish to see again. In a desultory fashion I tugged at the door of a wardrobe whose proportions resembled those of an upended sarcophagus from ancient Egypt. It was locked and therefore presented an open invitation, for me at least, to discover its contents. A sturdy Victorian piece, it tacitly repulsed all thoughts of assault and battery. Searching for the key, I drew a blank in the desk drawers, but in a moment of rare insight peered into an unpleasant-looking vase on the mantelpiece, and there it was—an unlikely facsimile, in brass, of a papal key.

The door of the wardrobe swung smoothly back into the room. I stared at the immaculate black uniform tunic of an Oberleutnant of the SS. On a shelf above lay the visored, high-crowned matching cap, the silver death's-head glinting; on the floor of the cupboard a pair of highly polished knee-length black leather boots stood neatly to attention.

The wardrobe was stuffed with Nazi military memorabilia. Three complete uniforms, two black leather greatcoats, caps, boots, gloves, even several sets of underwear bearing military markings and therefore probably authentic. A roomy cardboard carton contained a miscellany of weapons, pistols in cheap leather holsters, daggers, knives, bayonets, a *Feld-marschal*'s baton, a rubber truncheon, a bullwhip. . . .

In the light of so much authenticity there was something poignant in the fact that none of the firearms were genuine, but were of the type purchasable in toy shops and pseudo-military stores. George Mathews was probably a loner, a solitary, groping for an identity more rewarding than his own and finding it in the sinister accoutrements of an SS officer. Like an actor, I thought, he would stand before his mirror and gradually effect the transformation; unlike the actor he would start with the underclothes and, working outwards, assume each garment with a sensual, even sexual, appreciation until the man he longed to be gazed back at him complete to the last detail.

He probably even had a name, this figment of a desperate imagination, this

Hyde to Mathews' Jekyll. And when the performance was over the strutting Karl, or whatever, would be relegated reluctantly to the wardrobe and the gentler, ordinary, shambling George Mathews would take over where he left off. The wardrobe would be secured against inquisitive eyes, the door to his room unlocked, and life with little Imogen resumed, Mr. Gooding's tractor waiting for him at Poppit Sands.

A stud drawer in the wardrobe caught my eye. I drew it open slowly, knowing instinctively what I would find: photographs. The colour was uniformly muddy, the images blurred, but there he was, this Oberleutnant, slim, cool and arrogant, younger-looking than when I had last seen him. I flicked them through: the hand stiffly upraised in the approved Nazi salute; smiling and relaxed, a gun pointing indolently at the camera; lounging elegantly on a corner of the table, smoking a cigarette in a long holder, the black leather greatcoat unbuttoned revealing the immaculate uniform beneath; the coat removed altogether, straddle-legged, boots gleaming, the bullwhip grasped in black-gloved hands, the eyes glaring into the lens, theatrically—and stupidly —evil. And looming in the background the murky squalor of the room with its shadowy wallpaper of reality.

Returning the photographs to the drawer, I slammed it shut. I locked the wardrobe and, for a second, was tempted to throw away the key. Carefully I replaced it in the vase on the mantelpiece for others to find and wonder at: I could only hope that the police would be compassionate and dispose of the bizarre trappings of this secret man without malice—if only for the sake of his child.

When I returned to the kitchen, Imogen was immersed in a fairly inarticulate explanation of a painting she had perpetrated at school. With all the complacency of a proud mother, Julie looked up as I entered. "Just look at this, Mark; Imogen has painted a picture of her father."

I stared bewildered at the splodgy sheet of paper: a blue Guinness bottle on legs with stick arms and a pinkish lampshade for a head. "Ah," I said. "Yes, very good. I don't know your father but I'd recognise him anywhere from this. Very nice. . . ."

She was now wearing a blue school gabardine over her nightdress and looked demure and unbearably vulnerable. Normally I couldn't be doing with children, but this one I could have fallen for with no trouble at all. She was touchingly shy of my approbation, and her innocence made me feel like something the cat had brought in.

I met Julie's amused eye. "We ought to go," she said, getting to her feet. "Madam here must get some sleep." We shepherded the child upstairs, where Julie tucked her into bed. "Go to sleep now like a good girl."

"Will you come again soon please?"

"Yes, of course we will. Very soon." She stooped and kissed the small cheek. "We'll call in on Mrs. Thomas-on-the-Hill and tell her to get you up in the morning and give you some breakfast. All right?"

We stood at the door and waggled our fingers at the sleepy little figure.

Downstairs, Julie, with a heavy air of preoccupation, returned the blue gabardine to the hall stand, collected her things, switched out the lights and passed by me without a word as I waited at the open front door.

For several long and silent moments, we loitered, shivering on the doorstep, pulling our coats about us; then she muttered tetchily, "I wish to God we had never come."

"Join the club."

"We'd better go and find Mrs. Thomas-on-the-Hill," she said brusquely, "I know where she lives," and stalked off into the darkness, leaving me to catch up.

A kindly Mrs. Thomas was disposed to accept Mathews' absence with a *che sera sera* sort of shrug and promised to attend to Imogen's needs in the morning. "He should have told me—he usually does when he's going to be away; she could have spent the evening with us. But there, I expect he forgot. They're all the same, these men." She flashed a loaded glance at me through her gold-rimmed spectacles, and I stared fixedly at my feet with an appropriate display of masculine guilt. We had told her merely that we were friends of Mathews looking him up on our way north. She had expressed no desire for further enlightenment.

On the return journey through Cardigan I told Julie of my findings in Mathews' room. "Poor chap," she murmured when I had finished. "It must be terrible to have no one to share things with."

"Who have you got?" I asked almost brutally.

There was a second's hesitation before she leaned forward and snapped the heater on to full. "Dad shares things," she said shortly.

I looked at her for a moment and laid a repentant hand on hers. "I didn't mean to say that—not in the way it came out. It's just that I'm . . ."

"Incensed?"

"Could be."

"Me, too. But there's not a lot we can do about it."

"Not until someone turns up with that body. And even then . . ."

With the warm air circulating, we thawed out a little.

Julie said, "There's nothing that'll connect him with you, is there?"

"If the police discover where he was killed, plenty. As I said, my prints are all over the place. Our enquiries about him tonight would lead them to me too—to both of us. The kid will remember you particularly, and Mrs. Thomas will be sure to remember the couple who called in to see him on their way up north. When he's been missing for a couple of days she'll be the one who'll call them in."

She frowned. "What's going to happen to that child?"

"Aunt Amy, I guess, and Grandad. Great-grandad."

"With his head."

"Aunt Amy is massive and motherly; she'll cope."

"I wish to God we'd never gone there," she said again.

"Dragon coming up," she announced later, as we shot past a 30 m.p.h. sign at fifty.

Michael Davies, neither surprised nor particularly happy to see us, took the news of my departure stoically enough, and whilst I went up to the room to collect my things, he held on to Julie, asking after Bruno and busying himself with the task of preparing my bill.

The door to my room was slightly ajar. Gently I pushed it open.

On the great lumpy bed sat the great lumpy Emrys Williams.

"Saw you arrive," he wheezed without either introducing himself or getting up. "Wanted a word."

I moved warily into the room. "I believe I owe you," I said.

He shrugged. The bed creaked appallingly as he heaved himself to his feet. "You're in danger. We think you ought to go home."

"We?" He nodded. "What sort of danger? And who's we?"

"The danger of your death, that's what sort. And who 'we' are is not important."

"I think it is."

"Tough," was all he said, making for the door. "Go home, Mr. Savage, be safe. And don't involve the girl. Your danger could be hers. The enemy isn't selective."

I was at the door before him, my back to it, my hand on the gun in my pocket. "What enemy? Don't warn me off without explanations. Tell me, I might listen; you might even convince me."

There was garlic on his breath: I received the full benefit of it as he gave a loud theatrical sigh. "Mr. Savage, I am doing my best to save your life."

I said reasonably, "I'm not doubting it. But if you were in my position wouldn't you want to know why? You were there this morning—I saw you. Why were you up there?"

For a moment, I had the feeling he was about to tell me. The huge eyes narrowed, their intensity wavering for an instant, then they were wide again and staring as he came slowly towards me. "I can tell you nothing."

The gun was levelled at his chest. He stopped, looking slightly amused. He shook his head. "I'm not convinced, Mr. Savage. Put it away." He hesitated, raising an enormous hand, palm outwards like a traffic policeman. "Look, let me talk to someone. If he listens you'll get the answers."

"And if he doesn't?"

"Then go home. I'll contact you."

There was something in his manner which made me feel a trifle foolish. I have always despised the man with the gun; he can afford to talk big with a large-calibre bullet on his side, particularly if he has no qualms about using it. I had qualms and Williams knew it, so the Walther could have been a water pistol for all the impression it was making. Slowly I lowered the muzzle. "I am capable of using it, you know," I told him as a face saver.

He nodded. "I know that." I put the gun back into my pocket and removed myself from the door. "I shall expect to hear from you."

He was about to reply when there was a sharp tap at the door and Michael Davies walked in. His eyes flicked from me to Williams and back again. "Your bill, Mr. Savage." He handed me a paper. "I came to see if I could help." His eyes shifted to Williams. "Or perhaps I can do something for you, Emrys?" The voice was suddenly hard, metallic-sounding. I glanced at Williams. The great bulging eyes were positively blazing. He stood his ground for a second or two; then, muttering something in Welsh beneath his breath, he barged through the doorway and down the stairs, almost capsizing Davies as he did so.

"What did he say?" I asked mildly, turning away to gather up my modest belongings.

"What was he doing in here?" asked Davies, recovering himself quickly and choosing not to satisfy my curiosity.

"We were talking." I stowed the few things into my bag.

"He had no right to be here."

"I invited him."

I turned my head and encountered his eyes. They were disbelieving and hostile.

"Right," I said lightly, hefting the bag in my hand. "Here we go, then."

At the foot of the stairs, Julie waited. She had muffled herself up in her old Oxfam mackintosh against the cold night air and looked just as I had seen her for the first time, barely twenty-four hours earlier. Now we were friends, accomplices and, mentally at least, lovers.

I paid the bill and promised halfheartedly to see Michael Davies again. As he saw us off the premises I stumbled up the two steps. I snorted with sudden laughter and turned impulsively to share the joke with him.

On the gaunt bearded face there was no vestige of a smile.

"Oh, Lord," muttered Julie as we turned into her drive.

"What?"

"Dad's in the kitchen."

"Is that bad?"

"It's not good. At best he's trying to find something to eat—at worst he's trying to cook it." She gave me a slanting, oriental look. "Never share your wigwam with a brave who isn't house-trained."

She drove round to the back of the house and into a lean-to garage built alongside the barn, where I had left the Triumph.

I was first out of the car and stood riveted for a second, the familiar ominous prickling at the back of my neck. Something was wrong. I moved round to open her door as she doused the lights. I leaned in. "Don't move," I whispered.

In the garage it was pitch black; her hand sought mine. I heard only the stealthy rustle of her mack and her intake of breath. Straightening slowly, I peered back across the yard to the loom of the house beyond. A glow from a side window illuminated a narrow portion of the drive and its verge. The silence was almost frightening. A shadow crossed the pool of light and was gone. My pulses leapt. Julie sensed the sudden tension. Her whispered "What is it?" sounded like a shout.

I bent lower. "What's the light in the house?"

"The kitchen."

"There was a shadow just now."

"It was Dad, I expect." She was beginning to sound querulous.

I opened the door of the car without a sound and helped her out, her mackintosh crackling like a storm in a pine forest.

"What is it?" she asked again.

I was confused. "Something's wrong. I can sense it, but can't explain."

She stood quite still, trying to share my uneasiness. The shadow appeared and went again. "That's my father," she said decisively.

I nodded impatiently. "I believe you. But this is something else, something different."

The feeling was beginning to wear off. I slammed the car door suddenly in an effort, I suspect, to exorcise my hunch altogether. That helped, but remnants of it persisted as the shredded memory of a dream persists in the subconscious.

I spoke in a normal voice. "Let's get indoors; otherwise we'll be standing around here all night. Take no notice of me."

She unlocked the back of the Traveller and I collected my parcels, stamping around and slamming doors with more violence than was necessary, and when she finally banged the garage doors shut, we lay back on them and gave ourselves up to an attack of the giggles. Suddenly she was in my already-laden arms and I was kissing her. There was no holding back on her part, her body strained against mine, her arms tightly twined about my neck. And in the midst of it came that warning again. My laughter died, every sense alerted.

Silent and anxious, she stared up into my face.

Slowly I disengaged myself from her and placed my packages carefully on the ground at my feet. I put my lips to her ear. "Whatever it is, it's next door. Do you have a torch?"

She opened up the garage again and disappeared into the darkness, returning a moment later to press a rubber-cased torch into my hand. Taking the gun from my pocket, I eased off the safety catch and pushed Julie back into the shadows. "Don't budge," I whispered, holding a warning finger to my lips.

Noiselessly I turned to the barn. I squatted on my heels and peered cautiously into the gloom. I could make out the paler bulk of the Triumph looming in the darkness. For several seconds I remained motionless, painfully aware that my head was silhouetted against the glow of light from the house behind. It was just possible that I was hidden from him by the car. Wherever he was, he'd had his chance and missed it. Ducking into the building, gun in one hand, torch in the other, I scuttled like a ferret to the rear of the barn, where I took up a stance with my back to the wall. Snapping on the torch I swept a beam of light from wall to wall, from floor to ceiling. I was conscious of cold sweat congealing on my forehead and of a gradual easing of tension. The place was empty. Then the light of the torch touched the radiator of the car and strayed slowly upwards . . . my hand trembled violently and the sense of relief was gone. I snapped off the light.

Someone was sitting in the passenger seat staring at me through the windscreen.

My stomach griped. The light reflecting on to the glass had made it difficult to make out any details. I crabbed quickly around the vehicle, hugging the wall, and switched on the torch again. I held the gun well forward into the beam so that he couldn't miss it.

"Come out," I called in an unrecognisable croak.

He made no move.

When I directed the shaft of light at the passenger door, the window reflected it back and still I couldn't see. Clamping the torch beneath my arm, I lurched forward awkwardly and grabbed roughly at the handle; the door creaked open towards me. I saw him move slightly. Ducking sideways with the torch in my hand I thrust its beam into the car, the muzzle of the gun not two inches from his head.

The ashen, long-dead face of George Mathews turned slowly towards me as his knees buckled against the dashboard and the body settled a few inches into the seat. I stared dumbly into the empty eyes. The dried blood about the mouth was black and scabbed.

I switched off the torch.

"Mark . . . ?" She was standing in the doorway.

"No . . . don't come in. . . ."

She was at my side, easing the torch from my hand. Numbly I turned away, left her and wandered miserably out into the yard. I pressed my body hard against the doorjamb for comfort and closed my eyes.

Seconds later, she joined me. "George Mathews?"

I nodded wearily.

"Oh, the bastards," she whispered half to herself. "The rotten bastards."

7

Hamish Remington, veterinary surgeon retired, was a man still to be reckoned with. Massive and rangy-looking, he gave the impression that even now, in his late sixties, he could wrestle a steer, shoe a stallion or break in a colt. He was the kind of man whose presence made a room seem smaller, dwarfing those around him, demanding their attention, not by stature alone but by the impact of his personality. He should have been a leader of something, the president of somewhere, or the founder of the ultimate faith.

But he wasn't. He was a retired vet failing in health and somewhat addicted to the bottle.

The heavy-lidded eyes betrayed him. Red-rimmed and vague, they prowled aimlessly in their dark sockets, searching for answers beyond their focus.

I felt for him. I had been some way along that particular path. I knew the floating twilight of Limboland and the lure of promised oblivion which never came, no matter how many times one hit the deck.

He peered at me for some time before convincing himself that I actually existed, then he extended a hand and clasped mine with only the sketchiest show of acknowledgment.

Julie, after a noisy confrontation with Bruno, who had lurched precipitously in on three legs and attempted to bowl us over, tipped the pizza her father had burned into the waste bin and shepherded us all into the back room, where, without question or apology, she dispensed pure orange juice for the three of us and an outsize biscuit for Bruno. Hamish Remington, hunched in the chair I had occupied the previous evening, gazed gloomily at the beverage as if it were a personal affront. I perched on the arm of the sofa whilst Julie stood with her back to the fire, looking at her drink as if she, too, were wishing it were something other than fruit juice.

"Dad," she said quietly. "We have something to tell you."

For no better reason than that we felt he ought to know what was going on in his own back yard, we had decided to tell him about his unwanted guest outside. We had to do something about the earthly remains of poor unfortunate George Mathews, and the thought of lugging him around the countryside and dumping him into the river or under someone else's bush was unacceptable. This decision was irrespective of my own private belief that I was under the close scrutiny of some person or persons unknown for most of my waking hours and had I opted to pick up the body and move it somewhere else I would almost certainly have woken up in the morning to find it tucked up in bed beside me. So the best thing to do—

"A body?" echoed Hamish Remington, his glass of orange juice halfway to his lips. "What body?"

"A dead body," said his daughter.

"Whose?"

"We don't know," I put in quickly lest Julie become too expansive. "A man. Your daughter says he's not local. And he's been killed."

"If he's dead of course he's been killed." He frowned at me belligerently, his eyes narrowing slightly as they roamed by easy stages over my woebegone exterior. "What did you say your name was?"

"Mark Savage."

"You're not local either."

"No, I'm English. From London."

"Ah." He nodded knowingly several times as if that explained everything. He glowered at his daughter and said, "Ah," again with a slightest variation in tone which meant: you see what happens when you fraternise with foreigners.

"Dad," said Julie patiently. "What do we do?"

He blinked at her. "Do?"

"About the body."

"Get on to Owen the Police, of course. What else should you do?" He turned again to me. "Unless you want to take it back to London with you. After all, it's not ours, is it? We don't want it."

"I don't want it either."

"It's in your car."

"Someone dumped it there."

"Who?"

It was my turn to say, "Ah."

"Possession, you'll find," stated the old man, rolling the phrase impressively about his tongue, "is nine points of the law. That's what Owen will say." He looked with distaste at his orange juice. "However, the law is an ass, we all know that, and so is Owen." He took a swallow of the drink, made an agonised face and looked at his daughter, the glass raised beseechingly in her direction.

"No," she said firmly.

"Get on to Owen, then," he grunted, putting down his glass with equal finality. "Ask him round for a drink."

"I'll just ask him round."

"Before you do so, I would suggest, without offence I hope, that your friend here does something about his appearance. He's a bit ramshackle. Scratches on his face and so on. Not his fault, I'm sure. But if Owen sees him like that he'll arrest him as a vagrant if nothing else. I know Owen." He gave me a twisted smile. "Nothing personal of course."

"In other words," said Julie, taking me possessively by the arm, "welcome to our home. Come on, I'll show you where things are."

She opened a door across the hall. "You'll be comfortable in here." Gathering up my bag and parcels from the hall stand, where I had left them earlier, I wandered into the room and watched while she drew the curtains, switched on an electric fire and collected a couple of towels from a cupboard. "The bed isn't made up yet; I'll see to that later." She indicated a washbasin in the corner. "At least you can have a wash, which would be a great improvement. Have a bath if you wish, there's plenty of hot water. Bathroom and loo upstairs first on the left." She stood very close. "Change into your new finery. Give the old man a thrill." She stood on her toes and touched my cheek with her lips, running a finger along my stubbled chin. "Hobo," she whispered with a smile, and went out saying, "Don't be long," as she closed the door behind her.

I washed in blazing hot water, stared helplessly at my scarred face and dabbed at it tenderly, so as not to start up the bleeding again. Then I splashed Houbigant over my elegance and hit the roof as most of it burned its way into the open scratches. I clambered painfully into new denims, shoulders and ribs protesting at every movement; socks, shoes and sweater and I was ready.

I stuffed the discarded clothing into my bag—maybe I could pass it on to Oxfam after all—took the crisp black trench coat out to the hall stand, where I hung it lasciviously alongside Julie's elderly and redolent number. I was right—it did smell like old rubber tyres and I was fast coming to the conclusion that I liked the smell of old rubber tyres. In an unguarded moment I raised one of its sleeves and put my lips to it. I turned my head quickly. Julie was standing in the doorway of the sitting room, watching me earnestly. She said, "That's called fetish worship where I come from."

I blushed like a schoolboy.

Owen the Police arrived on a bicycle, his only concession to the force being a helmet and uniform overcoat with three stripes on its arm. The rest of him was in brown corduroy trousers topped by a highly coloured woollen jumper. In his helmet he stood about six feet; when he removed it, he was five feet six, a melancholy fact of which he was uncomfortably aware. He was flushed and important-looking and strutted on legs which seemed incapable of bending at the knees.

He was a ham.

Bruno voiced his poor opinion of this oddly attired representative of the law with a prolonged series of growls culminating in a lightning flanking attack at the policeman's left trouser leg, a sortie which might have had serious repercussions had not Julie hurled herself with a great shout between dog and man, startling Owen and me more than it did his attacker. With apologies, Bruno was withdrawn from circulation, and when Julie had returned from wherever she had banished him, we trotted the small sergeant out to the barn and showed him poor George Mathews. Since the barn was without light, torches were produced whilst Owen, having seen all the best films, placed his fingers—incorrectly as it happened—on the pulse at the base of the dead man's throat, and listened breathlessly for a heart beat. Then he tried to close the dead eyes without success—they popped open twice—and finally stood back and studiously recorded his findings whilst Julie and I, holding torches for him and feeling almost as cold as George Mathews, wished we had brought our warm clothes.

"Dead," proclaimed Owen eventually, snapping an elastic band around his notebook with the air of one who had just invented the sewing machine. "For several hours, I'd say. Cold. Cold as ice. Stiff, too." He leaned towards us and added in a low, confidential voice, *"Rigor mortis."*

Then he tried surprise tactics. Turning on me suddenly and standing very close, he flashed the beam of his torch up into my face—I must have looked like the Gypsy's Warning in that light. "Did you ever see this man before, Mr. Savage?"

"Never."

"What was his name?" Oh, clever.

"If I have never seen him before, I can hardly be expected to know his name."

He was unconvinced. Although only a sergeant, by exposing the killer that night he could be standing in line for an inspectorship before sunup. But he knew, and I knew—and he knew that I knew—that if he hadn't solved the case in the next half hour or so it would be snatched away from him by Homicide and he would probably remain a sergeant for the rest of his working days.

It would have shown a certain generosity on our part to help him out, but neither Julie nor I was in the giving mood, so we galloped back into the warm. There the sergeant stood primly in the centre of the room, heels together, and surveyed us loftily whilst the story was told. It was not a lengthy story; it took ten seconds flat: "When I arrived home this evening I discovered the body of a dead man sitting in the passenger seat of my car; he was covered with blood." That was it. But it was not the sort of thing to deter a policeman of his calibre. He produced that ominous little black notebook and settled down quite happily to a cross-examination which dragged on for the best part of twenty minutes.

The final question he aimed at me was what had happened to my face. I told him I had fallen down. He looked at me regretfully for a long, loaded moment as if I had just committed perjury and would I care to change my story? When I remained obstinately silent, he turned with a sigh to his notebook and, with elaborate mouthings of the words aloud, wrote, " 'I fell down,' said the witness."

That done, Sergeant Owen made a series of depressed telephone calls to various interested parties. He then cheered up, took off his overcoat, and joined us in his brown corduroys and coloured jumper and became a Welshman like everyone else.

Julie presented him with a bottle of beer and a digestive biscuit and we all sat around companionably waiting for what he jocularly termed the "meat wagon." The Triumph, it seemed, would have to be towed away for forensic examination and would remain in the custody of the police until such time as they saw fit to release it.

"So, how am I going to get back to London?"

"I'm afraid, Mr. Savage, you will have to remain here until such time as my superiors are satisfied that you had no part in the crime."

"Charming," I said sourly. "I would hardly have called you in if I'd done it myself, would I? Cheers," I toasted him in orange juice.

"Cheers, Mr. Savage." He drank deeply of his beer, watched enviously by all, and wiped his mouth with the back of his hand. "Tell me, Mr. Savage, what exactly is the nature of your business in this part of the world?"

"I have already told you. I am a private investigator."

"But what is the nature of your private investigation?"

I smiled obstinately. "As the term suggests, its nature is private."

He returned my smile. "Off the record, however."

"Off the record, however, I am at the moment not investigating anything. I am a messenger boy delivering a package to a client." He drew breath. "A private package," I added blandly.

"And have you done so?"

I shook my head. "Unfortunately my client appears not to be at home."

"Dead, perhaps?"

"Missing."

"So what will you do now?"

"Wait until you give me my car back, I imagine."

"And where will you be staying in the meantime? At the Dragon?" He reached for his notebook.

"Here," said Julie. He left the notebook where it was.

"Here?" Hamish Remington raised heavy eyebrows. "First I've heard of it."

"Yes, Dad. I should have mentioned it before. I've asked him to stay with us."

Her father looked at me fixedly. "Who is he?"

"Mark Savage," I told him.

"I know what your name is. But I would like to know something more than a name if you are going to stay under my roof."

"*Our* roof, Dad," said Julie gently, "and Mark is a friend of mine."

"You've never mentioned him before."

"You've never listened before."

The argument was too much for him and he withdrew into his orange juice, a few hollow rumblings reverberating in his glass.

"I wonder why," pondered Owen, and I groaned inwardly, having come to recognise that those three words inevitably heralded a question to which no satisfactory answer could be attached. When he repeated the phrase, he amended it pointedly. "I am *still* wondering why our hypothetical murderer should have chosen your particular car in which to dump his victim?" There was indeed no safe answer to that, so I attempted none but looked at Julie instead: she raised her eyes to the ceiling and crossed them slightly in sympathy. "It's not as if your car was standing by the roadside. To reach your car it would have been necessary for him to carry that body almost all of one hundred yards."

"Alternatively," I intervened drily, "he could have brought his own car down the drive and off-loaded the body in comfort and privacy."

He raised a dogmatic finger. "But Mr. Remington was here the entire evening and heard nothing."

Hamish Remington, alerted by hearing his name spoken, said, "What?"

"I said you heard nothing."

"When?"

"If a car had come down your drive you would have heard it, would you not?"

"No."

"No?"

"I make a point of not hearing anything I am not listening for. I am also slightly deaf. What were you saying?"

The sergeant eyed him for a short spell, clearly weighing the advisability of further communication in that quarter, then decided on a change of tactics.

"Where did you say you had fallen, Mr. Savage?"

"I don't think I did."

"A bad fall, I imagine, for your face to have come out looking like that. Damaged your shoulder, too, haven't you? I can see that. Very tender, is it?" He was maddeningly observant. "Where did you fall?"

"Down a bank, a steep bank. I don't know where. I'm unfamiliar with the landscape. I was walking and slipped."

"Just walking? Could you show me the place?"

"I doubt it. There was a lot of fog about."

"Might it have been somewhere in the vicinity of a house called Wanhope?"

I blinked at him. "Wanhope?"

His smile was bland. "I understand you were making enquiries as to its whereabouts in the Dragon last night."

"You're very well informed."

"That's my business, Mr. Savage."

I shook my head weightily. "The whereabouts of my falling down can surely have no bearing on the discovery of a dead body in my car."

"That is for you to tell and me to find out."

"Sergeant," I said politely, "I have given you a statement. There's no more I can add to it—nothing cogent. I could tell you what I had for breakfast this morning, but I doubt if it would help."

"I can tell you exactly what you had for breakfast, Mr. Savage, and you are right, it doesn't help."

I drew a deep breath and decided to head him off. "I can only repeat that I did not shoot him; I have never shot anyone in my life."

His little eyes snapped. "Who said anyone shot him?"

"Someone must have done it."

"I said nothing about shooting."

"You mean . . ." It was Julie, overacting like Monday night in repertory. "You mean . . . he wasn't shot!" She sounded like Jeanette MacDonald.

Sergeant Owen smiled at her smugly. "I take it you did not examine the body when you discovered it?"

"Of course not. We went straight to the telephone and rang you. We just took it for granted that he had been shot. We saw the blood."

He lowered his voice and leaned in dramatically. "The man was stabbed, Julie Remington. Stabbed to death. With a knife. In the stomach." *His* performance wasn't all that good either.

"Mr. Savage"—he rounded on me; shock tactics again—"do you, as a matter of interest, have a gun?"

"A gun?" I looked shifty. "Yes, as a matter of interest, I have."

"May I see it?"

"If the man was stabbed—"

"Please."

"But it's not even—"

"Mr. Savage."

I stumped across the hall and into my room, conscious that he was close at my heels. I unzipped my bag, and took out the Colt, his gimlet eyes following every move. I stuck my index finger into the trigger guard and as I turned back to him, spun the weapon adroitly several times as they do in the Westerns. Sergeant Owen retreated a step.

"Do you have a licence for that?"

"A licence? Good heavens no."

"No licence?" His moment had come. "Unlicenced possession of a firearm is a most serious offence. I am bound by law to confiscate that weapon."

"It's yours," I said, handing it over and switching out the light as I passed him on the way back to my orange juice. "But I honestly didn't know that I had to have a licence."

"I find that difficult to believe, Mr. Savage."

"For a toy?"

"A toy?"

"I bought it in a joke shop."

He held the weapon between finger and thumb and stared at it as if it were something which had just died. "A toy?"

"I keep it to frighten the burglars."

He was peering down the barrel as though contemplating suicide. "Mr. Savage," he said in a low, choked voice, "I do hope you are not holding the law up to ridicule."

"Certainly not. You asked if I had a gun. I have. There it is. It looks like a gun. I think of it as a gun. I'd almost forgotten it doesn't shoot anything."

"If no one's going to feed me," broke in Hamish Remington, suddenly heaving himself to his feet, "I shall go to bed."

"You'll do no such thing," cried Julie, leaping forward and pressing him back into his chair. "We'll eat now. At once. Sergeant, will you join us in a little something? Pot luck?"

"I am conducting an investigation," he pointed out petulantly.

"Bosh," said Hamish. "You haven't said anything worth listening to for the past twenty minutes. You've got all the information you're likely to get, so let's forget about the bloody body and have something to eat." He caught my eye and gave me a broad wink. "Look at this lad, will you, Owen? Do you really think he's capable of sticking a knife into anyone? If you want my opinion, and I'm sure you don't, someone is out gunning for him. But, then,

I am older and wiser than any of you so I don't expect to be listened to. So food, Julie, please."

It was like breaking-up day at school. Everyone relaxed.

"I think there are lamb chops in the fridge," said Julie, collecting glasses. "If not it'll have to be tins."

"I had an Auntie Gladys once," I said—a remark which riveted everyone to the tracks. I went on more slowly. "She used to say, 'If I haven't got anything on in the evening I open a tin.' " They looked at me. "She's dead now," I added lamely.

"Not before time," murmured Hamish Remington.

Sergeant Owen gave an uncharacteristic chuckle. "I like it."

"You shouldn't make fun of your Auntie Gladys," was Julie's opinion. "Come and give me a hand in the kitchen."

We had demolished the lamb chops with mint sauce and potatoes long before the "meat wagon" arrived to collect the late George Mathews. I watched him go with no regrets. At least he was now released into the proper channels and would eventually be disposed of with some sort of ceremonial seemliness.

With the "wagon" arrived a plainclothes police inspector, an Irishman named Donnelly, swarthy and unfriendly, who put the same questions over and over again and missed no opportunity to pull rank on the diminutive Sergeant Owen, for whom, in consequence, I began to develop feelings of fellowship.

Donnelly didn't even mention my face; he probably thought I always looked like that. He was all puff and blow; the guilty-until-proved-innocent type of cop. When he went off to take the car apart, neither the Remingtons nor I took up his invitation to accompany him. He had in tow a forelock-touching underling who went by the name of Detective Constable Pridthorpe and was pushed about by Donnelly like a corporation dust cart.

They were more than an hour examining the Triumph—to little avail if one was to judge by the returning Donnelly's grimly set features—and when, with a valedictory threat about holding ourselves in readiness for further questioning, he departed from the Remington living room, driving D.C. Pridthorpe before him and dragging Sergeant Owen in his wake, the rest of us breathed a prayer of deliverance and Julie actually offered her father a bottle of Guinness and a pewter tankard to go with it.

"At least he's not Welsh," she said, handing him the opener.

"Thank God," he grunted fervently, whipping the top off the bottle. "Aren't you joining me?" he asked, cocking an eye in my direction as the beer gurgled invitingly into the tankard.

I shook my head. "I don't, thanks."

"Choice or religion?"

So I told him a little about some of my past troubles, to which he listened with earnest interest, nodding devoutly every now and again.

"Know all about it," he sighed when I had finished. "Funny old business, isn't it? Always think you're stronger than the next man. Wonder why that is?" He frowned reflectively. "I'm a bit of a liability to the animals now, and I care about that. I like animals more than humans. Which is as it should be. Too many take animals for granted, turn 'em into hard labour and ready cash . . . like we did slaves. Too much slaughter, too little regard for creatures who have a right to live but can't claim it unless some of us give 'em a hand. We haven't come far over the centuries; spend our lives thinking in dollar symbols. It's a sickness." He stared morosely into his tankard, his hand shaking a little. "So's this, I suppose—some people would say it is. But at least I'm the only one it harms." Out of the corner of my eye I saw Julie stir uneasily; he, too, caught the involuntary movement. "You, too, my dear, it harms you, too, I'm aware of that."

"Dad, do shut up," she murmured. "Mark doesn't want to hear our troubles."

He nodded. "True, true, he's got enough of his own, if I'm any judge." His deep-set eyes turned on me, suddenly shrewd and very alert. "Am I right?"

I shrugged. "Enough to be going on with."

"Help needed?"

I hesitated for a long time before answering. "If I knew what I was up against, help might be appreciated. Something unpleasant is going on up here and I seem to be in the middle of it." I paused. "I have been—placed in the middle of it. Deliberately. Sort of catalyst, I think. To stir things up, bring the muck to the surface. Mathews was killed because of me, I'm sure of that."

"The dead man?"

I nodded.

"So you did know him?"

"No, that's just it, I didn't. I saw him die but I didn't know him."

Julie said, "We think Pithy might have killed him."

"*Bach* Pithy?"

"He was around at the time. Mark ran into him."

"I also ran into Emrys Williams," I reminded her.

"From the Dragon?" He thought for a moment, then shook his head. "Emrys Williams wouldn't use a knife, not with hands like his."

"Pithy's got a pretty useful pair too."

"But doesn't know how to use them. He's a child, a big, powerful child—and in a corner he'd be lethal, as a trapped animal would be. He'd charge his way out. And if there was a weapon handy he'd use it, not necessarily to kill, but to hack a way out."

He broke off abruptly, a heavy frown darkening his brow, his eyes suddenly narrow as they stared soberly at his daughter. "Are you mixed up with all this?"

Her hesitation was fractional. "Only insofar as I am mixed up with Mark."

"And how 'insofar' is that—if a father may ask?"

Her eyes met mine and held them, the ghost of a smile on her lips. I had never seen her look so appealing. "I'm not sure—yet," she said and added slowly, "maybe quite seriously."

He took a deep breath and expelled it slowly, the frown deepening. "Would that make *you* happy?" he asked, flicking a glance at me from under his brows.

"Very."

He stirred his big frame, put down his tankard and ran the fingers of both hands several times through his thick mane of hair. "You're not government, by any chance, are you?" he asked. "MI what's it—secret service and all that?" And when I shook my head he shrugged dismissively. "You couldn't say so even if you were. And I don't think I'd want to know anyway. But if that one," and he pointed a long, bony finger in Julie's direction, "is interested in you, I think I am entitled to know *something* of what you are up to. Don't you?"

I nodded. "As far as I'm concerned you're entitled to know all of it, although very little of it makes sense."

"What does nowadays?" His mouth twitched quirkily. "Go on, then; tell me."

And I did.

He sat like a stone throughout, motionless and without expression. At one moment in the half-light, his huge hands spread on the arms of his chair and his head thrust slightly forward, he took on an uncanny resemblance to the Abraham Lincoln of the Memorial in Washington. Like his daughter, he possessed that inestimable ability—rare among those with whom I habitually consorted—the ability to listen. The carved look of concentration on his face invoked confidence and invited frankness.

When I had finished, he nodded half to himself several times, reached again for his tankard and drained it decisively. "I can understand why you didn't come clean with Owen; you'd have been behind bars by this time." He examined the interior of the tankard for a time, placed it on the table with an emphatic thump and eyed it obliquely with an air of accusation. He said, "Now I shall tell *you* something." He then remained silent for so long that I began to think he had changed his mind. I glanced curiously at Julie, who winked encouragingly and drew down the corners of her mouth. At last he spoke.

"Some years back—before your time here, Julie—a young man called Barry Newman turned up in the village, suddenly, out of the blue. A student, he said he was, studying the Welsh language. He also said he was a member of *Cymdeithas yr Iaith Gymraeg*—the Welsh Language Society." His eyes twinkled in my direction. "Even in the fastness of your English insularity you may have heard of that. It is a nonviolent organisation, and if you care about Wales it's probably a good thing to belong to. But, like all such organisations on the fringe of politics, it's apt to attract hotheads and fanatics. And fanaticism is one thing the W.L.S. can do without—in one night it can destroy the work of years. Ground gained by compromise and negotiation can be thrown away by dolts who haven't the patience to wait or the intelligence to understand. And the violence they perpetrate puts in jeopardy the very cause they claim to champion. Unless they're nipped in the bud pretty smartly, the whole bloody thing's driven underground, where it's eventually pronounced illegal and terrorist. You only have to glance across the water to see the results." He stopped and shook his head. "I'm giving a lecture, aren't I? Anyway, this Barry Newman, like so many of his kind, bore all the signs of a troublemaker. People here were wary of him. Despite the evidence of your recent experiences, we're a fairly quiet sort of community and fight shy of trouble.

"To begin with, Newman took a room at the Dragon, where, needless to say, he soon tamed young Michael Davies, who was then barely in his twenties. Their liaison was something of a local scandal, but since no one wanted to prove anything, we all looked the other way and pretended it wasn't happening. Newman picked up a job at the Hazlitt-Martin farm. I don't know what he actually did, but it involved quite a lot of travelling. A car went with the job, and a lot of his time was, I think, spent abroad. I imagine he was some sort of agent or buyer. Whatever he did, he was well paid for it. He smartened himself up considerably, bought an outrageously expensive car of his own, and it wasn't long before he lashed out and bought a house. Then the two of them, Mike Davies and he, er—what do you call it?—shacked up together.

"Then came the first of the fires. A holiday cottage was burnt down—owned by an Englishman. As you may know, one of our pet hates in this part of the world is the buying up of smallholdings by wealthy foreigners—and that means you lot over the border—who then convert them, tart them up and let them out as holiday homes at exorbitant rents. Because of this, prices have soared beyond the pockets of our young people who want to set up homes for themselves. It drives the average good Welshman quite mad.

"The fire was proved to be the work of an arsonist, and when, shortly afterwards, two similar fires broke out within a couple of miles of each other, it was pretty obvious that some sort of extremist campaign was being mounted. The English, of course, pointed the finger at the W.L.S. But you know . . ." he paused for a moment, staring into space, "many of us up here, for some reason, believed it to be the work of Barry Newman. Michael Davies, too, possibly, since one rarely went without the other. I don't know how we arrived at that conclusion; but I do know that one night in the Dragon the two of them were suddenly set upon by what can only be described as a lynching mob. From all I heard they were lucky to get away with their lives. Davies collected a multiple fracture of his femur and was carted off there and then to the hospital. Newman, somehow or other, got clear away. But . . . in the early hours of the morning his house and his smart car were set alight and completely destroyed. And some hours later they found his body."

He sat frowning to himself, disquieted by the ghosts he had disturbed. Neither Julie nor I moved. The living-room fire was low, a log hissing slightly in the melancholy stillness.

He continued slowly, "You're wondering why I'm telling you this," and gave a short laugh. "I'm beginning to wonder myself. But"—he raised a long finger—"there's a common factor to your story and mine, and it may have some significance." He released his breath in a long sigh. "Wanhope," he murmured. "That's the common factor. Wanhope was the house Newman bought and the house that was burned down. And Wanhope was where they found what was left of him."

"How terrible!" whispered Julie.

"It gets worse," grunted her father quietly. "It wasn't the fire that killed him. His clothes were burnt, his skin charred—I saw the body, attended the post-mortem—but he didn't die by fire."

"How, then?" I asked. "What killed him?"

His eyes met mine. "Heroin," he said. "He was chock-full of heroin."

Five hours later I was still awake, tossing and turning in a strange bed, drifting now and then into a comatose state of shifting ghosts and shadows, restless featureless beings, tall and rectangular, like grey-painted canvas flats moving without visible means, silent on a darkened stage. Sometimes they loomed over me, blocking my way, at others they faded abruptly to let me through, and when they did I awoke again, aware of their grey shapes waiting, huddled in the wings. Twice I put on the light to banish them and lay staring blankly at the shadowy ceiling.

The house was quiet. The ponderous tick of a grandfather clock in the hall seemed to add to the silence—like a huge metronome marking the slow pacing of the night. From Julie's infirmary, at the rear of the building, came the occasional soft whine and whimper of a half-drugged animal.

"Oh, Christ," I said aloud suddenly, sitting up, turning on the light and thumping crossly at the pillows, causing shoulder and ribs to throb with renewed vigour. "Why bloody heroin?"

Barry Newman had been murdered, Hamish Remington had said.

"You mean, someone injected heroin into his bloodstream?"

"That's exactly what I mean."

"Why couldn't he have done it himself? He could have been an addict."

"He wasn't. There were no indications of addiction. One puncture in the arm. One only. The fatal one."

"He still could have done it himself," I had insisted. "By mistake, perhaps. Or even deliberately. Perhaps he wanted to kill himself."

With closed eyes and compressed lips, Hamish Remington had looked suddenly much older. "If he'd committed suicide, the hypodermic would have been there beside him, twisted and burnt perhaps, but it would have been there. The heroin in his blood was 90 percent pure; you can't get any purer. In the trade I believe they call it Number Four—they cook the opium four times. Morphine's produced after the first refining, so you can imagine what Number Four's like. He would have been dead before the needle was out of his arm. They then set fire to the house—and cooked him. If he hadn't been lying on a stone floor against a brick wall he would have been burnt to a frazzle and there wouldn't have been enough of him left to perform any sort of autopsy."

"Was there an enquiry?"

"Indeed there was. Not a public enquiry, however. *In camera.* Nothing was ever made public other than the fact that he had been found dead among the ruins. But behind the scenes all hell was let loose. The pathologist's report set a monster cat among the pigeons. The Drugs Squad was up here in a flash, customs, coastguards, the lot. The one thing they all wanted to know was where the stuff had come from. It was all very undercover and cloak-and-dagger—really rather laughable when I look back on it; the place was absolutely stiff with the most unlikely looking tourists. That's the way they work, I suppose. They don't disturb the nest until they're sure everyone's at home. The result of it all was that eventually they caught up with a dope ring operating out of Haverfordwest. Whether they got to the bottom of it all, we'll probably never know. These things run deep, go to earth for a bit and then reappear somewhere else, looking quite different."

When I had muttered something about being surprised that drug running could go on in a place like Wales, he snorted with something like hurt pride. "My dear boy, what's so special about Wales? Where've you been all this time? We've got a coastline, haven't we? And we've also got quite a record.

Two years ago, they found over fourteen hundred pounds of cannabis in Cardiff. Only last year, in Llanddwyn Bay, up in Anglesey, they picked up a yacht with one and a half tons of the stuff on board. And that particular covey of gentlemen-smugglers had put no less than six million pounds' worth of the rubbish on the streets already. Six million pounds' worth! Think of it!"

I had thought of it. I was still thinking of it.

Wanhope. Two murders. And had I not been fairly quick off the mark, three. Not a bad average for one house. But Hamish had been talking of events which had happened four or five years before. The house had been gutted and rebuilt since then; how could there be a connection? If Newman had acquired the freehold, it was now in the possession of a new owner.

Tomorrow, I reminded myself, I had to find out who that owner was. Tomorrow I had to ring Mitch, if only to set her imagination to rest. Tomorrow I would ring Sam Birkett. . . .

> Tomorrow and tomorrow and tomorrow,
> Creeps in this petty pace from day to day. . . .

Somewhere a bell was ringing, insistent, irritating. I unglued my eyes. I was still sitting upright in bed with the light on. A pale glimmer of sunlight slanted through the heavy curtains at the window. The bell belonged to a telephone somewhere in the house. I was on the point of crawling out of bed to do something about it when the sound ceased and I heard Julie's voice.

My watch told me it was eight-thirty. My shoulder ached, my ribs ached and the Nibelungs were hammering out their gold on the base of my skull. By easy stages I edged carefully out of the bed, stood swaying for a moment, then limped over to the window, where I took a deep breath, clung on to the curtains and heaved them open like Wolfit taking a curtain call. Pallid sunlight flooded the room and hurt my eyes; closing them with a gentle moan, I rested my thumping head on the cold glass of the window. It was a rewarding, if masochistic, sensation, and life began to crawl sluggishly back into my veins. I raised my head.

Five people, waiting at a bus stop immediately outside, were staring in at me with their mouths half open. One of them, a ferret in a trilby hat, gave me a loud wolf whistle, which greatly amused the other four. Two women on the opposite side of the road parked their shopping trolleys and rooted themselves to the pavement: then a bus pulled up and two rows of pale white faces joined in the general viewing. Had I thought it would have completed their entertainment, I would have dropped my trousers.

Only then did I realise I wasn't wearing any. I wasn't, in fact, wearing anything at all.

Hurling myself backwards into the shadows of the room, I snatched up my clothes and began clawing my way into them.

The telephone outside gave a ping; footsteps and a light knock on the door. I gave a strangled cry, and when she pushed open the door I was standing in a twist at the foot of the bed, looking like a guilty schoolboy caught in the act.

"Whatever's the matter?"

"I've just exposed myself to a busload of psychopaths." Her eyes opened incredulously. I nodded. "I've been standing at the window stark naked. Absolutely stitchless."

She approached the window, for some reason on tiptoe, and peered out cautiously. "There's nobody there now."

"There was a minute ago. It was like Cup Final Day at Wembley." Half in and half out of my sweater, I humped myself on to the end of the bed. She stood before me in a trim white surgeon's coat. "What are you doing up so early anyway?"

"Early? I've done a day's work already. It's nearly nine o'clock. I just looked in to see if you felt like some breakfast. I have to go out to deliver Harry Hawk's calf."

"I thought Harry Hawk had an old grey mare."

"Tom Pearse that was, wasn't it?"

I clutched at my aching head with a sharp whinny. "I'm breaking up. What a terrible way to start a new day, standing about stark naked in the front window. I'm turning the place into a red-light district."

She took me by the arm. "Come and have some breakfast."

A couple of minutes later, presiding over me in the kitchen, she asked, "Do you ride a bike?"

"I ride anything," I mumbled over a scalding cup of coffee. "Anything at all."

"Good. Then, if you need transport while I'm away you can borrow my bike. I'd take the bike myself, only I carry such a lot of junk around with me—"

"Bike will do fine. Thanks. How long are you going to be?"

She shrugged. "As long as it takes. Can't rush these Friesian ladies. Dad says he'll take surgery, which is something of a minor triumph." She nodded happily. "You're responsible for that. You made quite a hit. He hasn't talked like that in years. Another couple of weeks of that sort of treatment and he'll be right back where he was."

I grinned. "I'll see what I can do," I said, and felt ridiculously elated.

She touched my cheek lightly, her face clouding a little. "You'll have to go back eventually. Don't let's fool each other."

I got to my feet. "You'll be late for Harry Hawk's cow."

She had changed out of her white coat and was now shrugging into the leather jacket. "Come on," she said, "I'll show you where the bike is. She has a small house on her own next to the garage."

A couple of minutes later, with a sardonic glint in her eyes, she was watching my jaw drop. "You thought she was a li'l ol' pushbike, didn't you?"

With awe and immediate love I goggled at the gleaming silver Honda CB900 Supersport crouched majestically in her small house, breathing power as we mere mortals breathe oxygen. "She's quite beautiful." A wave of pure green envy swept over me. "Much too big and masculine for a girl. How in hell do you even sit on her?"

"With pleasure and a great deal of difficulty."

I wandered around the machine, touching this, caressing that, and finally stooped down to examine my teeth in the mirror. She indicated a collection of clothing hanging on the wall. "If you want gear, it's up there. Gloves, jackets, a couple of helmets. Should be something to fit you near enough." Reaching up, she pecked me on the cheek. "If you need me, Dad will know where I am. Incidentally, if I get a moment I'll make some enquiries about Wanhope—who owns it and that."

I waved her off and wandered, suddenly desolate, back into the Honda's hideaway, where I rooted out a black crash helmet with a black visor and a well-worn rubber Belstaff jacket which fitted me where it touched.

I washed, shaved and ran into Hamish Remington a couple of times. He appeared to be in high spirits and almost chucked me under the chin the first time. On the second occasion, wearing a white coat, he buttonholed me in the hall. "A propos of our conversation last night, you will remember, won't you, that the bit about the . . . er . . . heroin is—was—pretty classified? I don't suppose it matters much after all this time but, as I said, it was never publicly proclaimed and one doesn't want to stir things up unnecessarily, does one?" His eyes roamed vaguely at the wall behind me, then he shrugged. "Up to you, of course."

I returned to my room, took out the carton of cigarettes, emptied the packets and with a razor blade meticulously opened every cigarette. I ruined one hundred and ninety-nine perfectly good cigarettes and collected a pile of tobacco which I put on one side for Hamish to smoke in his pipe. If Hamish smoked a pipe. But I had to be certain about those cigarettes. The talk of heroin and cannabis had revived my interest in them. When I'd finished with the cigarettes I took the packets and carton apart, carefully and ingeniously. After that I had a small pile of useless pieces of cardboard as well. If I'd had the energy I would have shoved them into a jiffy bag and posted it off to George Morton.

In the hall I found, surprisingly, the complete works of the London Post Office Telecommunications. I dialled Sam Birkett's number.

Mildred Birkett answered and sounded delighted to hear me but was inclined to chat. I headed her off by mentioning that I was marooned in a call box somewhere in the middle of the Welsh mountains and was Sam there?

Sam's grainy voice took over. "Mark, nice to hear you. What can I do for you?"

"George Morton, Sam," I said bluntly.

There was the slightest of pauses, then he said, "Pardon?"

"George Morton?"

"Who's George Morton?"

"Oh, God," I murmured half to myself.

"Tell me about him."

"Late forties, fat running to obscenity, ginger hair what little there is of it; wears a Gannex mack and a hideous green tweed hat. Says he knows you and that you recommended me to do a job for him. Or am I talking a load of cobblers? True or false, Sam?"

"Gently does it, Mark. I don't know any George Morton."

"Think, Sam."

"I have and I don't. No one of that name."

"Or of that description?"

"No."

"Have you recommended me to anyone?"

"I mention your name occasionally, but only in passing. People don't usually come to me for recommendations. I'm old hat, remember? Dixon of Dock Green, rather than Starsky and Hutch. Anyway, you know me well enough to know that I wouldn't put you up for a job without first consulting you and finding out whether you thought you were capable of doing it."

"And even if I thought I was, you'd still rely on your own judgment."

"That's what I used to be paid for."

I breathed thoughtfully down the telephone.

"You still there?" he enquired.

"Listen," I said, "if you'd been sent on what you considered to be a wild-goose chase, and found yourself up to the eyeballs in something you didn't understand, with people shooting at you and trying to run you down on the Queen's Highway with intent to kill, *and* a dead body following you around like a fucking revolving door, what would you do?"

"Call a policeman." There was no doubt in his mind about that.

"Ah," I said with caution. There was in mine.

"A policeman *has* been called?"

"Yes."

"And?"

"Is not in full possession of the facts."

"And is unlikely to be?"

"Unless he can work it out for himself, most unlikely."

"You withholding evidence?"

"Yes."

There was a pause. "Shooting at you, are they?"

"Someone is. What would you do, Sam?"

He took time out to answer, then said, "How about reversing roles? Go hunting. Take the initiative. Find out what you're up against."

"I don't even know who they are. Where do I start?"

"At the beginning, where else? If you can't go on, go back to the beginning. I had an old mate who used to say that; it's quite sound. Start again, but this time open your eyes. Everything's a clue, remember: take nothing for granted or on its face value. Remember what happened the first time and look at it differently, keeping in mind what you've learned since. Something will break, I promise. If it doesn't, go back and do it again. Police business is patience on a rock cake." All this I digested in silence. "You still there?" he asked again.

"Yes. I was thinking. Okay, I'll do as you say. I'll find out who they are if it kills me."

He grunted derisively. "Which won't do you a lot of good. Where are you speaking from?"

"Wales."

"Good God, that old dragon. Had a bout up there myself once. Not very pleasant, as I remember. Snowed up in a loony bin, I was. Lovely views, though. Like bloody Christmas cards."

I grinned down the phone. "Written any good books lately?"

"Several," he chuckled. "You should read them. Might learn how to handle things."

"That'll be the day. Sam, I'm most grateful and sorry to have bothered you."

"Any time. And Mark . . . tread carefully."

Then I telephoned Mitch.

"Well," she said in her most semidetached sort of voice, "I thought you were dead."

"So did I."

"What?"

"Twice."

"Twice what?"

"Dead." That would give her something to bite on.

"What are you talking about, Mark?"

"Any post?"

"Nothing that can't wait."

"Phone calls?"

"None. We may have to close down."

"Don't despair, Mitch dear, I'm earning a fortune up here."

She said rather prissily, "Are you likely to be returning in the near future? Just so I can inform the clients."

"What clients?" She didn't answer that. "Hold the fort, will you, Mitch?"

A slight pause. "For how long?"

"Things have become complicated."

"Can I contact you?"

I gave her the number. Alarm, or something coolly akin to it, was beginning to sharpen the edge of her voice. "Are you all right?"

"At the moment, I'm fine."

"But that could change?"

"It could, yes, conceivably."

Now the coolness was gone and the voice went up a notch. "Mark?"

"What?"

"Did you mean what you said about being nearly twice dead?"

"Being twice nearly dead? Yes."

Another pause; then, "Please be careful, Mark."

The low urgency in her tone touched me. "I will," I said, and felt a heel.

The longest pause yet; then she said soberly, "All right, then, go and earn a pot of money. See if I care." She hung up.

I stood holding the telephone, feeling mean and unwanted. The dialling tone clicked on. I replaced the instrument and looked at it for a moment, wondering whether I should ring her back. I decided not to, but hovered uneasily, wondering why I had goaded her. Now she'd sit there in that dreary office and worry. I snatched up the phone and had dialled 01 for London again when Hamish Remington put his head round the corner. "Oh, sorry, lad, thought I heard the phone."

I hung up. "It was me messing about." As he was about to withdraw, I stopped him. "You—er—don't happen to have a pair of binoculars I could borrow, do you? And possibly an Ordnance Survey map of the district?"

"There's one somewhere. Come on in." He held open the surgery door. "Binoculars should be in that cupboard up there over the instruments. Have a root round. . . ."

A dozy white rabbit crouched, shivering a little, on the plastic-covered table. I touched the long, silken ears and scratched gently behind them. The shiver became an ague. I dropped my hand and went in search of the binoculars. I knew how it felt; I thought again of the soaring buzzard blocking out the sun.

The glasses were Zeiss Dialyt, 10×40—very classy. Hamish Remington was irritably banging the drawers of the desk one after another. I said, "Please don't bother, I can manage without it."

"Here." He produced the map with a flourish. "Knew I had one some-where."

I slid it into my pocket. He looked at me quizzically over his gold-rimmed half-glasses. "Going bird-watching?"

"Something like that." I nodded at the rabbit. "What's wrong with him?"

"Fear, mostly. Doesn't like this place. They sense it, you know. Most animals do. On the other hand, he's been eating something that doesn't agree with him. Turnips, I shouldn't wonder—*old* turnips." He smiled at me over the glasses. "Don't feed your rabbits turnips."

"I'll remember that." I grinned and waved the binoculars at him. "Thanks for these. I'll try not to lose them."

"Mark . . ." I turned at the door. He was standing by the table, his great hand buried softly in the soft fur of the rabbit. "Mind how you go," he said quietly.

I nodded, noticing as he turned away that the rabbit, beneath his gentle hand, no longer trembled.

8

With the unaccustomed necessity of wrestling with a quarter of a ton of thundering metal, my immediate problems were, for the moment at least, simplified. To be astride that great, gleaming monster, experiencing its awe-some potency pulsating through every fibre of my being, was sufficient to drive all other thoughts from my mind. The breathlessness of power and speed reduced the compass of my consciousness to a tingling revelation of a sensual body encased in rubber, a closely helmeted head and the freedom of the winding stretch of road before me.

They were following, of course; I was quite aware of that, but they would be no match for the Honda and me when we decided the time had come to shake them off. All things considered, they were doing quite well, I thought, flicking a glance at the mirror. I was touching seventy and they were still hanging on half a mile back, the sun flashing frantic heliographic signals from their windscreen.

I was heading almost due east on the A475, in the opposite direction from that I had originally intended. Edging out from the Remington drive, I had caught sight of the blue Volvo parked a couple of hundred yards away to the right. "Cheeky sods," I muttered aloud and slammed down the black perspex shield of my helmet in the hope that, accoutred as I was, they might not recognise me. But, the moment I joined the straggling stream of morning traffic, the Volvo also launched out into it and took up a position several car lengths behind. So I roared across the main bridge, turned east, towards Lampeter, and settled down to a protracted joyride whilst the Honda and I got to know each other.

She was a joy, and I made up my mind there and then that if and when this whole miserable shambles was over, the first thing I would invest in would be a Honda. Or a Suzuki. Or a BMW. . . .

With Lampeter behind me, I turned towards Aberaeron, branching off a few miles further down, at Temple Bar. For the next ten minutes I had no idea where I went, nor did I care. Momentarily out of sight of the Volvo, I swerved dangerously into a lane whose entrance, buttressed by a pair of sturdy cottages, was too narrow to allow the passage of a car. After that, I twisted and turned, ignoring any thoroughfare wide enough to accommodate a four-wheeled motor vehicle. I juddered through a thickly wooded area, splashed over a shallow stream, came almost to grief on a slippery two-plank bridge thrown over an evil-smelling ditch, and fell foul of a shepherd driving a flock of dispirited sheep, the former invecting quite splendidly in several well-chosen Welsh phrases which he then obligingly translated into English. I waved an ingratiating hand and sped on my way, thinking how much richer the whole thing sounded in Welsh than it did in English. No wonder they wanted to preserve their language!

Erupting eventually on to the A487 bound for Cardigan, I prowled off it again at the first opportunity at a tiny place glorying in the utterly unpronounceable name of Plwmp, and then, with the sun over my left shoulder, edged down in the general direction of Newcastle Emlyn. Beneath an enormous spreading chestnut tree I drew up and, whilst the Honda throbbed and grumbled between my legs, consulted the map.

A few minutes later, I had left the main road to Castellcraig and was freewheeling silently along a narrow track which, according to the map, would lead to, or was part of, the bosky ridge above Wanhope.

"Go back to the beginning," Sam Birkett had advised. "Start again." It was like snakes and ladders. So here I was, at the bottom of the board, shaking the dice.

A heavy iron gate bearing the message PRIVATE PROPERTY NO ENTRY was set between two trees and barred the way. I braked gently. Even if I ignored the notice, which I fully intended to do, the presence of two iron, fan-shaped frames splaying to right and left and attached in turn to spiked iron railings marching solemnly across the slopes on either side made further progress on the Honda impossible. Wheeling the machine on to the narrow grass verge, I heaved it on to its rest and took a close look at the padlock and chain securing the gate; recently applied oil came away on my fingers. The black dirt of the track bore fresh tyre marks, which continued on the far side of the gate.

Collecting the Zeiss glasses from the pannier, I replaced them with the helmet and wedged the Walther into the waistband of my already tight jeans, where it felt like a chronic case of appendicitis.

The gate was a piece of cake; no more than shoulder high, it presented no problem to an intrepid mountaineer like myself. On the far side, I stood for a moment breathing deeply of the clean, sweet air, wishing I could bottle some of it and carry it away with me to the Big Smoke. Staring out over the stunning view, I recalled something else Sam Birkett had said. "Tread carefully," he had cautioned. Mitch had repeated a cool version of the same sentiment, and Hamish Remington's final thought had been "Mind how you go."

I hesitated, the words moving in solemn sequence through my mind, imbued still with the same quiet warning as that with which they had originally been spoken. I closed my eyes and concentrated, reaching out for that sixth sense which had so often, in the past, come to my aid; that odd, pricking sensation which told of prying and watchful eyes.

If it could be relied upon, there was nothing; I was alone and unobserved. Nevertheless, I retraced my steps, clambered again over the gate and, with a great deal of effort for one so young, moved the Honda deep into the cover of the bushes, adding further to its invisibility by several handfuls of strategically placed brushwood. With my foot, I swept away its tyre tracks.

In the excitement of launching the Honda, the grinding discomfort of my hurts had receded, even my shoulder had behaved itself, but my third assault on the gate reminded me of my parlous condition.

A hundred yards up and along the spine of the ridge, I arrived at the stretch of ground immediately above Wanhope. With my back planted firmly against the bole of a tree, I focused the glasses and studied the house and the ground below, inch by inch, foot by foot. I saw no living thing, not even a bird or a vole. Lowering the glasses, I stared thoughtfully at the grey roof nestled among the trees. A frontal attack was all I could think of; plough my way down the slope, knock on the door and, if nobody answered, effect, as they say, an entrance; I had been prudent enough to slide my do-it-yourself burglar kit into the pocket of the Belstaff jacket.

The decision made, I stepped off the track into the waist-high undergrowth, and froze, my ears picking up the distant whine of an approaching car. Swearing impotently, I plunged further down the slope and finished up in an untidy heap and what could only be a blackberry bush. Easing myself painfully from one thorn to the next I found a moment to repine over my new jeans.

There was no doubt that the car was climbing the hill I had just negotiated on the Honda; soon it would stop and someone with a key would open the gate.

I strained my ears; the slightest squeal of brakes, the engine idling for a second or two, then the surge forward in first; again a pause for the securing of the gate, followed by the approaching crunch of tyres. Through the tight network of twigs and branches, a familiar light blue shape crept into view. I removed a thorn from my backside with a deft hand, and sank back into my prickly hide.

The Volvo came to a halt no more than five yards away and directly in my line of vision. Andrew Elliot and his top cameraman couldn't have placed it better. A hand which sported a black-stoned signet ring and rested on the window ledge swung out the already open door, and a man in a tan raincoat stepped out. It was Steve McQueen. He stood for a moment sniffing the air and swivelling a pair of watchful blue eyes in every direction, including mine, for he seemed to look me directly in the eye; I was already rehearsing a reason for sitting in a blackberry bush when he turned away, exchanged a couple of words with the driver and slammed the door. He really did bear a startling resemblance to Steve McQueen. I lowered my eyes and gave up breathing, and as he passed, two yards away, I hoped he did not possess, like me, a built-in radar device which bristled the hair at the back of his neck.

Listening to his departing footsteps, I turned my attention to the car. The driver had so far not emerged, but then I heard the door snap open and his head and shoulders appeared over the roof. Not a pleasant sight. I had met his sort of face in films about jail riots; he was the one who loomed up behind the wrongly convicted hero in the laundry uttering dire threats without moving his lips and later confronted him in the shower with nothing but a bar of prison soap between them.

I watched him as he lumbered around the front of the car; he was square and thick-set and walked with a nautical roll; he hitched his fat bottom against the near-side headlamp and lit a cigarette, tossing the still-lighted match into the undergrowth. It was someone like him who had set fire to Rome and then blamed it on Nero. Pushing himself off the headlamp, he ambled around to the rear window, reached in and from the back seat withdrew a rifle. I jerked up the glasses and, near though I was, focused on the weapon: an AK47, a Kalashnikov Assault Rifle. It would weigh anything up to ten pounds and he was tossing it around from hand to hand as if it were a peashooter. What the hell was he doing with a thing like that in rural Wales?

With a sudden growl he threw it up to his shoulder, traversed it around, aimed it in my direction and said, "Bang, bang!" and chuckled happily. "Hey, Champ," he called to his descending companion. "You're dead. I just shot you." The pleasantry was clearly received with a rude gesture, for the sharpshooter giggled like an idiot and returned the gesture vigorously.

Behind the man's head I caught sight of a bird. Not a buzzard this time but certainly a bird of prey. I peered through the glasses and drew a breath; rusty-brown plumage, streaky white head, forked tail. I knew enough about birds to know that I was looking at one of the rare ones: a kite. Fascinated, I watched the wheeling flight, the tireless circling, heard its shrill cry. As did the goon with the gun. Twisting his head, he registered the bird and, without further ado, slammed the butt of the gun against his shoulder. I grabbed for the Walther at my waist. "I'll kill him," I muttered.

Champ's voice came floating quietly up the hill. "Deakin, you shoot that bird and I'll blow your sodding head off." Deakin gave no sign that he had heard but continued to trace the flight of the bird through his sights. The voice came again, soft and deadly. "That's a promise, Deakin . . . don't try it, Deakin. . . ."

This time the quiet threat was followed by a sharp metallic click. Slowly Deakin's rifle was lowered. He stood motionless for a long moment; losing face was being difficult for him. Then, with a sudden spurt of sullen anger, he returned the gun violently to the car, and moving round the front of the vehicle, got in and slammed the door.

The kite wheeled away on silent wings.

Below me Champ's weapon clicked again and I listened to the resumed slither of his descending footsteps. I drew up my knees and settled back among the thorns. When I stretched my neck and glanced down the slope, it was to catch a quick glimpse of Champ moving purposefully across the drive to the house.

Wondering how long I would have to wait, and what I was waiting for anyway, I became aware of the heavy rubber redolence of the Belstaff jacket I was wearing. This put me in mind of old motor tyres, which then turned my thoughts to Oxfam and by this declension to Julie. It would seem an unromantic quirk that the smell of old rubber should conjure up a vision of the girl I loved; mimosa or orange blossom would have been more seemly, or the wafting in her wake of some exotic perfume of Arabia. But I grinned happily to myself, not without some sheepishness, and settled for a secondhand mackintosh.

Which brought me back inevitably to Mister of that ilk and the reason why I was now squatting so uncomfortably above the house to which his name had been so haphazardly attached. The feeling grew in me that I was not about to solve my problems by remaining rooted among the blackberry bushes.

Raising the glasses, I again studied Deakin. Slumped in the driving seat of the Volvo, he was glaring blankly at the windscreen, mouth pursed, underlip protruding moronically; a slight and rhythmic motion of his head suggested the presence of a car radio. There was no sense of impatience about him. He resembled an unwholesome cab driver waiting with his flag down for a fare to return.

I turned my attention to the house. What was going on? What was he doing down there? Curiosity seeped into me like the damp oozing through the seat of my pants. My eyes lingered speculatively on the path winding down the slope to the driveway. Since that side of the house was windowless it might be possible to descend without being overlooked, providing Deakin continued to sulk and Champ remained where he was. Action of any kind was preferable to sitting about doing nothing. I had, after all, little to lose. Except my life, of course.

I wriggled my way gingerly out of the bush, through another and on to the treacherous surface of the narrow path. I trod carefully, clutching the gun in one hand and flailing about with the other from one hold to another. Gaining the clearing in which my career had so nearly been brought to a close the previous morning, I paused to draw breath. With the house now well in sight, I determined, as a safety measure, to leave the path and take to the undergrowth, where I would present a lesser target should my luck run out.

At last I reached the drive and scuttled across to the side wall of the house, keeping close to the overhang of vegetation. I thought I could hear what sounded like the distant clatter of a helicopter, but nothing else, no thumps or bumps from inside the house, no suggestion of movement. I poked my head cautiously around the corner of the house, then followed it, moving swiftly to the first window, flattening myself against the wall to peek inside; I saw only my reflection. Ducking low, I crabbed over to the second.

A shrill whistle suddenly pierced the silence. I hurled myself back against the wall as if pinned to it by an assegai through the chest. A car engine started up. The Volvo? If Champ wanted a ride, now would be the moment for him to quit the house.

I eased off the Walther's safety-catch, pressed back against the wall and waited. Nothing happened. All at once I felt petulant. I was doing all this and nobody was taking the slightest bit of notice of me. Throwing caution to the wind and doubling back a few paces on to the drive, I put the glasses to my eyes and watched the blue shape of the Volvo merge slowly with the shadows of the overhang of trees and disappear. Without Champ. I turned and stared soberly at the house.

I approached the building warily.

Who had whistled? Champ? Why? Because he needed the car? The Volvo had taken off without him in the direction it had been facing, not back towards the iron gate.

I was at the door, trying the handle. No joy. It was only then that I realised that the damage done by the bullet I had put through it the day before had been repaired and the lock replaced. Very neatly. At the window to the left of the door, the same through which I had seen the dying George Mathews, I bent double, setting my eyes to the lower corner and shading the glass with my hand. The room was as I remembered it, the table reset with most of its ornaments but lacking its vase of plastic flowers, the chairs, the door through into the passage. I crossed my eyes and examined the glass of the window. It had been cleansed of the blood which had streaked it. Again I looked into the room, straining my eyes and ears for any sign or sound of movement. The room was empty and unchanged.

Or was it? I frowned to myself. Something was different . . . some little thing. . . . I cast my mind back to the first occasion I had stared through this same window, checking everything as I had then registered it. Something had been there then which was now missing. But what? The answer evaded me. I turned away.

Making a cautious circuit of the house, I found myself again at the side door. Cobwebs clung to the jamb of the door and meshed across the lock; a small drift of undisturbed dirt and dust begrimed the step. I brushed away some of the cobwebs and tried the handle; it wouldn't even turn. The door itself was solid and unyielding. A histrionic attack upon it with my shoulder would put me in hospital for a week. I also didn't fancy the narrow window of frosted glass beside it, so I returned to the front, where the windows were more approachable and, being of the sash variety, secured only by a lever catch. I could see no sign of any safety device to prevent that catch from being released by the adroit insertion of a knife blade between the frames.

My do-it-yourself burglar kit included my trusty Scout-knife and I had this out and in position before anyone could say Baden-Powell. The catch was rusted but yielded after a couple of efforts, as also did the window, crookedly but with hardly a squeak.

Stepping over the low sill, I stood listening intently. Nothing.

In a flash I was at the far end of the room, my back to the wall against which the china wasp had been splintered; its shattered remnants were nowhere to be seen. My eyes quartered the room. It had been cleaned meticulously; everything neatly in place. On the stone floor where the body of George Mathews had lain, only the faintest of shadows betrayed the whereabouts of spilt blood; the oak table had been wiped clean, the ornaments carefully arranged upon it.

A dull and distant thud brought me back to the present predicament. A car door? Stealthily I moved into the hall.

A great deal of my time seemed to have been spent prowling around this Godforsaken house with a loaded gun in my hand and my heart in my mouth. I was beginning to tire of it.

The bathroom was immaculate, the blood-stained mat nowhere in evidence. The bedroom was undisturbed. Cupboards, alcoves, niches came once again under my scrutiny. I drew open the kitchen drawer which had contained the murder weapon. The knife was there still. I peered at it closely. If there were traces of blood on the handle and blade, a forensic examination would now be necessary to reveal them.

I slid the folding ladder from the ceiling of the kitchen and mounted again to the tiny attics. Nothing and no one.

Standing again in the main living room, I stared moodily out of the window, chastened and frustrated. If Steve McQueen, alias Champ, had entered that house, he had also left it, because he certainly wasn't there now.

"The place was empty," I told her, crunching loudly on a potato crisp and eyeing her over my orange juice. "I was there less than ten minutes after he'd gone in and he was nowhere to be seen. Disappeared through a hole in the floor."

"Perhaps that's where he went."

"Where?"

"Through a hole in the floor."

She was being flippant, but I entertained the idea seriously. "If there was a cellar I didn't notice it."

"Mike would know." I glanced at her enquiringly. "Mike Davies. After all, according to Dad last night, he and that other fellow, the one who was killed, shacked up there together."

"It's been burnt down and rebuilt since then."

"They could have stuck to the original plans. Probably did. No harm in asking." She leaned forward. "Incidentally, I looked in at Primrose's this morning, the local estate agent. They don't have Wanhope on their books, but they think they know who has. I said I might want to rent it for a friend. They seem to think it could belong to an English syndicate who are busy buying up rural property for holiday homes and all that. They said they'll let me know."

We were perched on stools in the saloon bar of the Dragon. The clock over the mercifully silent jukebox registered one o'clock and, as I glanced at it, struck three ponderously. Outside, the sun was shining.

I had been tooling back quietly from Wanhope, immersed in gloomy thoughts and crash helmet, when she had drawn alongside in the Morris and shouted across through her open window. I didn't hear what she said, but the unexpected sight of her all but drove me into a ditch. Passing the Honda, she waved me to follow, and here we were, with the bar to ourselves, waiting for toasted cheese sandwiches.

"How was Harry Hawk's cow?"

"Mother and child both doing well."

I looked at her quizzically. "I don't see you delivering calves and foals and bunging those great billiard-ball things down horses' throats."

She grinned slyly. "If it comes to that, I don't really see you as a private eye."

I made a face. "I should have stuck to the acting. I don't know what the hell I'm doing up here. Suddenly I'm James Bond and Boysie Oakes rolled into one and the bullets are real." I leaned in towards her and lowered my voice. "That imbecilic Deakin was playing around with an AK47 as if it was a toy. A Russian automatic assault rifle. That thing is capable of 620 rounds a minute. What the hell is he doing with a thing like that in the middle of Wales? That's a terrorist weapon. The other one had a gun too. What are they frightened of? What are they protecting? Who are they working for?" I had lowered my voice even further, so that even she was finding it difficult to hear. "I'll tell you one thing: Emrys Williams knows exactly what it's about. And our young friend Davies is mixed up in it too somewhere."

She shook her head. "I don't think so. He's into something, all right, but I doubt if it's your thing. He's a militant Welshman, granted, or he used to be; everyone around here knows that. At the very worst he's one of those idiots who're setting light to things. But they're not gunmen or terrorists; they don't go around shooting people."

"Yet."

"All they want is some action instead of just sitting around doing the civil-disobedience bit every now and again. Wales for the Welsh and all that. But they're not the next-best things to the 'IRA baboons,' as old Hailsham once said they were. No, it's your lot, the man with the gun and the Steve McQueen character, who are the ones in the baboon category."

"Deakin's a baboon, certainly. I quite warmed to the other one when he put a stop to Deakin shooting down the kite. There must be some good in him."

"As there is in every Mafia godfather—or so we're led to believe."

At this point, two toasted cheese sandwiches were placed primly on the counter by no less a person than Emrys Williams himself, who, studiously avoiding my eye, added, beside each plate, a meticulously folded paper napkin. When I handed him a five-pound note and ordered a further round of drinks he took the money, supplied the drinks, and gave me change, all without uttering a sound. No one could say he was either talkative or pleased to see us.

He was turning away when the door behind us opened to admit some new arrivals. Emrys Williams caught sight of them over my shoulder and, for a split second, I could have sworn I saw a flicker of alarm in his eyes, and even as I did so they turned and met mine for the first time, holding them for a fraction longer than was necessary. The message they conveyed was quite clear: watch yourself.

He then turned his attention to one of the new arrivals, an enormous Great Dane whom I later learned was called Hamlet—which was fair enough, I suppose. The dog by this time had heaved his forepaws on to the bar, laid his chin between them, and engaged Williams in a fixed and meditative stare. "Well, hello, young sir," responded Williams solemnly. "And what can we do for you?"

The dog gave a short staccato bark.

"One Guinness, sir? Yessir, coming up." The dog growled. "A pint?"

"No," drawled a familiar voice from the door behind me. "Give him a half, Emrys, or he'll be peeing all over the shop."

I turned and found myself face to face with Colonel St. John Hazlitt-Martin. The narrow grey eyes encountered mine for a second and then turned to meet Julie's. "Hello, m'dear, nice to see you: don't often run across you in here." The eyes were back on me. "Oh, yes of course . . ." He pointed a gloved finger at me. "Chumley, that's it, isn't it? Thought I remembered you from somewhere. How's the feed business? Can I offer you both a drink? Gertrude." He called over his shoulder as if he were addressing a recalcitrant NCO. "What'll you have—as if I didn't know?" An enchanting-looking elderly woman slid out from behind him and I detached myself politely from my stool. "This is the wife." He jerked his head at me. "Chumley. In the feed business; up here on a reccy. Spratts, wasn't it?" The mistake could have been perfectly genuine.

"Spillers," interjected Julie, a trifle too hastily, I thought. The mistake could have been perfectly genuine. "Hello, Mrs. Hazlitt-Martin. Spratts are no longer with us, you should know that, Colonel."

"Oh, m'dear, I can't keep up with all that nonsense. Spratts were all the rage at one time. Remember their logo. Little Scottie dog made out of the letters of the name. You remember that, Gertie, don't you, little Scottie dog? Ingenious, I always thought. What are you drinking?"

In the midst of all this, as well as refusing a drink, I managed to say hello to Gertie and offer her my stool, which she declined regretfully, indicating that they would be sitting in their usual place, in the window. She was a small, neatly boned woman in her middle sixties or thereabouts, with shrewd, sparkling blue eyes and the shyest smile I had encountered since grammar school. She wore her iron-grey hair in what used to be called a pageboy and carried herself with such effortless grace that I was inclined to suspect her of being a one-time ballerina.

Whilst her husband and Julie made desultory conversation, I collected from Emrys Williams a large bowl of frothing Guinness, and under the grateful supervision of Gertie, deposited it on the floor by the table at the window. Hamlet came and stood over it proprietorially, regarding it with a melancholy stare and making no attempt to drink. The faintest of whines escaped him. The colonel glanced across from the bar. "All right, old lad," he nodded, "fall to, fall to," and Hamlet, lowering his head, slurped away noisily in the dreamy-eyed manner usually to be seen only in television advertisements.

"I've never seen a dog drink Guinness before," I told Gertie, for want of something better to say.

"Oh, he was weaned on it." She waved an airy hand. "The horses, on the other hand, won't touch it—simply won't touch it. They prefer Whitbread, so I give them that; a pint every day stirred up in their gubbins. And there's quite a to-do if they don't get it on time, I can tell you." She treated me to a lengthy examination, the shrewd blue eyes roving over me questioningly as though searching for hidden blemishes; then she said in a sharp, accusatory tone, "Are you a horse person?"

"I like horses, yes, but I don't actually own one."

"Everyone should own a horse."

"I live in a flat," I pointed out. "In London."

The dreaded word "London" produced the usual effect. "Ah, yes," she nodded, suddenly gloomy. "I see. Well . . . that's a problem, isn't it?"

The colonel arrived bearing drinks and, excusing myself, I rejoined Julie and my cheese sandwich at the bar. Emrys Williams had gone, presumably to the public bar, where his services would be more in demand. "Ever tried Bruno on the Guinness?"

"I have, yes. The creature prefers whisky. So we settled for water."

I stole a glance at the mirror behind the bar. The colonel and his lady were sitting bolt upright by the window. Gertie looked bright enough, but beside her the grey shadow of her husband loomed, grim and uncommunicative, frowning to himself as though wondering what unfortunate circumstance had brought him to this particular moment of his career. I wondered too. About him. About his career. I tried to imagine him in uniform. Impeccable he would be, I thought, though khaki was too warm a hue; grey would have suited him better. Field grey.

Smirking at my bitter jest, I suddenly realised that he was as intent upon me as I was upon him. The cold grey eyes were fixed upon me like those of a basilisk, and as I became conscious of their regard they crawled across the back of my neck; my hair bristled. Shifting focus, they encountered mine in the mirror.

Resisting the desire to break contact, I received the full force of a remarkable and mesmeric power. Before I was aware of what was happening I had been drawn into a contest I had not sought, and whilst a small part of me ridiculed the situation, the rest strove manfully not to falter. Raising his tankard to his lips he took a leisurely draught, his eyes never once leaving mine. When he had finished and before lowering his glass, he raised it an inch towards me in a silent and mocking toast. The corners of his mouth twitched, the eyes glittered with sudden malice.

Julie was speaking, her voice tinged with concern. "Mark? You're as white as a sheet. You look as if you'd seen a ghost."

My eyes fell away in confusion; "Not a ghost," I muttered. "The bloody enemy."

"What enemy?"

I closed my eyes wearily. "In the mirror."

She was silent for so long I began to wonder whether she had left me. Opening my eyes, I turned my head towards her. "I don't believe it," she whispered.

"You'd better, because it's true."

"How do you know?" The question was querulous, and far too loud.

"He just told me. He looked at me in that mirror and told me."

There was a further lengthy silence, during which she stared at her capable hands outspread on the bar before her; she then said quietly, "I think you're being fanciful."

"Fanciful or not, I've got to follow it up."

"How?"

I shrugged. "God knows." I flicked a look into the mirror. With his hands on his knees, the colonel had reverted to his recent reverie and was staring stolidly in front of him. Beside him, Gertrude had not moved. She seemed to take her cues from him, and I wondered if I should feel sorry for her.

I said in a low voice, "Let's get out of here. I've got to think."

We finished our drinks and slid off our stools. A sudden burst of sound from the public bar indicated the return of Emrys Williams, who stood in the open doorway, a look of enquiry on his face; I shook my head. He turned to go.

"Mr. Savage." The clear, metallic voice came from behind me. The three of us, Julie, Williams and myself, grew roots. Williams, the first to recover, slowly turned his head, his great eyes resting for a second on mine, then shifting onwards over my shoulder.

"Mr. Savage," repeated the colonel.

What was the point of denying it? He had never been taken in by Chumley of Spillers for one moment; he had known of my true identity from the first second he had seen me, yesterday evening on his own farm after our brush with the Volvo. If Deakin and Champ were his men, not only had orders for my destruction by then been issued but two attempts had already failed.

As I turned slowly to face him, I was aware that Williams had faded discreetly from the scene. The colonel was regarding me with a sardonic smile on his lips. Gertrude was also watching, loyally sharing his amusement. Between them lay Hamlet, drowsy head between paws.

The colonel went on, "We were wondering whether you would care to dine with us this evening, you and—er—Miss Remington. Quite informal of course, potluck and all that, nothing fancy. What do you say?"

I was bereft of words. I think I might have behaved more intelligently had he been brandishing a Colt .45, rather than a half-consumed light ale. I had been through all this before—on the stage, lines forgotten, feet glued to the floorboards, with the prompter desperately attempting to make contact from the wings. . . .

"Please come, Mr. Savage," pressed Gertrude gently, "we would just love to have you both."

Julie was no help and obviously waiting for some sort of cue from me.

The colonel was going on: "Get to know each other, eh?" and since I still made no answer, added, "good, that's settled, then. Fine. Around seven, then, for aperitifs?" A *fait accompli.*

He then returned to his glass, lowering his eyes as he drank. I watched his Adam's apple moving up and down with each swallow.

"That *will* be nice," said Gertrude brightly while the clock ticked on as if nothing had happened.

With a sudden burst of energy, I snatched the Belstaff jacket from the counter, turned abruptly on my heel and left the bar, Julie grabbing at her unfinished sandwich and falling in—somewhat irresolutely, I thought—behind me.

"Why didn't you refuse?" she demanded, the moment we reached the open air.

"My tongue," I told her, "was stuck to the roof of my mouth, where it usually is in moments of crisis."

I led the way to the little courtyard at the rear of the building where we had left the car and the Honda.

"He knows who you really are," she told me, galloping gamely alongside and munching on her sandwich.

"Which proves who he is, and doesn't surprise me."

"We'd be mad to go."

"We're not going. I am. You're too busy. Harry Hawk's cow's had a relapse. I'll make your excuses."

"I'm going."

I stopped at the car and turned to her patiently. "You just said it would be mad."

"But I didn't say we wouldn't go."

She broke off as a crunching of gravel turned our heads. Emrys Williams was approaching, a heavy cask, supported by a huge arm, balanced on his stooped and massive shoulders; everybody's idea of a smuggler.

"Lie low, Mr. Savage," he grunted as he came alongside, breathing heavily. "And don't accept that invitation." I stood defiantly in his path. "Tomorrow, Mr. Savage," he growled, glaring at me, "I promise," and moved off to transfer his cask to a waiting truck.

Becoming suddenly very tired of being continually swept under the carpet, I started off after him. I didn't hear the approaching car until, with a squeal of brakes and the tearing sound of tyres on gravel, it came to a halt not six inches from my left kneecap. I heard an involuntary gasp from Julie but was too engrossed with the car's radiator to reassure her of my continued good health. Not six inches from that same left kneecap was a small metal badge, a black Maltese cross on a red-and-white ground.

Slowly I raised my eyes and met those of Champ, who was leaning negligently from the driver's window, eyeing me mildly. "People have been killed that way," he reproved quietly and waved me across with a polite hand. I took a step back instead and jerked my head in silence. The car surged forward gently, passing me so closely that I caught a whiff of his after-shave lotion. He grinned up at me, pursing his lips mischievously. "Nearly had you that time," he murmured.

I offered him a screwed-up smile. "Don't give it another thought," I said.

I stood and watched as he swung the car around and backed it dextrously into a parking bay alongside the gleaming elegance of a dove-grey Mercedes.

With the excitement of almost being run down yet again, my irritation with Williams had partially subsided and I shot a quick glance at him as he and another man occupied themselves with loading up the truck. I had no intention of taking his advice, and for the rest I decided to let it go for the time being. Until tomorrow, anyway. Tomorrow was as good a day as any. Providing I survived the night.

Julie was beside me. "You all right?"

"I'll live."

"But not for much longer if you go on like that."

"See who it was?" I asked. "Perhaps it's no longer open season for Savages." To make a show of it for those who might be interested, I took her hands and lounged intimately against the side of the Morris whilst covertly watching Champ disembark from the Volvo. There was no sign of Deakin.

"He's left the pretty one behind."

She didn't seem to mind about that. "I see what you mean about Steve McQueen," she murmured approvingly. "He's quite a dish."

"Ever seen him before?"

She shook her head and smiled slyly at me. "I would have remembered if I had."

Having locked the Volvo and checked the boot, Champ strolled over in our direction, presumably on his way to a pint. I detached myself from Julie just in case he wanted to try anything untoward and shrugged into the Belstaff, watching him as he undressed Julie in the approved manner of the male chauvinist pig and acknowledged me with a lascivious wink.

When he'd finally gone, I stared longingly at the Volvo. She read my thoughts. "It'll be booby-trapped and you'll get blown up."

"Doubt if he's left anything of importance in it anyway. He's cleverer than that." My eyes slithered along to the Mercedes-Benz. "I suppose that little old heap belongs to Éminence Grise, inside." I opened the Morris door. "Let's slum it for a minute and take the weight off our feet."

She settled herself with a loud sigh as if she hadn't sat down for a week. "How long have you known the colonel?" I asked.

She shrugged. "Ever since I came here. Nearly four years."

"Who is he?"

"Apparently respectable English farmer; by this time part of the landscape, and that, considering his nationality, is no mean feat. He's filthy rich of course, which might have something to do with it. And he runs that farm like a military operation. Wouldn't be surprised if they didn't have Reveille and Lights Out." She paused thoughtfully. "You know, you may be right about him. It's an extraordinarily self-sufficient sort of farm. One rarely sees any of the hands on the loose, for example, and if they *do* have days off for gallivanting, they never do any of it around here. They all have accommodation on the farm. In the stables, for instance, there are three grooms and a head man. All of them live on the premises. Mind you, that's not unusual for stable people; they like to be near the horses in case of emergency. But the odd thing is that I have never yet met one of them *outside* the farm, and I get around quite a bit."

"Does he race the horses?"

"They have a couple in training at Newmarket. This is just a stud. The horses are Gertrude's department, really, and it's more of a hobby than a business; she certainly doesn't need the money. But she's got some very nice animals, wildly expensive, and dear things. They're the light of poor old Gertrude's life."

"Poor?"

She frowned. "They're an odd couple. I've often wondered what she sees in him. But I suppose there's not a lot she can do about it now—at her age—even if she wanted to."

Silence fell for a minute or two; then I said thoughtfully, "For a military operation that farm's pretty lax on security, isn't it? You roared in there last night like a bat out of hell with no trouble at all and finished up cheek by jowl with a bloody great Range Rover—worth a king's ransom all on its own. Anyone could knock it off. He must have gates and fences, locks and bolts surely. Burglar alarms?"

"We were a bit cheeky last night. I took a shortcut through his next-door neighbour's farm. There's a sort of communal corridor. A few acres of the colonel's pastureland are marooned in the middle of the other fellow's property, so they've come to an amicable arrangement, but since the other chap invariably leaves most of his gates open, it's less amicable than it might be. So, if you know where to look for it, there's free access to the colonel. I use it all the time when I'm on call to both farms, as I am during the lambing season and such times. Neither of them seems to mind and it does save a pint or two of petrol."

I gave her a rueful smile. "In the light of what we think we now know, we drove straight into the spider's parlour last night. When Deakin and Champ arrived back at home base, hot and sweating after having lost us, they were probably regaled with the news that we had already been and gone. I can just hear the colonel, can't you? 'Dressed up as this shifty lookin' hunchback feller, he was, name o' Chumley or something equally idiotic, worked for Spratt's, *she* said.' " I snorted. "It must have made his day. Obviously that's when he sent them back to park poor old George Mathews in my car. I suppose he hoped I might get stuck with the police."

"Or warned off."

"He probably just wanted to get rid of the bloody body. Who wants a bloody body? Not much future in a dead body, is there?"

"None at all—especially if it belongs to you," she added, giving me a loaded look.

She glanced suddenly at her watch. "I must go, can't sit about here gossiping all the afternoon."

"More calls?"

"A sick pig, a distempered Welsh collie, and a lame mare, all at opposite ends of the globe, so the sooner I get away the sooner I'll be back. Thank you for a disturbing lunch. What are you up to this afternoon?"

I pondered for a moment. "A word with Mike Davies, for a start. Then, perhaps, your friend Mr. Pithy. He might come up with something. Beard him in his den, if you'll tell me where it is."

"Don't forget to go armed." She became suddenly serious. "Don't frighten him, Mark. He's a child. Tell him you're from the Admiralty or the Ministry of Food or something; he's terribly impressed with titles. You go up Beacon Hill past Wanhope. The road peters out into a sort of parking area and just beyond, up towards the beacon itself, you'll see his place. You can't miss it. It's a sort of caravan without wheels and flies the Royal Standard at all times." She forestalled my interruption. "Yes, I know, but she's rarely in residence. Officialdom is pretty hoity-toity about it, but I don't expect ER would mind. Anyway, treat him gently."

I opened the door and prepared to depart. "Is that it, then?"

"Dinner at the colonel's?"

Half in and half out of the car, I turned and looked at her over my shoulder. "I'll see you back at the homestead. We'll talk about it then."

I left the car and she watched with amusement as I buckled on the helmet and strapped myself tightly into the Belstaff. Her lips moved, but I couldn't hear what she said through the helmet. Misjudging the latter's bulk, I leaned in at the window and almost knocked myself out. My head rang like a bell. "What did you say?"

"I said you looked very butch."

When I had kissed her clumsily on the lips, I became aware that her eyes were fixed on someone or something over my shoulder. They were full of love. I screwed my head around. She was looking at the Honda. She spoke again, again inaudibly. "What?"

"I said, mind my bike." She started her engine, sat regarding me thoughtfully for a moment, then beckoned me in again. "If you are going to talk to Mike Davies, why have you put all that gear on? He lives here, you know."

And before I could reply, she smirked at me, let in the clutch and drove directly at the parked Mercedes in a burst of speed which stood my hair on end. With an inch to spare, she slammed on her brakes, executed a wild three-point and with a mischievous flash of teeth was gone.

9

Michael Davies, in a blue-and-white-striped butcher's apron, was in the kitchen supervising the sandwiches and keeping an eye on those in residence, who consisted of the birdlike female in the enterprising auburn wig, the

Dragon herself—she of the square head and the earrings—plus an extra pair of hands surmounted by outsize bosom and perspiring brick-red face, the latter rammed into a complicated turban cleverly devised from a pictorial tea towel. This mountain of flagging flesh answered to the name of Maisie, a fact I gleaned during a brief contretemps between the four of them when Davies demanded to know the whereabouts of a certain Mr. Griffith's shepherd's pie.

However, when Davies caught sight of me lounging negligently against the doorjamb, Mr. Griffith's shepherd's pie became a thing of no interest and he smiled brightly—too brightly, I thought—and came over.

"Hello. Anything wrong?"

"Not a thing. Just interested to see how the other half lives. It all looks very hot-making."

"No more than usual. Shepherd's pie and toasted sandwiches; that's all we do. But it's enough."

I looked casual. "Buy you a drink if you like."

He was obviously grateful for any excuse to get away, for he had his apron off and hanging on a hook in the steamy kitchen before I could draw another breath. "Let's go through to my place."

I bought the drinks at the public bar and carried them ostentatiously to his cosy hideaway, our progress through the crowded room being accompanied by only the slightest falling away of sound and the turning of a few curious heads, nothing like the reception we'd had on the previous occasion. The evening clientèle, I suspected, was of sterner stuff than that of lunch time. Williams was heaving a huge cask into position as I passed, and I countered the brooding frown in his protruding eyes with a pert wink.

Davies sank into his armchair with a protracted sigh. "Who would run a bloody pub? God knows what it must be like to manage a four-star place."

"You'd have more help."

"And more responsibility."

He watched me closely as I unbelted the Belstaff jacket. "You look good enough to eat in that thing," he told me with sudden and disturbing candour. "Very butch."

"Julie Remington's own words," I said, wondering why the sudden hand of friendship.

"A discerning lady."

An awkward silence fell between us as we had a go at our drinks. I had lashed out on yet another orange juice but craved suddenly for alcohol.

"You used to live at Wanhope, didn't you?" I asked abruptly, deciding there was no point in beating about the bush. He looked startled at the suddenness of the question, his eyes flickering involuntarily in the direction of the photograph on the table. I glimpsed an unfathomable depth of private misery and despair in the shadows which closed over them. I knew the cause and understood.

He nodded silently and, I thought, had decided to leave it at that, but then he spoke. "I wasn't entirely frank with you the other night, was I? You obviously know that now. Did Julie tell you? No, she wasn't here in those days. Hamish, then?" He nodded again. "Yes, Hamish knew. . . ."

"Do you want to talk about it?"

He shook his head. "Not particularly. It's all in the past. I should have got over it, but haven't. Yes, I used to live at Wanhope. Why?"

"Who owned the place, do you remember?"

He nodded at the photograph. "He did. Barry. Barry Newman."

"And when he . . . ?"

He shrugged. "It was burnt down, wasn't it?"

"But rebuilt."

"True." He frowned slightly. "He died intestate, of course; I knew nothing of what went on. Somebody must have bought what was left of it, I suppose."

"You don't know who?"

"No idea. Insurance people? They do sometimes. I only know they were an unconscionable time rebuilding it."

"Did the house have a cellar in your time?"

"If it did, we never used it. Barry was fond of wine, kept a large stock of it in a cupboard in the kitchen. He was always complaining about it never being cool enough. A cellar would have been the obvious place to store it if there'd been one."

"Apart from the front door and the side entrance, was there any other way in or out of the house?"

"None. It was jammed up against solid rock."

"Rock?"

"Well, whatever it is. The side of the hill. What's the mystery?"

I hesitated for a moment, wondering how much I need tell him. "Someone went in there this morning and didn't come out by either of the recognised exits. When I went in after him, the cupboard was bare." His eyes had narrowed slightly. "So I fell to wondering if there was somewhere else he could have gone, like down into the cellarage or through a hole in the wall. Otherwise he just disappeared into thin air and I don't believe in that sort of thing."

My solar plexus gave a jolt. I had answered the question myself. Why hadn't I thought of it before? Not down a cellar at all. Through a hole in the wall. There was a hole in that bloody wall. Into the hillside. And that was only a ridge, not the side of a mountain. You could tunnel right through that ridge and come out on the other side. Perhaps that's why rebuilding took such an "unconscionable time." I thought of the car and Deakin waiting on the ridge; the whistle; the car drawing away—and no Champ in the building. It had to be the explanation. He had gone through the house, through the ridge and out the other side, and Deakin had picked him up in the car. But why?

Michael Davies was watching me intently, aware that a penny had dropped somewhere. "You've thought of something."

I gave a shifty grin, then improvised. "The obvious explanation has just occurred to me, that's all. I've been talking a load of rubbish. There was one moment when he was actually out of my line of vision. It was brief but long enough for him to have left by the side door. Simple as that. I'm an idiot." He was staring at me quizzically. I broke off. I was protesting too much. I launched off at a tangent. "I was sorry to hear about—er—Barry, was it? Must have been a terrible blow." I glanced at the photograph. "He looks very —" I searched for a word—"butch?" I finished with a lame smile.

I had turned the conversation successfully but could never have foreseen the result of my strategy. By this time he had become wholly absorbed in the photograph. "He wasn't butch at all, really. He was—oh, I don't know—it's such a long time ago now; he was what people sometimes call a sensitive. A gentle person—loving. We had similar thoughts, cared about the same things . . ." He flicked a look at me. "How much did Hamish tell you?"

"Not much." I took up my drink. "I mentioned that I had met you and he said that things hadn't been all that easy for you, and so on and so forth, you know?"

I stopped, realising with some uneasiness that his eyes were brimming with tears. He brushed at them irritably with the back of a hand.

"I'm sorry," I mumbled. "I didn't mean to start up painful memories. It was simply that—" I broke off.

He was staring at me fixedly, his face crumpling in anguish. Before I knew what was happening he was at my feet, his head against my knees, his hands clutching convulsively at my arms, upsetting my drink over his own head. I watched the sticky orange juice seep into the silky brown hair; he didn't seem to notice it. Irrelevantly I thought tonight would have to be shampoo night. I put down the glass. He was muttering something into my knees but nothing intelligible.

I pried gently at his hands. "Come on, Mike," I urged quietly, "take a hold of yourself." I placed a soothing hand on his head. It was a mistake. At the touch, he dragged himself up on to his knees, threw his arms about me and buried his head on my chest. I struggled for release, heaving myself to my feet, bearing his full weight as I did so. He clung to me desperately, as if I were some kind of final hope. "Mike," I growled, impatient now and doing my best not to be violent with him. "Let go of me, for God's sake. Pull yourself together."

For a second, I held him hard in my arms, sensing his terrible and urgent need for comfort. I spoke gently. "Come on, now, have another drink. Let me go. And come and sit down . . . come on . . ." I guided him over to his chair, made him sit and reached for his glass. "Here, have a swig of this . . . it'll make you feel better."

In a sudden and inexplicable paroxysm of anger he lashed out wildly at the glass and sent it spinning across the room. I reached out a hand in a futile effort to prevent its flight, but like a homing missile it struck the photograph of Barry Newman with a great splintering of sound. Glass, frame, photograph seemed to explode. He knew what had happened without looking. With a final, long-drawn-out shudder, the paroxysm faded. For a brief moment he was utterly still; then slowly he raised his head, eyes inflamed and tear-stained, hair dishevelled, and stared at the debris, quite quiet.

The silence preceded a long, low, animal whimper. On his knees he shambled across the room to the shattered fragments and, heedless of the splinters, scrabbled with his fingers to unearth the photograph. Slivers of glass bit into his hands; blood, welling from several cuts, oozed on to the carpet; it dripped on to the picture and slid glutinously down the stiff card; he brushed at it with his hand. A long, dark ugly smear disfigured the portrait. I started towards him, thinking to save him from further hurt, but before I could reach him he had dropped the photograph and snatched up handfuls of the broken glass; blood poured from between his fingers as he ground the glass masochistically into them. He was raising the sharp splinters to his face, almost as if to wash in them, when I hurled myself upon him, holding him from behind, forcing his hands away from his face. He struggled like a maniac. I yelled for Emrys at the top of my voice, hoping that someone would hear above the general babel of the bar outside. As Davies collapsed beneath my weight, I rolled over on top of him, holding him down, pinioning his wrists and shouting to him to let go the glass.

Behind me I heard the door burst open. "Help me, for Christ's sake," I cried. The huge bulk of Emrys Williams came into view. My relief must have loosened my hold, for Davies rolled over suddenly, slid from my grasp and jerked his knee viciously into my groin. Lurching to his feet, he staggered for a second before launching himself at Emrys. It was a second too long. Emrys' fist shot out and contacted Davies' chin with a report like a pistol shot.

On my knees now and holding on to my bruised groin I watched as the head jerked back and the feet seemed to leave the ground: he flew slowly, or so it seemed, and landed on his back in the armchair, where he buckled like a ventriloquist's doll. His head slumped down on to his chest; the limbs rolled and flailed and subsided into stillness.

I sank down again with my head almost touching the floor. I groaned once, very loudly.

I heard Emrys say, "Jesus Christ," under his breath and raised myself with difficulty. This time I really did think my collarbone had gone. How much more could it take? I wondered. No mere body should be allowed to take the sort of beatings mine had sustained over the last twenty-four hours. I lifted my eyes and encountered those of Williams, who was standing over me, staring as if he had never seen me before.

When he held out a hand to help me to my feet I shied from it like a frightened mare, then reluctantly clutching at it, I climbed up it like a sporting geriatric. I leaned heavily against him as he trundled me over to a chair. "I'll get you a drink." I sat obediently while he helped us both to a healthy tot of alcohol from Michael Davies' personal collection of bottles. Alcohol, I thought, was exactly what I needed, and to hell with it!

From the open doorway I became aware of a confused mumble of voices, clients from the bar having gathered together to take in the fun. As Williams came over with the drinks, he kicked the door shut in their faces. "Piss off," he told them without rancour. "Nosey buggers." Then, having handed me one of the glasses, he jerked open the door again and called through. "Ned, see if Dr. Jenkins is still around, will you? Mike's had an accident."

The whisky burned my mouth and I realised with some surprise that my lip was bleeding.

Williams was busy rearranging the prostrate Davies in the armchair, lifting the limp limbs as if they were stuffed with sawdust. Over his shoulder he turned his great eyes on me.

"What in the name of God was all that about?"

I took another drink and slumped forward, elbows on my knees. "He just went bloody mad."

Williams straightened up. "He'll be all right. He saw a couple of stars, that's all."

"I'm not surprised," I muttered, blinking blearily at his fists, which looked like a couple of cauliflowers. "Coming up against one of those things, I wonder he's still alive."

"Only gave him a little pat, didn't I? He'll be okay, I expect."

I stared solemnly at the slack figure in the chair. "Poor bugger," I whispered. "He's in a hell of a state. Wound up like a clock spring. He'll end up in a loony bin if he's not careful."

I massaged my groin with caution and became aware that Williams was eyeing me doubtfully. "He stuck his knee in my balls," I informed him, since he appeared to be in need of an explanation.

Standing over me like the Colossus of Rhodes, he took a swig at his whisky and rolled the liquid appreciatively around his teeth. He winked at me and grinned, not caring a damn about my groin. "So what else happened?"

While I gave him the details, I limped over to Davies and took a closer look at his hands; they were in a terrible state. As best I could, I probed the larger pieces of glass from the lacerations and, snatching an antimacassar from the back of one of the chintz chairs, wrapped it around both hands in the forlorn hope of stanching the blood.

Williams wagged his head from side to side. "He never got over it, did he, poor little sod? It's years back now; he ought to have bloody got over it; no good brooding over these things." With a groan, he bent double and retrieved the damaged portrait from the floor; he raised it to within a foot of his eyes and studied it critically for a second or two. He wagged his head again. "Well, I'm never likely to understand this sort of thing, am I? But he certainly seemed to have gone a bundle on this one. Doesn't look much, though, does he? Weedy, I'd say. Still, no accounting for taste." He snorted suddenly and tossed the photograph aside.

I grinned. "Well, don't knock it just because you don't understand it."

Michael Davies was breathing heavily, almost snoring. I closed his mouth deftly and the noise subsided. Turning back to Williams and exploring my tortured ribs with a tender hand, I uttered the sixty-four-thousand-dollar question. "Did you talk to you-know-who?"

"Who?"

"I don't *know* who, do I? I don't know a fucking thing. You said you were going to talk to someone and if he listened I'd get the answers."

"I *told* you," he said soothingly, "tomorrow. You'll get the answers tomorrow."

"So what am I supposed to do in the meantime? What am I supposed to do tonight, for instance? And why am I bothering to talk to you, anyway?"

"Look!" He suddenly turned his head and fixed me with a glare like a gorgon's. "I'm not your bloody keeper. I'm just someone who's being paid to do a job. I'm the one who takes the orders, see? If you don't understand what you've got yourself into, it's not for me to enlighten you. I was told to keep an eye on you, right? I've done that and I'm doing it, but I'm not your bloody keeper. You get asked out to dinner with the gentry. Fine. Whether you go or not is entirely up to you. But I happen to know a couple of things which you don't and I say—I suggest—don't go. For what it's worth, that's my opinion. I think it's dangerous and if you go you'll probably never come back. Neither you nor your pretty girlfriend. You're treading on someone's heels and he's not liking it one little bit. And if you're not careful, you'll go the same way as young Mike's boyfriend there." He stabbed his stubby finger at the photograph on the floor. "He died in a fire, they said. An open verdict. Well, nobody has to believe everything he hears. Barry Newman was slugged, pumped full of dope and then chucked on to that bloody fire like a lump of garbage. And that"—his finger stabbed again, this time into my face—"is fact. And if you don't believe it, keep your flaming appointment with Colonel bloody Hazlitt-Martin tonight, but don't say nobody didn't warn you."

By the time he had finished, I was as breathless as he was. I sank on to the arm of the chair. "Okay, okay," I nodded. "I've got the message. But just to put my mind at rest, what's so different about tomorrow? Would you mind telling me that?"

His breath hissed between his teeth. "What is so different about tomorrow," he growled with exaggerated patience, "is that it isn't today, that's what's so different. And I'm not telling you any more than that. I can't tell you any more than that." But he did, because he added, "D day, that's what tomorrow is; D day."

I raised my hands in surrender. "Right. Right. Right." And as he turned away with an ungracious grunt, I found myself looking into the wide-open eyes of Michael Davies. How long he had been conscious I had no way of telling, but he still looked pretty dozy.

"Hi," I said, giving him a winning though painful smile. "Feeling better?"

Emrys Williams swung back into the room, exchanging a warning look with me as he did so. He stared down at Mike. "I had to clock you one," he mumbled in the nearest he could get to a conciliatory tone. "Sorry, but you were doing yourself no good."

The injured man paid no attention but stared instead at his shrouded hands. I said hastily, "The doctor'll be here in a minute. You've probably got some glass in them."

His puzzled eyes shifted to the mess on the floor and then to the crumpled portrait of Barry Newman. Comprehension seemed to be returning only slowly. "I flipped, didn't I?" he whispered hoarsely.

There was an awkward silence. Williams cleared his throat. "I'll go and see what's keeping that doctor." He opened the door and came face to face with what had to be that doctor in person, a distinguished, comfortable-looking individual in his fifties and an ill-fitting tweed suit.

"Ned says there's been an accident." He greeted us with a cheery smile and then, catching sight of the wan figure over my shoulder, bustled in with his bag, brushing Williams and myself aside as he passed. "You were lucky to catch me; I was just off." Putting his bag on the floor, he removed his gold-rimmed half-moons and polished them with a spotless folded handkerchief. "And talking about being off," he called to Williams' departing back, "I'd take a look at that shepherd's pie if I were you. I have the feeling that's a bit off too."

Replacing his glasses, he took in the shambles around him with an incurious eye and, pulling up a low stool, squatted with a contented sigh before his patient and began unwinding the antimacassar. "So what have you been doing to yourself, young man?" Frowning slightly as the damaged hands were revealed, he dropped the blood-stained antimacassar fastidiously into the hearth. Slowly he straightened out the clenched hands, his spectacles glinting first at Davies and then at me. "What happened?"

I concocted an unlikely story about Mike having come a cropper with the picture frame and a glass of whisky in his hands but I could see he didn't believe a word of it. Mike looked more convinced than he did. During the improvisation, the worthy doctor delved into his bag, produced cotton wool, antiseptic solution and a small pair of tweezers and was now peering intently through his gold-rims whilst deftly removing small splinters of glass from the still-seeping wounds.

"Well," I said, backing away and feeling a trifle *de trop*, "I'll be getting along. I'll call in later, Mike, see how you are."

Mike looked at me blankly as if wondering who I was. "What's that funny smell?" asked the doctor suddenly, sniffing the air loudly. I thought for a moment he was referring to me. "Oranges?" he queried. His eyes fell on Mike's bowed head and he leaned in cautiously, wrinkling his nose. "And you've got orange juice in your hair, old fellow, did you know that?" He wobbled a bewildered head at me hovering in the doorway. "He's got orange juice all over his head."

There was nothing I could add to that without confusing him further, so I smiled glassily and firmly closed the door.

The sun which had gladdened the morning had gone, retreating behind the lowering overhang of cloud that loomed in from the northwest, where snow had already been reported. A keen wind had sprung up too, bending the treetops and whipping dirt and dust into my face as I turned once again on to the road leading to Wanhope. I slammed down the visor of my helmet. My spirits were as cheerless as the weather.

Tomorrow, Williams had said, was D day. A launching, a first night, preceded as always by the recurrent nightmare of all actors: alone on the stage, in the wrong play, wearing the wrong costume and unable to recall a single line of script. The sweating terror of it made my skin crawl even now. Of tomorrow I knew nothing other than the strong possibility that I might not live to enjoy it. Emrys Williams appeared to know what he was talking about.

I assumed it was money which kept me from going back to London, but what money? I had been handed one hundred pounds for expenses with the vague promise of more. And the understanding between myself and my obese employer assumed the delivery of a dubious package that I had instead destroyed. So it couldn't be the money. What, then? Excitement? Doggedness, stupidity, pride?

How about Julie Remington?

I drew into the side of the road and, with ninety-five horsepower grumbling away on the leash beneath me, thought quietly about J. Remington.

That I was in love with her I had no doubt. That she was in love with me was a realistic possibility. She lived in Wales. Her occupation was highly specialised and intrinsic to the well-being of the community. Time, money and scholarship had been expended that she might achieve the position she now enjoyed. She had brains, beauty and a body I lusted after; in short she was the one with whom I would be content to spend the remainder of my life. That was Julie.

Mark Savage? He lived in London. He had lost the position he once enjoyed and was flirting with a profession—if profession was the correct term for it—about which he knew little. He was reasonably intelligent, passably personable—at the moment a cripple—and had a few hundred pounds stashed away in one of the more reputable building societies. His future looked unpromising and, with the sort of earnest application he had already lavished upon it, could well be nominated for an Oscar as the most successful failure of the year.

Suicide was the obvious solution.

The first flakes of snow fell gently on my visor. I shivered. The sky was dark and ominous. I let in the clutch and pressed on.

On the approach to Wanhope I slackened speed for a moment or two, wondering whether to call in there first, but then I decided to get Pithy off my chest and do Wanhope on the return journey.

Only a couple of hundred yards further on, the road stopped and broadened into the sort of terrace one might expect to find overlooking a beauty spot, a place to park the car and crouch over cucumber sandwiches and a flask of metallic tea whilst appreciating the outlook. On this particular afternoon the space was empty, but the view was still there, darkly wooded hills and ferned ridges marching away into the scurrying flurries of snow. It was here that the Volvo must have waited, with dead George Mathews in the back, before hurtling down and driving me off the cliff.

I switched off the engine and raised my visor. Ice-cold wind whipped at my face, a snowflake flicked at my eyeball and another touched my lips. The silence was awe-inspiring. Only the scurrying wind disturbed it. This was a world I had so often craved and never achieved: a world devoid of people and screaming children, a world without self-service stores, multistoried parking, central heating and the internal combustion engine. . . .

A thin mewing threaded its way through the falling snow. I raised my eyes but could see nothing. A bird of prey hovered somewhere up there beyond my sight. This, too, was a world of the hunter and the hunted, survival of the fittest, red in tooth and claw—so perhaps it wasn't so different, after all, from the one we had all hammered out for ourselves. It was a sad and sobering conclusion.

I climbed off the machine and heaved it on to its rest and stuck my helmet in the pannier. I checked on the Walther nestling in the pocket of the Belstaff. I had no intention of shooting Pithy, but I was beginning to appreciate the sense of security that small lethal piece of ironmongery gave me. That, too, was a thought I cared not to dwell upon. I had always despised the man with a gun, but what could you do when the other man had one bigger and better than you—an automatic Kalashnikov for instance—and it was important, to you at least, to survive?

Hunching myself against the cold into the comfort of the waterproof jacket, I headed off into the wind. The snow was establishing itself fast now, a thin white coating of it dusting the ground and turning the trees into a filigree of shimmering lace.

I had walked only a hundred yards when I came upon Pithy's homestead. It was, as Julie had described, a hybrid structure, somewhere between a caravan and a potting shed. It had begun as a caravan, from which the wheels had long since been removed; various ramshackle attachments now clung to it like barnacles on the hull of a ship. It gave the impression of being marooned in a surging tide of nettles, vetch and saxifrage. Above it, snapping proudly in the wind and attached to a broomstick, flew the red, blue and gold of the Royal Standard. I found myself grinning at his presumption. Somebody had said—Cobbett, was it?—*Set a beggar on horseback and he'll ride to the devil.*

An ill-defined path through the tangle of weeds and nettles led me to the door of the bizarre structure. At any moment, I expected its owner to leap out and confront me—probably with a double-barrelled shotgun levelled at my chest. Whilst not looking forward to a second head-on confrontation with Pithy, I had decided, if only for my own peace of mind, that I must face him with what I knew of the events of Tuesday morning and extract from him, in turn, what part he had played in them. It was highly unlikely that he would confess all without a struggle, but with any luck some sort of relevant information might be forthcoming, even if it was only what George Mathews had been up to at the moment when he was so lethally interrupted. If, that is, the assumption of Pithy's guilt was correct.

The mass of wild growth encroached almost to the walls of the caravan, leaving a narrow skirting passage of trampled vegetation between the tide of weeds and the structure itself. The door hung slightly askew from one hinge, the other having been inexpertly replaced by what looked like the twisted remains of a wire coathanger. In place of a lock or handle was a knotted rope, dangling from a round hole. Just such a device, I remembered, was used by my paternal grandfather to secure the entrance to his chicken run.

I punched at the door with my fist, the other closed firmly about the butt of the PPK. The entire edifice shook beneath the onslaught, but no answer came from inside.

Above the doorway, nailed crookedly to the woodwork, was a board into which had been scorched with a hot iron the words *Home Sweet Home*.

With my blood beginning to coagulate in the cold, I made a circuit of the shack, peered into a couple of windows, saw nothing, knocked at the wooden walls and called, "Mr. Pithy," at intervals—all to no avail. Finally I pulled on the knotted rope and raised the latch.

"Mr. Pithy . . . ?" I pushed open the door and went in.

It was dark inside, and for some moments I could see nothing at all. He had obviously never heard of electricity, and I possessed neither matches nor cigarette lighter, so I stood around until my eyes became accustomed to the gloom. Then, catching sight of a hurricane lamp with matches alongside on a table by one of the windows, I set light to the wick and peered around.

What I saw surprised me. The place was as neat as a new pin. Its furnishings betrayed what I hesitated to describe, in the light of what I knew, as a feminine touch. I settled instead for the presence of an unusually fastidious and exacting taste—whatever its sex. The interior of the homestead had a warmth and homeliness which suggested enormous care and pride. Even the tiny section set aside for the kitchen—a cylinder of bottled gas supplied essential heating—was meticulous in the disposition of its meagre equipment.

Of Pithy himself there was no sign. I found myself guiltily harbouring a suspicion that I might discover his body, poisoned, stabbed, beaten or even suspended from the ceiling; but he was nowhere in evidence, dead or alive. As I turned to go, I noticed, hanging on the back of the door, the black oilskin jacket he had been wearing when we had met on the hillside. Its presence was vaguely disquieting. If he was out in that weather, he surely should have been wearing it. I extinguished and replaced the lamp. There was no reason to suppose that the oilskin was the only protection against the elements that he possessed.

I let myself out and pulled the door to after me. The latch snapped into place. For a second or two I stood contemplating my next move. The snow was falling quite heavily and the wind had freshened. Should both continue in that vein, bad drifting would occur and the roads would rapidly become impassable.

I wandered around to the rear of the hut, staring out over the desolation beyond. There was nothing much to see, just whirling snow and a wooded valley. The shack, I realised for the first time, was perched on the summit of a promontory—what they called the Beacon, perhaps—the ground plunging away less than fifty yards distant, and quite precipitously if one was to gauge the depth of the valley by the writhing treetops well below my eye level. Even against the speedily settling snow I could discern a trampled section of undergrowth leading directly to the edge of the descent. I stared at it for a moment, turned away, then slowly turned back again, frowning to myself.

Leaning against the wind, I trudged through the whitening vegetation to the brink of the precipice.

The wind gusted the fine snow into my eyes. Shielding them with both hands, I stared fixedly downwards into the valley. I lowered my hands, raised my head and stared blankly at the sky.

I had found Pithy.

I assumed it was Pithy. Reluctantly I looked again. A body lay sprawled on its front against a tree, legs twisted, arms splayed in cruciform, the head invisible and at one with the dark bole of the tree. There was no doubt that whoever it was, was dead.

Searching along the ridge for a possible path, I was able to make out, a short distance to the left, a narrow track which plunged steeply down the face of the precipice.

I tramped across to the spot to take a closer look. It was even worse close to. However, recalling that I had already contemplated suicide once that afternoon, I decided that this perhaps might be the moment to put my money where my mouth was. I sat in the snow and dangled my legs over the edge and then proceeded to slip, slide, crawl and clutch my way downwards. It was not at all the sort of thing I had been accustomed to portray on the bright Technicolor screen, romantic and tight-lipped with nary a hair out of place. The last ten feet I slid ingloriously on my bottom and finished up at ground level, sprawling like a starfish.

Clambering guiltily to my feet, I took a look upwards to measure the magnitude of my achievement. The Matterhorn was a molehill by comparison.

I was some distance from the body. Twenty paces, in fact. Who measured the ground? I did. Deliberately. For one thing was certain: had he fallen accidentally, it would have been well-nigh impossible for him to have come to earth on that particular spot.

I knelt beside him. The body was cold and stiff; it looked as if it had never lived, never breathed. I was tempted not to touch it, but it was impossible to ascertain whether, in such a position, it was Pithy or not. The gorilla-like framework was like Pithy, but then, Emrys Williams was built like a gorilla too.

Straddling him I hauled lustily at the massive shoulders. With ribs creaking and arms trembling, I was beginning to feel the whole operation was beyond me when the great frame budged an inch or two. I redoubled my efforts and slowly he came over, the face jerking finally and abruptly into view. I stared at it, my stomach turning, horror rooting me to the spot. Then I was lurching away from him, staggering drunkenly to the next tree, where I vomited up my lunch.

When it was over, I clung desperately to the tree, embracing it like a lover, pressing my face violently against the hard, rough bark. Over and over again I found myself wishing I had not disturbed him.

The heavy jaw was recognisable as Pithy, but the entire upper half of the skull had been crushed to a pulp; there was no nose, no eyes, no brow, nothing but the awful sickening glisten of blood and bone and brains . . .

I have no idea how long I remained there, hugging that tree and moaning to myself. Eventually it was the cold, I think, which prompted me to bestir myself: if I didn't do something pretty soon, I would be discovered frozen to the tree like some survivor from the Ice Age.

Finally I let go and stared up at the black overhang of cliff. I knew intuitively what had happened, and how. In my mind's eyes I saw it as clearly as if I had been a witness to it.

Two men—Deakin and Champ?—had carried him unconscious between them from the shack. They had stood up there on the edge of the cliff, each taken an arm and a leg and one, two—"try to hit the tree with him"—three! he had sailed through the air and thudded head first against the tree. . . .

I shuddered and my empty stomach heaved painfully.

I closed my eyes and wished poor Pithy well, wherever he might be.

I opened them and damned Deakin and Champ to every suffering that could be devised—now and for ever. . . . Amen.

Pushing myself away from the tree I wandered off, leaving Pithy in his pitiful welter of blood.

Set a beggar on horseback and he'll ride to the devil.

As I approached the path of ascent I could almost hear the beating of hoofs at my back.

I was becoming fanciful.

10

By the time I had struggled back to the Honda, after coping with the uncongenial elements and the sheer physical sweat of the climb, I was on the point of calling it a day. Every bone in my body ached. Even my brain ached.

Pithy's needless death, to say nothing of the manner of it, had affected me badly. That it had been needless was born out by what Julie had said about him. At Wanhope, clearly he had seen something he shouldn't have. But the locals looked upon him as little more than the village idiot, and had he elected to tell any of them about it he would have had a hard time convincing them. Then, too, were he guilty of the death of Mathews, it was unlikely, even dim as he was, that he would go wandering about the place blabbing about other people's misdemeanours, when his own offence was distinctly more culpable.

Whatever it was that "the enemy" had tucked away in their pipeline was obviously considered worthy of a death or two, as was amply demonstrated by their sniping in my direction. But, then, I was fair game; I was snooping among their souvenirs and prepared to snipe back. Pithy wasn't, no matter how much Mathews' death might suggest the contrary.

In a tight corner, and given an available weapon, even a child will kill. Only an adult, and an intelligent one at that, will assess the desirability and possible consequence of such an act; and if he's that intelligent, he will hire henchmen to do it for him. Such henchmen were Deakin and Champ.

And the intelligent one? It could only be the double-barrelled Grey Eminence himself. I didn't have anyone else. And upon him I was about to let slip the dogs of war. I shivered at the prospect.

Having determined to keep my appointment with him that evening, I now found myself in need of further grist, more information. I needed evidence of what Wanhope contained. Mathews had presumably been killed because of it; Pithy must have seen it and suffered the same fate. And now Aunt Sally was limbering up to offer herself as a prospective third victim.

I leaned wearily over the Honda. I remembered watching as a child an Aunt Sally at a fairground. He had been a tall, grim-looking man, in black frock coat and top hat. With hands patiently folded behind his back, he had marched tirelessly to and fro behind a net of close mesh; only the hat was unprotected by this net; the object of the exercise was to knock his hat off with wooden balls, as in a coconut shy. Success would be rewarded by a doll or a lollipop. Although pressed to do so I could never bring myself to join in the fun. The man was so sad and vulnerable and, even as a child, I wondered what had brought him to such a pass . . . up and down and to and fro, like an animal in a cage, a target for sport and greed, with the added possibility of being hurt.

I watched the snow falling on to the backs of my hands outstretched on the saddle of the Honda; each flake lay for a second and then began to melt; before it could do so completely, another had added itself to the remaining fragment, as gradually the hands were hidden beneath a layer of snow.

There would be no protection. No net. And no sport in the accepted sense of the word. No top hat either. The target would be my head and the missile no wooden ball, but a bullet.

I straightened up, shook the snow from my hands, drew on my damp gauntlets and looked disconsolately at the sky. Against the leaden, slablike expanse of nothingness the falling snow swirled and flurried, smothering the earth with its blanket of silence. I had never liked snow.

About to lift the Honda from its rest, I had second thoughts. The silence of the snow could perhaps be of service to me. I decided not only to leave the machine where it was and walk the few hundred yards to Wanhope, but also to approach the house head on, so to speak, and without circumspection. If the place was under surveillance my presence would be noted whether I marched up the aisle or slipped in quietly through the door of the side vestry.

So I tramped down the centre of the road, clambered over the fallen branch and crashed my way up the drive to the front door, which I then proceeded to belabour with true Wagnerian aplomb. Only when I looked over my shoulder and registered the great black footprints of my progress through the snow did I feel a qualm or two. But only for a moment. The snow was coming down heavier than ever, and with luck would obliterate the prints within a quarter of an hour.

In the unlikely event of someone opening the door, I had prepared a small speech about how I was making enquiries as to the possibility of renting the establishment for a month. Of course, should that someone happen to be carrying a gun when he opened the door, I most likely wouldn't bother.

There was no answer to my summons.

Almost as if it were a prescribed condition of my being there, I drifted again to my favourite window and peered into the room beyond. The table, lumpish shrouded furniture . . . I hovered at the window. As before, that same subtle difference nagged at my memory; something was not quite as it had been on my initial visit. Table . . . ornaments . . . vague humps of furniture. . . . It was impossible to see further into the room, the interior was too dark; it had always been too dark. So what else could I have seen? Something lighter, obviously. A light? And then I had it. There had been the reflection of a picture or something hanging on the wall opposite the window; certainly a glint of light. I shaded my eyes with both hands and stared again very carefully. I couldn't even see the wall, let alone a picture.

Whipping out my Scout knife, I let myself in through the other window as before, closed and rebolted it, gravitated towards the centre of the room, and stood with my back to window number one. I was looking through the door of the room and across the narrow strip of corridor to a completely featureless wall. No picture, no electrical fitting disturbed the bland grey plaster surface.

I moved to the doorway; to the left lay the kitchen, an extension of the corridor itself but built a further three or four feet into the hillside. Daylight was supplied by the frosted glass of the side door and the narrow window. To my right lay the master bedroom, beyond the front door, served by the remaining front windows. At the far end of the corridor were two doors; the nearest was to the bathroom, and next to it a narrow slip room which could, if necessary, serve as a spare bedroom; the slip room and bathroom were single-storey, lit only by skylights. The bathroom door would not be visible from the window behind me, so even had it been open on that first occasion —which it probably was, since Mathews was busy pouring his life's blood over the bath mat—I would have seen no light thrown through it on the grey wall facing me.

I moved in and stared intently at the wall, going over it inch by inch like an art dealer assessing a questionable old master. To right and left and about four feet apart were heavy oak uprights—a touch of the mock Tudors— sturdy as railway sleepers, and these in turn supported a massive beam which spanned the full length of the corridor and seemed to take most of the weight of the encroaching hillside; the uprights were repeated every four feet or so on both sides of the corridor and down into the kitchen itself.

When I had first looked through the window, what I had seen was not the reflection of a picture glass—there were no indications that a picture had ever hung on the wall—but a light or the reflection of a light beyond the wall; this section of the wall had just not been there. It was a door, I was convinced of it, and the door had been open.

I examined every inch of those uprights, pressing, prodding, twisting, looking for knotholes or blemishes, anything which might prove to be a hidden catch or button by which a mechanism could be set in motion.

I stood back from the wall muttering crossly to myself. It was there somewhere. It had to be. My questioning eyes fell on the flagged floor. Even from where I stood I could see the dark stains similar to those made by Mathews' blood in the sitting room. Kneeling down, I examined them carefully, peering into the crevices and scratching with my knife blade between the flagstones and the wall in the hope of finding a gap where a door might meet the floor. Once more I drew a blank.

Then I noticed, immediately against the wall, a curiously kidney-shaped stain, and I stared at it for a full minute before I realised what it was: the imprint of the heel of a palm. A handprint. And the other half of it, the fingers, were under and on the far side of the wall. Of the door.

With my knuckles I pressed down on each flag in turn, and when I reached the one on the right beyond the oak upright, also blood-stained, I felt it give a little. I pressed harder. It moved again, but not in the way a loose stone moves: the movement was controlled. And the stone was shinier than the others, more worn, perhaps. I leaned more heavily, and with a whirring whine the wall swung smoothly inwards.

I stared into the black void.

Before launching myself into the cavity with an abandonment I might later regret, I brought my mind to bear on the mechanism of the wall. Releasing the pressure of my knuckles, I was gratified to find that the wall remained open; a second pressure, the cavity closed, a third opened it again: as precise and simple as a ballpoint pen.

Rising quickly, I fumbled for and found a light switch; a single, low-wattage bulb in the ceiling gave forth a meagre light. Just such a light as I had seen from the window—before Mathews had heard me, that is, and dragged himself from the bathroom, closing the door as he passed, in some last desperate access of caution.

With the same sort of curious wonder as Alice must have experienced when she stepped through the looking glass, I moved cautiously over the threshold. The same flagstone that operated the door on the outside projected under the wall to give similar service on the inside. So, just in case some busybody like Mark Savage should turn up and peer rudely through the window, I allowed the wall to swing shut behind me. It closed with a pneumatic gasp and a slight click. I almost panicked at being thus walled up, but, after communing sternly with myself, I turned to examine my surroundings.

A narrow and quite lengthy chamber, not much wider than the corridor outside, it was lined with shelves from floor to ceiling, and these bore boxes and parcels and canvas bundles varying in size and shape. For the moment, I ignored these, my first thought being for the second door, which I knew must be somewhere. This time there had been no attempt at concealment: it lay at the far end of the passage-like room and seemed to be a perfectly ordinary door—until I attempted to open it and discovered that it weighed a ton. I put my shoulder to it and it swung outwards on oiled but reluctant hinges. When I peered out at the snow-cluttered landscape, I realised why they had been so reluctant. The outer surface of the door was part of the hillside and had been ingeniously camouflaged with earth and grass—to which nature had now added her own small benison of snow. When closed, it would be indistinguishable from the natural slope of the hill. Immediately in front of me the tyre-marked dirt road from which I had been shot at continued its descent. Up there to the right, above and beyond the building, lay the gate I had climbed over that morning.

As I suspected, this curious room was hardly more than a tunnel, running from inside the house, beneath the ridge, and out to the far side. I took my hat off to them, whoever they were. It was a perfect hideaway or emergency exit, and only a minor genius like myself, actually looking for it, would be likely to find it. Before closing the door, I noticed that there could be no access through it from the outside: it was strictly a one-way door.

I shut myself in and found another light switch, and this time, after preliminary flickerings and splutterings, white fluorescent strip lighting bathed the chamber in a baleful radiance. Also baleful were the blue barrels of a rackful of rifles glinting against the wall and facing me as I turned from the door. There were eight of them: three Mausers, two Lee-Enfields, and three AK47 assault rifles. Beneath them, on a horizontal rest, lay a Uzi submachine gun, squat and ugly, its metal stock folded away. Behind it lurked a Thompson 700.

I raised the lid of a green metal box. Ammunition, hundreds of rounds, was tucked away in careful compartments according to calibre. Another box displayed three neat rows of hand grenades. On the opposite wall, a comprehensive selection of pistols and revolvers lay in pigeonholes, along with the requisite ammunition; Lugers and Mausers, Colts and Brownings and a couple of others I didn't recognise. The bloody place was an arsenal. I quailed at the firepower contained within these four claustrophobic walls. I held on to my figurative hat when I discovered several packets of C.7 plastic explosive looking like plasticine wrapped in greaseproof paper, complete with detonators and several timing devices.

What the hell was he running up here in the middle of Wales, a private army? Or did he just ship the guns over to Ireland and similar centres of unrest? As my tour of inspection progressed, so my quailing turned to sick horror. The remainder of the hidden chamber contained what I knew to be the *raison d'être* of the operation: narcotics. Pounds and pounds of the stuff were tidied away into the metal equivalent of shoe boxes, each containing a specified one kilogramme. Quite recently, I had read somewhere that a kilo of heroin was worth in the region of £40,000, selling at a street price of £100,000—and that was a conservative estimate. Gazing around, I boggled at the riches surrounding me. I was not Alice Through the Looking Glass, I was Ali Baba in the Cave of the Forty Thieves. What I was looking at was several million pounds' worth of misery. Having had some traffic with them during the less enlightened pages of my life, I recognised both cannabis and heroin as I peered into one or two of the containers. Each bore, in an elongated handwriting, details of its country of origin, date and varying degrees of quality. Additional signs and symbols offered further information to those with eyes to see and understand. The street market was represented too: a metal box packed with marijuana cigarettes; a padded circular container offered narrow phials of liquid—probably oil of cannabis; folded-paper packages looked like Beecham's Powders but weren't.

My forehead was damp with sweat. All at once, in that bright, sinister chamber I wanted only one thing: to destroy, obliterate, annihilate.

I turned again to the armaments.

Part of my mind was already recalling and rehearsing a sequence from a film, called *War Games*, in which I had been required to blow up a bridge somewhere in Germany. Andrew Elliot had taken me step by step through the preparation of the plastic explosive, inserting the detonator, explaining the simple mechanism of the timing device. "It's a close shot on your hands; they must be neat, precise, like a surgeon's—no fumbling, no hesitation. You know exactly what you're doing and the audience wants to know that too."

I thought I might have forgotten most of it, but, having unearthed the explosive and the timing device, the method crept back to me; I just hoped it crept back correctly; there would be no retakes this time. Someone had thoughtfully provided some elementary instructions with the packet of explosive, and I followed them slavishly, checking and rechecking with my sketchy memories.

As I worked I found myself justifying my behaviour. Real live bullets had been shot at my head; real live explosive was my return gesture. It might, of course, I thought wryly, eyeing the timing device with trepidation, be my last.

I remember Andrew Elliot thumping merrily away at the plastic explosive as if it were plasticine. (On that occasion, of course, it *was* plasticine.) "You don't have to treat it with kid gloves," he pointed out. "Until you shove it full of fuses it's just like plasticine." He was welcome to his opinion; I treated it as if it were nitroglycerine. What I knew about the wretched stuff could be printed on the head of a pin.

Whatever it was, I was plastering it warily over the inside of the box containing the hand grenades when suddenly those useful hairs at the back of my neck began to stir. My sweating hands became still, every sense stretched to its limit. There had been no sound, no sign of movement, but something had alerted me and I was taking no chances. As I straightened up, one of my knees cracked like a starting pistol. I reached for the Walther and slid off the catch. Dousing the fluorescent lighting, the click of the switch was like thunder and the lights went out with a roar. When it had all quietened down again, I stood in the dim chamber, head bent, listening: nothing, not a sound. I moved to the inner door and, with closed eyes and a prayer, noiselessly coaxed up the second switch. Inky darkness engulfed me. For a moment I contemplated a safe retreat by the other door but dismissed the thought: I wanted something to happen, for God's sake, and now was as good a time as any. My foot found the operating flagstone and, flattening myself against the wall shelves, I pressed down on it. The machinery purred. As the door swung inwards, I watched the narrow cleft of daylight widening. There was the slightest of *clunks* as the door reached its open position. Nobody sprang at me brandishing a weapon. Quite right, too. If he had any sense he would be on the other side, flattened against the wall, waiting for me to come out, just as I was waiting for him to come in. It was stalemate. I strained my ears. Unlike me, he seemed to have stopped breathing.

Taking courage and gun in both hands I executed a textbook canter through the doorway in the crouch position, swinging the gun fast through an angle of 180° as I erupted first into the passage, then into the room beyond. The place was empty. I felt a little foolish. I continued the move swiftly to the window on the left of the front door and peered out, still with exaggerated caution. Nothing. I drew open the door. My footprints led blackly through the still-falling snow, up the drive, on to the step where now I stood, and then to the window.

Too blackly. My stomach slowly turned over. Other feet had been planted meticulously in those prints, bigger feet, blurring the original outlines.

I turned slowly into the living room. A trail of still wet footprints crossed it to the entrance of the darkened chamber, then broke away to the right to lose itself in the shelter of a huge armchair shrouded in a dust sheet. Moving quietly, I skirted the chair with care; then, putting a foot against it, shoved it hard across the stone floor. As it collided violently with the far wall I was crouched again, gun pointing at an empty bookcase. No one was there, but a sinister glistening pool of melting snow indicated where he had been.

I glanced hurriedly around the room. No other possible place of concealment presented itself. My eyes returned again to the black doorway of the narrow storeroom I had just vacated and sensed, rather than saw, a darker shape looming in the depths of it.

My gun probed into the shadows. "Come out," I whispered hoarsely. My throat was so dry I could barely utter the words. A growl came from the darkness like that of an animal sitting in his lair and daring anyone to go in and get it.

"If you put that thing away, I will."

There was a click and preliminary flickerings as the fluorescent lighting got under way. It was an ill-judged action on his part: only my own juddering fright prevented me from emptying the Walther's magazine into him.

Emrys Williams glared at me from the far end of the room, his great globular eyes pulsing with the lights overhead and almost as phosphorescent.

"You're an idiot," I snarled, relief seething up inside me. "You nearly got yourself killed." Turning away, I stamped over to the front door, slammed it shut, and put my back against it, mainly to keep myself upright.

"And if I'd been the opposition you'd have been dead long ago. So don't let's call each other names."

"What the hell are you doing here?"

"Bill and Ben have gone to Haverford to pick up supplies. Deakin and Champ, that is. Watching them leave the Dragon, I thought I'd trudge up here and have a poke around. It's an impressive tidy-up job they've done. . . ." His eyes travelled slowly down to the box of grenades I'd been working on. He touched it with his foot. "You weren't thinking of putting a light to that lot, I hope."

"Of course not," I replied peevishly. "You just happened to catch me in the middle of an initiative test."

"Mr. Savage." He was full of patient weariness. "I'm on your side."

As he switched off the lights and moved towards me, my reflexes jerked and I lined up the Walther with his stomach. "And please," he murmured, disregarding it and making his way to the chair I had displaced, "put that bloody thing away before one of us gets hurt."

With one huge hand, he rolled the chair back into position, then went and peered out of the window. "Bloody weather," he growled. "Hate snow." He glanced at his wristwatch. "We'll be all right for a bit. With any luck, Bill and Ben will get snowed in." He turned and faced me, a hulking silhouette against the dirty grey rectangle of the window. "You really were going to set light to that stuff, weren't you?"

"I can't think of a better way of disposing of it."

"Then it couldn't be used in evidence." He lumbered away from the window, hunching himself aggressively into his fur-lined anorak. "Could it?" He stamped his feet to keep the circulation going. "How did you find it?"

"Brains."

He nodded approvingly. "You're better than we thought."

"We?"

"Since talking to you earlier I've had words with you know who. . . ."

"No, I don't know who, actually."

". . . and there's been a change of plan."

"You mean there was a plan in the first place?" I hooted rudely. "No one would ever have guessed. This place is like Hammer Horror with knobs on. Ever since I arrived, people have been going down like flies; Mathews dead,

Pithy dead, me nearly dead—and you only survived by the skin of your teeth.
. . . And I've only been here since Monday."

"Pithy dead?"

The question stopped me in my tracks. "Don't tell me you didn't know
that?"

"Where?"

I told him angrily, sparing none of the gory details. When I'd finished, he
lowered himself wearily on the arm of the shrouded chair and sat shaking his
head despondently at the floor. "I should have warned him somehow. He
didn't know the danger he was in, poor sod. He was always wandering about
on his own like a blasted zombie. The locals were scared of him; still in the
Middle Ages, most of 'em. I suppose he was a bit creepy, but I didn't mind
him; there was no harm in him."

"Not unless you call sticking a bloody great knife into Mathews harm," I
pointed out sourly.

He raised his head. "How d'you know that?"

"Well, didn't he? We haven't got anyone else." I bared my teeth at him.
"Except you, of course. You were up here. What were you doing, lurking
about in all that weather?"

"Trying to stop you falling foul of Mathews and Deakin, if you want to
know. In all that mist it seemed perfect for them to be up here shifting out
some of that junk in there. I missed you at the hotel and came after you on
foot—a shortcut over the rough—and managed to get here before you did."

"How did you know where I was going?"

"God Almighty, the whole village knew where you were going."

"And did you actually see what happened?"

He shivered suddenly with the cold and, reaching into a pocket, produced
a leather-bound brandy flask, flipped up its top and offered it to me. I shook
my head and waited while he downed a considerable amount of its contents.
When he'd finished, he smacked his lips, burped loudly and snapped back
the top.

"Too late to see it, but I heard it. Mathews was in there, as I'd thought,
sorting the stuff out ready for Deakin to pick up from the back entrance, and
Pithy must have walked in on him—just the sort of daft thing he would do.
Mathews probably left the front door open; silly bugger. Anyway, from the
noise I'd say Mathews went for him and Pithy picked up the knife in the
kitchen and that was that."

"Then he bolted."

"Almost into my arms. I was on the doorstep by then, so he made off like a
lunatic up on to the ridge. I found Mathews in the bathroom dead as a
doornail—or so I thought—blood all over the place. Then I heard what I
took to be your car grinding up the hill and dashed on down to head you off;

no one wanted you mixed up in murder. Well, I missed you again, didn't I? I went on down to Will Evans' to use his phone and was still talking when the shooting started. When I got back, Deakin was humping the body into his car; you, I s'pose, were still farting about up on the top somewhere."

"Deakin did the shooting?"

He shrugged. "He was up there in the car. He had a gun. He always has a gun. There wasn't anybody else."

I thought about the green tweed hat but kept my counsel. "He must have moved pretty sharpish," I said. "The body had gone when I got back. He could never have made it in the time—not from way up there."

"There's a way down if you know how and have got the nerve. It's a one-in-five gradient and comes out on the road below Wanhope. He managed it all right, 'cos I saw him. So then his car was facing in the wrong direction, wasn't it? He had to go up to the Beacon to turn round. And hung about up there waiting to see which way you were going to jump. I was so busy keeping an eye on him I didn't spot you 'til he was actually running you down."

"Why the hell didn't you shout?"

"I did."

"I didn't hear you."

"That's life, isn't it? Anyway, he knew he hadn't hit you, so he came back to finish you off, saw me and scarpered—with Pithy and you heading his list for early disposal." He raised his eyebrows in lugubrious humour. "One down, you to go. So if you do happen to survive this evening, keep out of his hair. He's the one who shoots first and then forgets to ask the questions."

"How did he know *I* didn't kill Mathews? Why blame poor old Pithy?"

"Why should he care? You were both up there when he was doing the shooting. My guess is that Pithy went back for another snoop, probably when he and Champ were tidying the place up. Champ would have been in on it too. They got rid of him 'cos he couldn't keep his mouth shut about anything, silly old sod. We won't know for sure 'til Champ and Deakin are reeled in—if then."

"And where does Champ fit in?"

"Replacement for Mathews. Brought in from Fishguard. Transferring the stuff's a two-man operation. One keeps watch on the ridge till the other gives the signal to drive down to the back entrance. Champ's only a heavy, like Deakin. Unlike Deakin, he's got a bit of a brain."

I thought of something. "You didn't go to the police, I notice."

He eyed me unenthusiastically. "Neither did you," he observed.

There was a long silence. I watched the snowflakes, silent and dark against the window, drifting gently earthwards; each one was fragile and aimless, yet stick them together and they bring man and most of his works to a standstill.

"We'll be snowed up ourselves if we stay here much longer," I muttered.

Apart from a dismal creaking from the chair arm labouring beneath his weight, he made no comment.

"Is that all you're going to tell me?" I grunted. "I worked out most of that on my own. What about all that junk next door? Why don't we do something about it?"

"Like blowing it up, for instance?"

"Why not? It'd be a lot more fun than sitting about here like a couple of superannuated gargoyles." I made a move in the direction of the storeroom, but his voice pulled me up.

"Mr. Savage." Now he sounded really tired. "It wouldn't be just a question of blowing up this dump—I'd be only too happy to help if it was—but you'd be blowing up an operation of ours which has taken the best part of eight months to set up." When he climbed to his feet, claustrophobia moved in. "And I couldn't allow you to do that. Could I?"

I tried to stare him down, but with eyes like his he could have outstared Argus. And since his question was presumably rhetorical I didn't bother to answer it. I said instead, "It's getting dark."

"I've got a message for you," he said abruptly, as though he had just remembered it. "Go to the colonel's tonight for dinner."

"Who says?"

"That's the message."

"Is that the change of plan you mentioned just now?"

"Part of it. If you want to know, I don't go along with it."

I nodded sympathetically. "That's how it is when you're not the boss."

"Right."

"So who *is* the boss?"

"You can take the girl with you if you like."

"Whatever happened to all that concern over our welfare?"

"That was *my* concern, not his. I've just given you the message." He took another swig at his flask.

"Any reason why I should obey it?"

Staring at me blankly, he wiped his mouth with his sleeve and stowed the flask away in his pocket. "You're still a free agent."

I snorted derisively. "That's a laugh."

Moving across me to the storeroom, he placed an outsize foot on the flagstone; the machinery whirred, the door closed and we were staring at a blank wall. "Clever buggers," murmured Williams, running an exploratory finger down the wooden upright. "Never know, would you?"

"You know," I said. "I know."

He grinned suddenly and gave me a wink over his shoulder. "That makes *us* clever buggers too, doesn't it?"

"Where does all that stuff come from?"

He shrugged. "Everywhere. The world." There was a bitter finality in his tone. "Via Amsterdam, Ankara, Marseilles."

"And goes where?"

"Wherever there's a distribution point. Which is most places, believe it or not. All over the country."

"What about the hardware?"

He gave a grunt. "That's only a sideline. Northern Ireland, mostly; aid to our friendly neighbours. They ship 'em out of Fishguard and Holyhead, even Barmouth, I'm told; destination Rosslare, Cork, Dublin, wherever they want 'em."

"And the colonel's the big wheel?"

"The colonel's only a cogwheel—quite a big one but still a cog. Narcotics are like a plate of spaghetti; everything's twisted. Follow one lead, you stumble up against another; there's no end to it. That junk in there is only the tip of the iceberg." He stood for a moment in silence; then, shaking his head hard, he made for the front door, passing me on the way. "I've got to go; I got work to do."

"It was just getting interesting."

"The rest can wait."

" 'Til *Der Tag?*"

"What?"

"You want a ride?"

"On the back of that bike?" It was his turn to be derisive. "I'd sooner walk. Thanks all the same."

"Listen. If I go to the colonel's tonight it's because I'd already made up my mind to go and not because you-know-who has graciously given me permission. I'd like him to know that."

"I'll be sure to tell him."

He opened the door and stood in the draught, zipping up his anorak and jerking the hood over his head. Behind him, I felt small and frail in my thin jeans and Belstaff jacket. "I say." He didn't hear me inside his hood so I poked him in the back with a finger and gave him a start; he almost put his hands up. "Why don't you tell me who he is?"

He swung his head, pulling the hood away from his ear. "What?"

I repeated the question.

"Because he told me not to," he said reasonably.

"Do I know him?"

He stuck out his lower lip. "I don't know. *Do* you?"

And he departed down the drive, breasting the elements like a snow-plough.

I watched him until he had disappeared around the bend; I thought he raised a hand as he went, but the approaching dark and the falling snow made it difficult to be certain—in any case I didn't acknowledge the gesture. To hell with him. I had already decided upon my next move and it had nothing to do with the preservation of the contents of the storeroom for future evidence.

I closed and bolted the door.

A moment later, I was squatting on my haunches peering apprehensively at a boxful of copper-coloured detonators and various timing devices, some of which looked like domestic electric-cooker clocks; these latter bore some resemblance to those I'd handled in *War Games*—except that these were Japanese, which did nothing to help. I crossed my eyes at the mysterious Nipponese characters and a couple of crude instructional line drawings which looked like something out of an American comic. Eventually I was thrown back on the vague recollections of my studio exploits, and selecting a detonator at random, I played with it for an anxious moment, offered up a prayer and planted it gingerly into the explosive; I wired four batteries together; my watch told me it was almost four thirty; I set the clock for midnight—only pumpkins would be around at that time of night; dead pumpkins didn't count.

Realising once again that I knew absolutely nothing about real live explosives—plastic, TNT or dynamite, you name it, I knew nothing about it—I made the connection. A needle below the clock face flickered alarmingly and then was still. My gulp of fright was the only sound; nothing went up.

When I rose to my feet, sweat slid down the inside of my jeans. "Silly sod," I muttered crossly. "Why don't I mind my own business."

At the front door I hesitated and stared back at the blank wall hiding all that violence and misery; I crossed my fingers.

I closed the door behind me and floundered off through the snow. It was now quite dark.

I had trouble with the bike. By that I mean I fell off twice in the first couple of efforts to get the thing airborne. It didn't seem to be able to cope with the snow at all. When finally I got the hang of it I rolled steadily downhill with the satisfying assistance of its powerful engine.

Ten minutes later, the headlamp picked up the muffled mass of Emrys Williams toiling manfully down the centre of the road. I hooted and without turning or slackening his pace he moved over to the side, waving me on. I drew up alongside. "Come on," I bawled above the din. "Don't be proud. I'll drop you at your door."

Half expecting a rude retort, I was surprised when he ambled over and, with several grunts and groans, climbed aboard; he'd obviously had his fill of winter sports for the day.

"Dragon?" I yelled over my shoulder.

"Right."

At the dangerous bend on to the main road, we both fell off. Fortunately there was no other traffic. Sprawling messily on the road, Williams said, "Shit," loudly and waited with patient resignation whilst I wrestled with the snarling machine.

Eventually I delivered him to the Dragon front door.

"Ta," he said and, turning at the door, raised a limp thumb. "The best of British for tonight."

"Hey!" I called, switching off the engine. "How's Mike?"

He turned back. "Mike? No idea."

"Haven't you seen him around?"

He shook his head. "Not since you did."

I clambered off the bike. "You're an unfeeling sod, aren't you? I'd better come in, see if he's all right. He could be bloody dead for all you care."

He shrugged wordlessly and passed through the door: I was delighted when I heard him stumble down the two steps inside. Serve him bloody well right. Heaving the bike on to its rest, I followed him through to the silent and gloomy bar, behind which he disappeared with only the slightest of valedictory grunts. I went on to the closed door of Mike Davies' room.

I knocked gently. There was no reply, but I could hear music. I turned the handle and put my head round the door. The music was Isolde's "Liebestod."

The room was in shadow, only a flickering glow of a low fire relieving the darkness. For a moment or two I could see nothing; then, all at once, eerily, I caught the glitter of his eyes.

"Mike?"

He made no reply. I reached for a switch, and a single warm-shaded lamp glowed in the far corner of the room.

He was huddled in a chair, eyes wide and wet, his mind submerged in the soaring music. I hesitated, not knowing whether to go or stay; people are apt to be touchy about music—particularly this sort of music. The fact that the piece was nearing its end persuaded me to stay. Stepping into the room, I closed the door quietly. Berlioz glowered at me from the wall.

I padded noiselessly across the room. He made no move. His bandaged hands lay on his lap side by side, like small wounded animals. Kneeling on the hearthrug I stirred up the fire a bit, replenishing it with a nearby log, which snapped cheerily as the flames caught at it, and produced an irritable shift of position from the listener in the chair. I replaced the poker. He was watching me now; he blinked once and a tear rolled down his damp cheek. I began to wish I hadn't come.

In dem wogenden Schwall, in dem tönenden Schall, sang Isolde. . . .

I stared morosely into the fire; not, I thought, the sort of thing to make a chap get up and go.

. . . *ertrinken, versinken—unbewusst—böchste Lust!* . . .

The waves of tone widened, hung endlessly, it seemed, in the quiet room, oboe and cor anglais clinging to the resolving passion of the theme, then, together, fading poignantly into a silence louder than music.

The cassette deck clicked as the tape ceased to roll. I got up, peered closely at the knobs and switches and turned it off. On the table beside it lay the crumpled portrait of Barry Newman, streaked with dried blood.

"Just looked in to see how you were," I said, by way of clearing the somewhat portentous Wagnerian atmosphere. He made no reply. "Can I give you a drink?"

I poured a stiffish whisky, gave it a short burst of soda and stood over him until he raised his head to focus on the glass, six inches from his nose. His wounded hands caused me a twinge of guilt. I balanced the glass on the arm of his chair. "Can you manage?"

He took the glass between swathed fingers and eyed it fixedly as if about to embark upon a new experience. "Aren't you having one?"

I shook my head. "I'm visiting the sick. And driving, to boot."

"Where's Boot?" he asked which made us both giggle inanely.

I nodded at his hands. "How are they?"

"They'll live." Swallowing most of the drink at a gulp, he leaned back in his chair and eyed me with a certain amount of quiet amusement. "How do you dig Wagner?"

"With caution," I said, and added tentatively, "I'm not sure *Tristan*'s altogether the right thing for you to wallow in at the moment."

"Self-indulgent." It was a statement, not a question.

"Could be."

"We used to listen to it for hours."

"Which is how long it takes," I nodded, wryly remembering a fearsome performance I had once endured at Covent Garden some years back; Charles II wasn't the only one who had been an unconscionable time a-dying. "Well," I shrugged, "I'll be off. Just wanted to say hello, make sure you were all right. It's not good to brood, you know." I sounded like somebody's auntie. "If you must listen to music a touch of the Beethovens might help. Uplift guaranteed."

I was about to make my escape, had the door in my hand in fact, when he said, "Mark," using my Christian name for the first time. I turned. "What Williams said—is it true?" I put the door back in its place. "He said Barry was slugged, pumped full of dope and chucked into that fire like . . . garbage. That's what he said. You heard him. I heard him too—he'd hit me hard, but not that hard. All I want to know is—is it true?"

"Look." I went and sat on the arm of the chair opposite him. "I don't know if it's true or not, do I? I wasn't there and I have no way of finding out and neither has anyone else after all this time. The coroner passed an open verdict. Julie's father will bear that out. If Barry had been pumped full of heroin it would surely have been worth a passing mention by the coroner, don't you think? In addition to which, there was also the small matter of the postmortem."

"Hamish Remington muscled in on the postmortem, didn't he?" His voice was low and tense. "That's it. He was told about the heroin and he told you." I tried to interrupt him but he overrode me. "Williams said 'dope,' you said 'heroin.' "

"Oh, for Christ's sake, Mike, dope, heroin, what's the difference? Forget it . . . let it be."

He was holding his glass between bandaged hands, staring into it as though watching something horrifying taking shape. "Barry was into drugs, wasn't he —in a big way? He was supposed to be working up at that farm for the Hazlitt-Martins. But he was always going abroad. Buying, he said. Farming equipment? Why go abroad to buy farming equipment?" He emptied his glass. "Later on he became odd—secretive. Used to fly off the handle for no reason at all. Talked about going abroad to live. Said he'd been offered a super job on the continent somewhere, Marseilles I think it was, and he was going to take it because they were breathing down his neck. When I asked who 'they' were he just said Hazlitt-Martin and that gang." He looked up at me, his eyes almost translucent. "Hazlitt-Martin killed him, didn't he? It could only have been him."

I stared at him steadily for a couple of seconds. "Barry Newman died in a fire. That's all I know."

"But you could find out."

"Find out what?"

He rose abruptly, shoving past me. "You're a private detective—it's no use denying it, everyone knows it. Find out how Barry really died and I'll foot the bill, however much it may be."

He was wrestling with the whisky bottle and accomplishing nothing. Getting up, I snatched it from him, uncorked it and poured a large measure into his glass; his bandaged hand tipped up the bottle further and he smiled as the liquor gushed clumsily into the glass, and overflowed on to the carpet. He gave a loud, unnatural laugh. "Tonight," he squawked, "I shall get well and truly stoned."

"You do that thing," I growled crossly, grabbing at a paper napkin and drying the bottle and my hands. I watched him as he half emptied the glass.

"Well, will you take the job?" he asked, wiping his mouth with a bandaged hand.

"No, I bloody won't," I told him curtly.

"Why bloody won't you?" He was almost shouting.

I took a deep breath. I said quietly, "If you want someone to investigate Barry's death, then get someone local, someone who knows everybody and can talk to people without arousing suspicion. You'll find plenty of names in the Yellow Pages. Under Detective Agencies. Right?"

He said nothing but continued to stare at me over the rim of his glass, a slightly wild look in his eyes. Then, throwing back his head, he knocked off the remainder of his whisky and reached again for the bottle.

"You really meant what you said, didn't you?" I remarked, heading once again for the door and wondering if I would make it this time. "About getting drunk, I mean."

"Mark." I hauled myself to a standstill. "If you don't do the job I'll do it myself." There was a note of desperation in his voice.

I stood quite still for a moment, then slowly turned towards him. "You'll be a damn fool if you do. You might even be a dead fool. You have no idea what you could be up against. If Barry was killed . . ."

"Murdered."

"If Barry was murdered, then whoever was responsible is hardly going to sit on his backside waiting for you or anyone else to prove it. Let it alone, Mike, or you'll get hurt. Really hurt. We've enough trouble going on up here without you launching out on a personal vendetta. Go and talk to the police. That's what they're there for. But you keep out of it at all costs. And that's the best advice I can give you." I pushed past him, snatched up the bottle and filled his glass to the brim. "Now you get yourself well and truly stoned and then go and sleep it off. Tomorrow you'll feel a whole lot better." I went back to the door. "Maybe." In the doorway I paused to look back at him.

He was standing in the centre of the room, limply, like a puppet waiting to be manipulated; he was clad in black from head to foot, only his face, streaked with sweat and tears, gleaming pallidly in the uncertain light; chalk-white stumps hung where the hands should be.

11

"Perhaps you could get out and walk in front with a lantern," Julie suggested, her nose close against the windscreen in a gallant effort to interpret the various humps and ridges which heaved monotonously out of the darkness into the yellow glare of the headlights.

"Alternatively," I said, "*I* could drive and *you* could get out and walk in front with a lantern."

I had been outside three times already, unclogging the wipers and knocking snow off the headlamps; my shoes were ruined, my socks were soaked and the legs of my jeans clung to my calves like the skins of a couple of dead haddock.

Which was a pity, because I'd put in a lot of time and trouble trying to make myself presentable for the enemy. Not that there was much I could do about clothes. I only had one set. Have jeans, will travel. Jersey, jacket and splendid black raincoat completed the outfit. But I had shaved with more than usual care, been painstaking with my hair and splashed Houbigant around with praiseworthy prodigality—enough at any rate to make Julie's nostrils flare a little when she passed me on the way to the bathroom.

She had poured herself into a close-fitting woollen number in soft yellow and beige stripes which made her look like a shapely stick of Edinburgh rock but had then ruined it all by climbing into a pair of muddy Wellingtons and that ineluctable mackintosh from Oxfam. Parrying my protests, she said, "I'll take it off for dinner, I promise." The Wellington situation she overcame by bundling a smart pair of tan leather shoes into an International Stores carrier bag. I gave up.

"Can we go your private way?" I said, emerging from my reverie. "Through the other bloke's property?"

"Why not?" A moment later. "On the other hand, why?"

I didn't know why. "They won't be expecting us by the back door. It might confuse them." I brooded over my wet feet for a moment or two. "I hope we were right to tell your dad where we were going. He won't jump the gun or anything, will he? Go ringing up Owen and the like?"

I had told neither of them about my latest discoveries in Wanhope, nor about my demolition plans. They had enough on their plates without all that. But the last thing I wanted was the idiot constabulary poking around up there at midnight and getting itself blown to smithereens.

Julie shook her head. "Not Dad. He's not the panicky sort. He'll wait up for us, like he said."

"At least he'll know where to start looking."

"I could end up in some oil sheik's harem, couldn't I?"

"Only if you're lucky."

"And what about you?"

"Oh, I'll be somewhere in the Tregaren bog, I shouldn't wonder—with a weight at each corner."

"I don't think we should be having this conversation," she murmured quietly, peering intently through the falling snow for an expected turning. "Seriously, though, I do wish I knew why we had been invited."

"Know your enemy, perhaps."

With a decisive slap on the gear lever, she stopped the car, pulled on the brake, leaned on the wheel and looked at me. The dashboard lights glinted in her worried eyes. "I also wish I knew why we're going. The snow would be a lovely excuse to get out of it. You could be walking into the most awful danger. Barry Newman killed, Pithy killed and they've already had a couple of goes at you. . . ."

"Listen." I took her hand. "No one's going to get killed. Not tonight, at any rate. They've got to be cleverer than that. Williams knows where I am, his boss knows, your father knows. . . ."

I gave her back her hand. She released the brake, hesitated and then put it back on again. "Why don't you give me the gun?" To my protests she said, "Stuck down the front of your trousers it looks as if you're about to drop a foal. It would be safer with me."

I had to admit she had a point. With an excess of lascivious rustlings I groped around beneath my raincoat, eventually producing the Walther. I handed it to her. "What do I say if I need it in a hurry? 'Please can I have my gun back?' "

"Can I borrow a handkerchief?"

I offered her the only clean one I had left. She sighed. "That's what you say. 'Can I borrow a handkerchief?' Which will give me a legitimate excuse to burrow around in my bag. All right?"

She stowed the gun away in her bag, released the brake and let in the clutch; we churned off once again—at all of eight miles an hour.

A jaunty trundle across the remembered cattle grid alerted me to the fact that we were approaching our destination. I scrubbed at the window. "I think the snow has stopped."

"It has." She switched off the wipers. Another twenty yards and a low building loomed ahead; a careful left swing of the wheel and again we drew up alongside the impressive Range Rover. She cut the engine and doused the lights.

We sat for a moment staring at the dark windscreen. She gave a long groan of relief that the drive was over. The uneasiness I had been holding at bay began to crowd in on me. "I wish you hadn't come," I said, more for something to say than for any great need to repeat a sentiment of which she was already aware.

"I'm here," she said quietly.

"All right, then." I took her hand and kissed her glove. "Here we go. And you'll have to lead the way."

At the point where I had first met the colonel, we stood looking up at the sky. The air was clean and pure; fast-moving clouds were breaking up, and, through the ever-widening rifts, stars glittered, and a gibbous moon stared down moronically at the crystallised landscape.

Beside me, Julie shivered suddenly and drew the high storm collar of her mackintosh closer about her ears. "Somebody walked over my grave," she whispered. "Come on." She slid her arm through mine.

An untidy sprawl of farm buildings lay a quarter of a mile or so away, surrounding an imposing centrepiece. Beneath its recently acquired layer of icing sugar and gleaming in the fitful scurry of moonlight, the scene took on the dreamworld aspect of a Christmas card.

We crunched through the snow, Julie healthily booted and dry, with me tagging gamely alongside, the icy dampness seeping between my toes.

"This is the west side of the house," she volunteered suddenly, probably in an effort to rouse my flagging spirits. She pointed away to the left. "Barns and stables over there behind the main building; that long low shed with the steep roof is the dairy. A large and profitable property, as you can see. Most of the staff have individual cottages on the far side, but the stud groom, of course, and most of the stable lads live cheek by jowl with the horses."

I almost came to a halt as the hairs on the back of my neck stirred. We were being watched, every step under surveillance. Whilst Julie talked, I glanced warily to right and left. I could neither see nor hear anything untoward.

"Have you actually been inside the house?" I asked in a lower voice.

"Only the morning room; east side, right of the main entrance. Otherwise not."

My eyes quartered the ground ahead of us. "You don't know the whereabouts of the dining room, then? Just in case we have to make a run for it."

She was silent for a moment. "We're not thinking of making a run for it, are we?"

"Nothing is impossible."

Another silence. My ears strained for the slightest sound.

"Life seemed so much less complicated before you came," she said softly, and I glanced at her quickly, trying to see the expression in her eyes, but her face was almost invisible behind the all-enveloping storm collar. There had been a disturbing wistfulness in her tone.

"I'm sorry," I said.

She stopped dead. I had seen it a split second before she did. A few paces ahead, a deep set of fresh black footprints lay across our path, then lost themselves in a cluster of bushes and trees on our right. I heard a stealthy rustling in the undergrowth. After a moment or two, we went on. We trod more carefully. I can't think why. We had, after all, been invited to dinner, and anyone prowling the grounds in this sort of weather would most likely be staff and expecting us.

We found several more sets of footprints, newly made and crossing each other—at one point converging into a small trampled area; some sort of conference, perhaps.

A sudden flurry of sound made us turn. Across our own tracks a few yards back lay a new trail. Julie's hand tightened on my arm. I stared into the silvery darkness. Less than a dozen yards away a black form stood, frozen and motionless. It could have been the stump of a tree, but something about it . . . I could have sworn it shifted infinitesimally. My eyes followed the footprints; where the form stood, they ended.

I detached Julie's hand from my arm, laid a warning finger on my lips and indicated that she should remain where she was. Without haste I moved off in the direction of the still figure. As I closed on it I could see it was a man; I could even make out the white clouding of breath around the head. There was an unmistakable metallic click. The barrel of a rifle glinted momentarily in the moonlight. I froze in my tracks. With barely four yards between us, I watched the barrel slide slowly upwards until it pointed at my head. If I rushed him I'd be dead before I'd gone a yard. I remained rooted. The figure moved slowly backward, away from me, the gun raised and threatening.

A cloud passed over the moon. Mesmerised, I made no move. When the cloud had gone it had taken the ghostly figure with it. The footprints led to a black clump of bushes and undergrowth; there they merged with the shadows and were lost. Only the warning lingered.

The sweat had frozen on my forehead.

Slowly I backed towards Julie. She was standing just where I had left her. As I returned to her side I heard a slight click. I glanced down. The Walther was in her hand; she had just slid on the safety catch.

"I would have killed him," she said in a dead voice. My gaze moved up to her face. Her eyes glittered in the cold light, and her mouth was a hard line, grim almost to the point of ugliness.

As she replaced the gun in her bag I registered her trembling hands, an icy tremor, almost of nausea, seeping into me. She had been prepared to kill. I took her arm gently. "Let's get on. It's unhealthy hanging about here."

At a slightly quicker pace we moved off, my mind brooding unhappily on the shadowy figure. Who was he? An armed guard keeping an eye on the property? The tracks suggested that there were four of them at least. Armed guards ranging an English gentleman's farmhouse in the middle of Wales during a blizzard? It made sense when one remembered what this particular English gentleman was up to.

"Straight ahead is the tradesmen's entrance," Julie said suddenly.

"You all right?"

"Fine." Her voice was crisp and dry.

"Then, let's go and bang on the tradesmen's entrance," I said lightly. "I'm not proud."

Suiting the action to the word, I belaboured the sturdy door with its sturdy iron knocker, then rang sturdily on an electric bell set into the wall beside it. In no time at all, the door was opened a few inches by a startled swarthy face which peered around its edge and was surmounted by a tall white chef's hat.

"*Oui?*" it said and Julie astounded me by bursting into a flood of French. "*Oui, oui,*" said the face again, a flash of gold teeth glinting beneath the heavy black moustache. With a flourishing Gallic gesture, the door was flung open and we saw for the first time the butcher's cleaver in his other hand.

Ushering us into a brightly lit kitchen, he propped us in a corner like a couple of playing cards, reached for a house telephone on the wall and began shouting at someone in an urgent and quite incomprehensible patois, waving the cleaver encouragingly in our direction from time to time.

Two men in white aprons and a dour-looking woman wiping utensils at a large stainless-steel sink gave us a casual glance and went on with what they were doing. A delicious odour of roast duck and herbs titillated my nostrils.

"Aaaarrhh!" cried the chef testily and replaced the receiver with an emphatic clatter indicating that whoever had been on the other end was an idiot. He raised a long, beckoning finger. "Come. Follow, *s'il vous plaît.*" Disposing of the cleaver, he swept through the kitchen like a guide in a picture gallery ignoring the exhibits you most want to see. We trotted in his wake down a dimly lit corridor, up some stone steps, through a baize-covered door and finally into what turned out to be the main reception hall, warmly lit and richly carpeted.

A broad-shouldered, portentous man in a dark and impeccably cut suit took us off the chef's hands without once glancing in his direction or attending to a word of the vociferous stream which poured from his Gallic lips.

Eventually the chef gave up and withdrew behind the green baize door, still waving his arms and fulminating.

"Miss Remington and Mr. Savage," the new man murmured sedately, steely grey eyes taking in every detail of our dress. "Colonel and Signora Hazlitt-Martin have been expecting you." Another accent. Italian this time. Tito Gobbi as Scarpia.

As I handed over my raincoat, the man's eyes crawled disdainfully over my jacket and jeans. They were utterly unprepared, however, for the spectacle of Julie's calamitous mackintosh; he removed it from her shoulders with two strong and fastidious fingers. I can't honestly say that I blamed him; it did give off a certain air of geriatric decline.

Julie perched herself on a nearby Chippendale, removed her Wellingtons, took the tan shoes from her International Stores carrier bag; put them on and stuffed the bag into one of the boots; these she handed to the man, whose eyes by this time had quite glazed over.

As he turned away into a small lobby to dispose of our finery, I noticed that his suit was not so impeccably cut as to conceal the shoulder holster he wore beneath it. My eyes shifted to Julie's bag, which contained the Walther, and then up to her face; she smiled and winked mischievously. Happily, she appeared to have regained her normal spirits.

Poised primly on her Chippendale, she looked ridiculously like a million dollars, but when the butler, or whoever he was, returned to us, he remained pointedly unimpressed. Silently indicating that we should follow him, he made off grandly down the softly carpeted hall. Julie took my hand and squeezed it gently.

"*Bon appétit,*" I whispered.

He knocked at a door on the left, opened it without waiting for a reply and stood aside, allowing us only enough room to squeeze through. "Your weapon's showing," I told him quietly as I edged past him into the room.

"My dear, how nice of you to come." It was the diminutive Gertrude, dressed in a stunning full-length creation in mauve shot silk which had leapt straight out of the pages of a 1950 *Vogue.* She took Julie in one hand and me in the other. "And you, Mr. Savage. I do hope the journey hasn't been too frightful. We were beginning to think you might not be able to get through."

Her hand was small and dry and encrusted with rings, her smile bright and welcoming. The perfume wafting about her was delicate and expensive, and her diamond bracelet and neat, diamond-studded choker would have kept me in small change for the rest of my life.

"Thank you, Cesare," she told our Italian guide with the gun. *Cesare,* indeed! He hovered for a moment, then withdrew.

"Here they are, John," she went on comfortingly to her husband, as if he had been out searching for us and had only just returned. He had, in fact, been there all the time, rooted to the hearth rug, his back to an enormous fireplace, watching me with what can only be described as a cold eye.

He offered neither word, smile nor hand, but with the slightest of nods did at least stand to one side as we approached the blazing fire. He, too, was in evening clothes, an immaculate grey velvet smoking jacket being his only gesture to the promised potluck informality.

His wife had called him "John," I noticed, having presumably cohabited with him long enough to discount the relevance of the "St." which preceded it.

Beyond the fireplace I became aware of a third person tucked away in the shadowy depths of a large wingchair. The colonel's cold grey eye shifted momentarily as he registered my glance.

"You already know the general, of course."

No, I thought. I don't know any generals.

The occupant of the chair heaved himself into the light and got to his feet with an ungainly lurch.

"The late Mr. Savage, I believe," wheezed George Morton, extending a fat wet hand in my direction.

12

Dinner took on something of the nightmare quality of Macbeth's banquet. It would have come as no surprise had the ghost of the blood-boltered Pithy appeared in the empty chair opposite.

The shadowy dining room did nothing to rule out such a possibility. Two seven-branched candelabra six feet apart on the narrow rosewood table and one more on an adjacent sideboard supplied the only illumination. As host, the colonel took the head of the table, with Morton on his right and Julie opposite. At the far end sat Gertrude, with me on her right; the unlaid place and empty chair across the table was only occasionally occupied by the spectral figure of my vivid imagination. Had Julie and I each cared to make a long arm, we might just have touched fingertips. I felt marooned.

The actual meal was produced by Cesare and a diminutive maid in a disturbingly short black silk skirt—a peccadillo of the colonel's, perhaps?—

which helped, periodically, to take my mind off the saturnine features of Cesare, who hovered above me like an expectant undertaker.

My initial curiosity concerning his operative villainy was reawakened by the sight of an enormous gold ring on the third finger of his right hand, occupied at the time with pouring a delicate rosé wine into Gertrude's glass. Glinting eerily in the golden flicker of candlelight, the ring caught my attention not merely because it was the size of a snail's shell but also because of the embossed and enamelled replica of a bull upon it, which I took to be a family crest and which seemed familiar. When, a moment later, the hand crept over my own right shoulder, I attempted to take a closer look at it but was frustrated by the wine bottle. Only when my glass was actually to my lips did my recalcitrant memory give me a jolt which all but decanted the wine into my lap.

With rock-steady hand and fluttering pulse I replaced the glass carefully on the table. If they imagined for a moment that I could be persuaded to touch a drop of anything from a glass set by the hand of some Italian Mafioso who answered to the name of Cesare, they needed their heads examined.

The bull, I had just recollected, was the crest of the Borgia family.

"Is the wine not to your liking, Mr. Savage?" asked an anxious-sounding Gertrude, noticing my abrupt change of mind.

I grunted and cleared my throat. "It's fine, thank you, fine . . . very nice."

She smiled a little quizzically over her glass and took a delicate sip. "Oh, yes," she murmured. "Just right, I think."

One man's meat, I thought moodily, remembering the ingenious things the Borgias had been able to do to the rim of a glass. I peered suspiciously at my smoked salmon and the sinister little chunk of lemon reclining beside it. What if . . . ?

I shook myself and flicked a glance along the table. Julie was in the act of replacing her slightly depleted glass, and her plate betrayed the fact that she had also sampled the salmon. She caught my eye and gave me a gloomy smile.

Maybe she was right. Would they be likely to spoil a perfectly good dinner by disposing of two of the guests during the first course? Far better to wait for the arrival of the cheese board. That way, even the condemned man could eat a hearty meal. To hell with it, I thought. Raising my glass, I lowered a draught to my hostess's bright china-blue eyes. It was, as she had intimated, an extremely good wine, well worth my bending my teetotal principles.

Nonetheless my taste buds lurched a little as I encountered the watchful eye of Cesare from the shadowy refuge of his candle-lit sideboard. I returned the look boldly, and almost immediately lowered my eyes significantly to his ring to indicate that I, for one, was on to him. I think he must have miscon-strued the message for, turning away, he furtively checked his flies.

Gertrude chose that moment for the opening gambit of her dinner-table conversation by apologising for the "potluck" fare we were being offered. I didn't see a lot wrong with smoked salmon—provided it wasn't laced with hemlock, of course—and if this was her notion of potluck she obviously had no idea how the other half lived. However, she was not all that insistent upon it and, having mentioned it and begged our communal indulgence, she dropped the subject and turned back to her plate, wondering aloud as she did so whether the despoliation of our rivers was worth the somewhat limited pleasure she experienced in the eating of fish.

She must also have experienced one or two uneasy qualms that she was doomed to share the next hour or so with an unusually bovine dinner com-panion, for my polite grunts and occasional eyebrow-raising would have dis-couraged the most dedicated of conversationalists. Things, however, were due to perk up quite a bit later on.

Having subdued my queasiness with regard to Cesare's ring, I turned my attention to the other end of the table. George Morton was even fatter and more obnoxious than I had remembered, and my dearest wish was to upturn his soup plate over his head. (Smoked salmon, he had declared loudly, was not for him nor he for it, so tomato soup was sent for and produced.) I could hear him slurping away at it even as far below the salt as I was.

I hadn't yet recovered from the shock of his appearance in the drawing room. How I had taken that fat damp hand in mine and endured the effusive bonhomie that went with it without shoving two healthy forefingers into his piggy red eyes, I shall never know. I remember once nodding over a school-master's homily on the art of restraint. Restraint, he had maintained, was one of the cardinal virtues. Which may well be true. It is also one of the greatest stockpilers of adrenalin, wrath and homicidal tendencies known to red-blooded man.

He had squinnied up into my face, winked, blinked and breathed garlic over me, and I could happily have blown his head off there and then, but for the impossibility, at that precise juncture, of asking Julie for her handker-chief, since she happened to be blowing her nose on it.

"You didn't tell me he was a general," hissed Julie over her Croft Original a moment or two later. We had drifted slightly apart from the others, who had engaged themselves in desultory conversation about the weather and the well-known fact that the Hazlitt-Martins always, but always, dressed for din-ner.

"General, my foot!" I growled. "Just keep your handkerchief handy and your powder dry—we may just need it."

Before we eventually trooped into the dining room, I had gathered that though the colonel and his wife had often talked with Morton on the telephone, neither had actually come face to face with him until that moment—an overdue occurrence, I thought with malice, which must have given them both a nasty turn. Gertrude had gone on to say how surprised they had been to learn that he was even in England. They should have asked me, I could have told them.

Now, having disposed of the smoked salmon without keeling over, I picked at the main event of our potluck collation—roast duckling with green peas and apple sauce—and turned my most immediate thoughts towards the problem of self-preservation. I cheered myself with the thought that the unexpected, and as yet unexplained, advent of Morton had somewhat improved our chances of survival; whatever plans the Hazlitt-Martins might have laid for our eventual disposal (I had by this time exonerated Cesare Borgia and his ring; his hasty preoccupation with his flies had endeared him to me for ever), those plans would presumably now be in need of modification. After all, to all intents and purposes, I was on the payroll of their guest of honour. I just hoped they realised that it was not now a question of Them and Us: we were all Them together. And I still had some of Morton's money in my pocket to prove it.

To dissemble was the only course open to us. Run with the hare, hunt with the hounds. To play along with them might well produce handsome dividends—though what possible use they could be to us in our present predicament I failed to see. To whom would I be allowed to report my findings? At the moment, clearly, George Morton trusted me. But that trust would quickly disintegrate if I were discovered muttering mysteriously into the nearest telephone. And anyway, whom could I call? Emrys Williams? Williams was the only friend I had, but—

"Do you care for Bach, Mr. Savage?" asked Gertrude Hazlitt-Martin out of the blue and apropos, it seemed, of absolutely nothing at all.

I looked at her blankly. "Bach?"

"Johann Sebastian." She was batting with fortitude on her extremely sticky wicket.

"Ah . . . Bach, yes . . . that one. No, I can't say that I do actually. Not a lot, no."

"Oh, good. Neither do I." Which surprised me a little, for she was just the sort of person I'd have thought would have gone for that ancient and tedious old master—except that she kept horses, of course.

"Frightfully boring, I find him," she confided, nodding her encouragement of my views like a canvassing lady MP with her foot in the door. "I'm so glad you agree. People are always afraid to express an unbiased opinion nowadays, don't you find?" She chewed on her duckling for a ruminative moment or two; then, taking a small sip of wine—it was Chablis by this time—she leaned in gently towards me, a conspiratorial smile twitching mischievously at the corners of her mouth. "A great friend of mine recently came up with the most divine description of harpsichord music. . . ." She glanced with furtive amusement at the others and lowered her voice even more, so that I too was obliged to lean in to hear this special gem. "The sound of the harpsichord, she said, made her think of two skeletons copulating on a hot tin roof."

My spontaneous yelp of laughter turned all heads in our direction. Gertrude lowered her eyes demurely and daintily continued to dismember the leg of her duckling.

"What was that, dear?" enquired her husband, an expectant half smile on his face. "Won't you share the joke with the rest of us?"

"It was nothing, John dear," she said blandly, glancing at me with the merest flicker of a wink. "Nothing at all. Mr. Savage was merely taken unawares, that's all. My fault. I do apologise."

There was a silence during which her husband considered whether to press the point. In the diffused golden glow of the candles, he seemed to have lost something of his remote greyness. He was a handsome man—typically military, of course, but no less handsome for that. He sat his chair as one might expect him to sit a horse, upright, contained and no lounging. Good hands, too. Deciding against further elaboration of the episode, he raised his glass in a toast instead. "To you, my dear."

There was something achingly olde-worlde about them, and I caught myself wondering whether there had been some mistake and they weren't really evildoers after all. I glanced at Julie as we joined in raising our glasses. She gave me only a token smile, her mind elsewhere.

Only Morton ignored the gallant toast. He didn't even raise his piggy eyes from his plate. Hunched monstrously over the table, he stuffed food into his face with the kind of frenzy one might have expected from the repatriated Ben Gunn after his three-year stint of berries and oysters, plying his fork like a steam shovel. As I glowered at him, he picked his plate finally clean. With his mouth still full, he gulped down half a glass of wine, mopped his face with his napkin and, with cheeks bulging in a silent belch, pushed away his plate and leaned back in his chair. Aware of my gaze, he jerked his head round, winked and then began a noisy exploration of his teeth with his tongue.

I turned away my eyes.

If my survival depended upon his good offices, I was ready to offer Gertrude my head on a platter. I gave her a surreptitious glance. She, too, had been following her guest of honour's feeding habits. Our eyes met. For her, too, the performance had been something of an experience.

With a suppressed sigh, she laid down her knife and fork, leaving the remainder of her meal untouched. There was a moment of uncertainty, hesitation, as if she were contemplating an unpleasant course of action.

"Are you a policeman, by any chance, Mr. Savage?" she asked at last, her eyes fixed resolutely on her plate.

The sudden question was nothing if not disconcerting, but her uneasiness had half prepared me for it.

"No, I'm not a policeman."

"For whom, then, do you work?"

I nodded towards the head of the table. "For him, up there. The messy eater."

Her eyes flickered in my direction. "Do you really expect me to believe that?"

"Not really, no. Even I find it difficult."

The corners of her mouth drooped cynically. "From what I hear, you appear to be hell-bent on destroying his organisation; a strange way to work for a man."

I followed her gaze as she stared at Morton for a couple of seconds with blatant distaste. He and the colonel were mumbling together whilst Julie sat neglected, staring bleakly at her wineglass. My heart went out to her.

Gertrude was saying quietly, "It all seems such a stupid waste: I feel we have so much in common, you and I. We could so easily have become friends . . . little Julie, too—I've always been fond of her—such a pretty girl."

"Julie has nothing to do with all this; you know that as well as I do. She's here simply because I'm here and for no other reason."

She said simply, "She's here because the general insisted on her being. On the phone he was most insistent; he wanted both of you here."

"Why?"

She hesitated. "I have no idea. I would like to say that he wished to make you some sort of offer—a proposition, perhaps."

"An ultimatum, I think. Join us or else. Couple found dead in burnt-out car. . . . Two die of exposure in fifteen-foot snowdrift. . . ."

She looked startled. "Oh, dear me no, nothing so drastic, I'm sure." The fact that she didn't deny the possibility was disturbing, to say the least. "If you really do work for the general," she went on steadily, "you must surely be prepared to accept the consequences of . . . defection. In the Army they would shoot you for it."

She leaned in. "We're in a most sensitive and complicated line of business, Mr. Savage. It is simply a question of having to protect our interests. You must surely see that." She made it all sound so reasonable, as if she were running the cake shop on the corner.

"Then, perhaps you should change your interests," I suggested in a gritty undertone. "I personally would find it difficult, if not impossible, to conceive of interests more repellent and more corruptive than yours."

"Oh, come, come." She made a small dismissive gesture. "That is nothing more than the standard moral censure of an already corrupt society. We supply a need, Mr. Savage, a deeply felt need, no matter what you or our detractors may say, and we're only a small part of an enormously able organisation. What would change if our particular group withdrew tomorrow? Nothing. A war cannot be stopped by a handful of conscientious objectors. I admit that those against us amount to something more than a handful, but that doesn't necessarily prove that the war is wrong. Certainly there are sinful elements, there are in every war; both my husband and I would be the first to agree with that. Occasionally he has to concur with certain . . . minor irregularities, which he openly admits to finding irksome, but first and foremost he's a military man, you must remember that. He's accustomed to obeying orders, however uncomfortable they may be at times. Orders have to be obeyed or there would be anarchy. Now, that's true, isn't it? You can't possibly disagree with that."

The quiet reasoning of her argument filled me with dismay. I stared at her with growing disbelief, the bile rising in my throat. I leaned closer to her, my face a few inches from hers. "Mrs. Hazlitt-Martin, I find it difficult to believe you quite realise the enormity of what is going on here. You of all people. What you've just said, for instance—about obeying orders at any cost—that went out with Nuremburg. Nowadays such an uncompromising attitude is looked upon as an almost indictable offence." I had touched an exposed nerve. I could see the sudden pain in her eyes—pain and something else, a flicker of comprehension, perhaps? I pressed on hastily, "I'm not just concerned with drug-trafficking, though Heaven knows that should be enough in itself. It's murder I'm talking about, cold-blooded murder. During the past couple of days your husband has made several attempts to have me killed. If I've understood you correctly, you're prepared to condone that. But who *ordered* him to do it, can you tell me that? And who, in God's name, *ordered* him to kill Pithy?"

She looked at me almost stupidly for a moment. "Pithy?" she repeated slowly. "The simple one? Simple Pithy?"

"The very same." She really hadn't known. Her defences began to crumble.

For a further second, she stared into my face blankly, as though not seeing me; then the change began. When her eyes eventually turned towards her husband, they were filled with such latent violence that the colour seemed to have drained from them. There was a whiteness about the irises which was frightening. I saw the bunching of the flexed muscles of her jaw. "I don't believe it," she whispered softly, her gaze still fixed on her husband. "I simply don't believe it. . . ."

"Would you like me to take you to the body and let you see for yourself?" I asked brutally. "They smashed his head to a pulp—against a tree."

"No!"

The single syllable echoed round the room, and again all heads turned in her direction. Out of the corner of my eye I saw Cesare's hand make an instinctive movement towards his gun. The colonel, half rising to his feet, remained transfixed by the sudden malevolence in his wife's eyes.

"What *is* the matter, my dear?" he murmured, with a fine show of amused curiosity. His gaze, shifting slightly, crawled over me as if I had committed some sort of impropriety.

"You've killed Pithy," she said in whisper. "Why did you kill Pithy?"

"Pithy?" For a moment, he was at a loss. I could almost see him thinking, Pithy, Pithy, who the hell's Pithy?

Gertrude ploughed on. "What possible reason could you have for killing someone like Pithy, poor pathetic creature that he was? What harm could he possibly have done to you, to any of us?" Her voice grew strident.

The colonel said loudly, "Gertrude, I did not kill Pithy."

"But you were responsible for killing him. You had him killed." Now she was on her feet, screaming at him.

Morton stirred uncomfortably, glancing over his shoulder at Cesare and the maid. "Steady on now, steady. This can be discussed at another time, surely—in a more civilised manner . . ."

"Civilised manners!" Gertrude rounded on him furiously. "What would you know about civilised manners? Kindly hold your tongue."

Even Morton was cowed by the sudden vehemence of the attack.

After a moment during which she made a supreme effort to control her anger, she said, in a scarcely heard whisper, "Margaret, Cesare, will you be so good as to leave the room?"

The maid needed no second bidding but departed with precipitate haste. Cesare, a heavy frown on his face, shot an uneasy glance at his employer. After a moment's hesitation, the colonel sent him away with a curt nod. The Italian padded from the room, closing the door loudly behind him.

Some of the candles guttered and went out in the sudden draught, and the room became slowly permeated with the acrid pungency of smoking wicks.

The colonel reseated himself, casting an anxious sidelong glance at Morton. Eliciting no response from that quarter, he sighed and stared bleakly at the table.

Gertrude's small, blue-veined hands twitched nervously at her napkin, folding it this way and that, tugging at its hem as if to tear it into shreds.

The silence became intolerable. Reluctantly her husband cleared his throat. "Perhaps, my dear, you would care to explain your . . . unseemly outburst. And incidentally apologise to our guest." He spoke in a gruff monotone, making no effort to look at her.

The hands steadied, occupying themselves now in an almost fastidious attempt to fold the napkin, and having done so, placed it neatly on the table exactly parallel to the place mat. I glanced up at her. She was having trouble controlling the muscles about her mouth; tears brimmed unshed in her eyes. I could sense the effort she was making to hold them back, knowing that their release would be seen as a sign of weakness and penitence.

At last she spoke, her voice low and unsteady.

"The reason for my 'unseemly outburst' as you are pleased to call it should be fairly obvious to you, John. Mr. Savage here has just informed me of Pithy's death . . . and the manner of it." She raised her head and stared at him with intense distaste. "I can see no purpose, no possible reason for an act of such . . . obscenity. Who killed him? Deakin and Champ, I suppose. But without *your* word they would not have moved." She paused. "A small part of me understands why you wanted him dead. But who, John, who would have listened to him, whatever he might have said? We've all *heard* his stories, but which of us has actually *believed* them? All those wild things he was so fond of telling people he'd done and seen. Nobody listened to him, John, nobody. So why did you have to kill him?"

Now the tears welled over. I tried to understand her and failed. All the immeasurable human misery for which she and her husband were responsible, and she was weeping over Pithy. The silence seemed to go on and on. With a deep, shuddering breath, she continued.

"I understand you less and less as the years go by, John." She made a vain attempt to stanch the tears with the heel of her hand. "If this affair should by any chance blow over—and I doubt it will, because too many people know about it"—and here she took in Julie and me before turning back to her husband—"but if, as I say, this should blow over, then I'm finished, John. You of course must do as you please, as always, but I, personally, will no longer be part of it. Never. Ever again." She took up her small, jewelled purse, which lay on the table beside her plate. "Now if you will excuse me. . . ."

With a soft rustle of draperies, she moved behind me on her way to the door, pressing me gently back into my chair as I half rose to my feet.

Behind Julie and facing Morton she paused. "General Morton, I apologise for my . . . unseemly outburst. For the rest, for what you have just heard and I hope understood, you must act according to your own lights. I will not betray my husband, ever, nor will I betray you. Perhaps you will remember that when you are making your report to your superiors. If indeed you have superiors. But I expect you have. We all have them, don't we . . . for better or for worse. Good night, General, and may our paths never cross again."

She turned away.

"Gertrude. . . ." Her husband seemed genuinely moved. He held one hand to her in a last, desperate appeal. "Gertrude . . . *please.*"

But she ignored him and left the room with the most awesome display of dignity I had ever seen. At her departure the candle flames flickered again, but this time it was almost as if they were applauding.

The colonel rose shakily to his feet.

"Stay where you are," growled Morton.

"I must go to her. . . ."

"We have important business to attend to. You can talk to her any time."

The colonel opened his mouth to speak, thought better of it, then turned, as if for support, to Julie. She lowered her eyes. Finally he sank back into his chair. He had aged ten years.

The candles flickered and were still. Morton's morose and evil eye rested speculatively on Julie.

"You, however, Miss Remington, are at liberty to leave us whenever you wish."

"I'm delighted to hear it," she answered evenly. "But I intend to stay."

He shrugged. "Your choice entirely. But I will thank you not to interrupt or interfere."

It was high time I took part in the proceedings. I started angrily to my feet. "Now, listen. . . ."

"No," said Morton mildly, raising a fat finger and stabbing it in my direction. "*You* listen." He held my eyes steadily. "You are here to learn. And you will learn only by what you hear."

I glared at him long and levelly. "Julie," I said quietly. "May I borrow a handkerchief?"

I registered her intake of breath and without taking my eyes off Morton was aware of her lifting her bag from the floor and rummaging among its contents. No one else moved. I held out my hand. The Walther was placed in my palm. I grasped it, slid my finger into the trigger guard and pointed the weapon steadily at Morton's head.

The colonel shifted uneasily and cleared his throat. Morton stared into the muzzle of the gun, then slowly raised his gaze to mine. The heavy lips puckered with faint amusement. "Well . . . a persuasive performance, Mr. Savage."

I lowered the barrel of the gun, dragged my chair alongside Julie's and sat down again, placing the weapon on the table in front of me. "Just to remind us," I explained, "that all the advantages are not on your side of the table. Now, you were saying. . . ."

Never had I contemplated pulling the trigger—not then, at any rate. He of course knew that. But the will to kill was clearly present, and the squeezing of the trigger simply a matter of the cessation of my restraint. When the moment came, he would be dead. He knew that, too.

It was some time before he stirred. Hunched in his chair, breathing heavily through his nose, his slitted eyes were intent on the untidy remains of his meal before him. To his left, the colonel, fiddling unhappily with a silver napkin ring, was still having trouble with his throat. Julie remained a motionless and silent spectator. Somewhere outside a small avalanche of snow slid off the roof with a muffled roar.

Morton spoke at last. "Some years back . . ." The effort sent him into a wheezing paroxysm of coughing. Reaching for his glass, he emptied it at a gulp. "A young man, one Barry Newman, was killed up here by an injection of heroin. An abortive attempt was then made to incinerate the body. The result of that spot of bungling was catastrophic to the network and caused the shutdown of the Haverford cell. Several thousand kilos of merchandise were seized and millions, and I mean millions, of pounds sterling went down the drain." He swivelled his eyes towards the colonel.

"And you were responsible." He raised his voice to override the other's protest. "The buck stops here, Colonel. I'm not suggesting that you, personally, were responsible for Newman's death, but one of your minions was— Deakin, was it?—and that, according to your precious army code, places the onus squarely on your shoulders. Right?"

The colonel shifted uncomfortably.

"Was it Deakin?" asked Morton softly.

The other shrugged stiffly. "I sometimes think Deakin isn't quite all there."

"Yet he's still on your payroll."

"He has his uses." The colonel glanced coldly in my direction. "And one takes what one can get."

Morton flipped up the lid of a silver cigarette box at his elbow, peered at its contents for a second, selected one, delved in a pocket for a match, lit the cigarette and, true to form, flicked the spent match over his shoulder. I watched the colonel's eyes narrow with distaste as they followed the progress of the match.

"I wonder if you realise just how near to disaster you yourself were during that little Newman fracas," Morton went on, exuding a dense cloud of smoke. "It was only by a miracle of quick thinking on our part and botched police work on theirs that you survived at all." He blinked at the glowing tip of the cigarette. "P'raps you'd like to tell us just why Deakin chose that somewhat bizarre method of disposing of Newman. If anything was likely to hit the fan it was surely that. You might as well have advertised the stuff in the local press."

"I can't answer for Deakin."

"I think you should try, don't you?"

The colonel sighed heavily. He had threaded the napkin ring on two of his fingers and was turning it slowly, as if winding up a clockwork toy. "Newman was an unpleasant man at best—rarely missed an opportunity to ride the less fortunate and less intelligent. Deakin loathed him. I don't know what actually happened. So long ago. All hearsay. A brawl in the pub. Newman got a bang on the head or was drunk. Deakin was seen getting him to his car. Brought him back here, I suppose. The merchandise was stored in a barn here in those days. No idea how he did it. Can't be all simple injecting the bloodstream. Someone gave him a helping hand perhaps—my guess would be George Mathews. Why that particular method? Who knows? To make him look like an addict, probably. Then the body had to be got rid of. Presumably he bundled it into the car, took it to Wanhope—Newman's property in those days—and set fire to the place. It's guesswork of course. But there's no doubt in my mind that Deakin was responsible."

For a long moment, Morton eyed him with distaste. "Get rid of him," he said at last. "Fast. Because it's all about to happen again, and this time no one but you is going to foot the bill."

I made an involuntary growling sound at the back of my throat. Morton looked across at me and gave a snort of merriment. "We are none of us, Mr. Savage, playing games. You must bring yourself to understand that or go under." Again he turned to the colonel. "Three days ago I sent someone up here to check your security. That someone had no knowledge of what he was doing or what he was after. But in those three days—three days, Colonel—he has blown you wide open. There is almost nothing about your organisation he doesn't know. He's met both your dead bodies head on, knows your bully boys by sight, narrowly escaped being killed himself—but what I find somewhat more interesting is the fact that only a few hours back he was standing in Wanhope examining your highly secret store of merchandise, to which he gained access by common sense and the smallest amount of ingenuity." He pointed a finger at me. "And there, Colonel, should you need to know, is the man himself, Mr. Mark Savage. And if Mr. Savage, who is as yet a trifle wet behind the ears and has no more than average intelligence, can pull off such a coup on his own, then I shudder to think what short work the Customs people will make of it." He stubbed out his cigarette in the mess of bones on his dinner plate. "What a bloody tangled web it all is. Mathews' body is in the hands of the police, so there's nothing we can do about that. But if the loony's body is discovered you'll have them crawling all over the place like meat flies." He almost spat. "Get rid of it. Bury it, burn it, drown it, but get rid of it pretty damn quick."

With an effort of will, I detached myself from the sound of his voice. Something he had said had struck a warning note—what was it? I picked my way back through the welter of words . . . Deakin, Mathews' body, Wanhope . . . Wanhope a few hours ago . . . that was it. A few hours ago, he had said, I had been in the storeroom at Wanhope.

My heart took a dive. Who but Williams knew that? No one. Only he could have reported my movements to Morton. So he and Morton were together. Morton was his boss. Mine, too. Despair stirred in me like a sickness. There was no "You Know Who" on the side of the angels. No one to turn to. No hidden and mysterious ally prepared to ride in with the cavalry and save the day. Williams was Morton's man and had been from the beginning. Piece by piece, the jigsaw puzzle of the last few days fell into place.

I groaned inwardly, appalled by the situation I had got myself into, a situation now shared by the innocent Julie. She had sat here tonight and heard and understood every word. Possessing that knowledge, she could be offered one of only two alternatives, neither of her own free will, and both unthinkable.

I felt the adrenalin begin to flow, the anger choking all restraint as the will to kill overpowered me. I closed my hand over the gun. . . .

The door flew open with a crash. The candles guttered in the sudden draught. The colonel swung around in his chair as I started to my feet. Gertrude, wild-eyed, stood in the doorway. "The stables are on fire. The horses are burning."

A strident alarm bell clamoured; running feet and upraised voices added to the commotion. The colonel was the first to move, overturning his chair and hurrying to his wife to calm her panic: she beat him off violently and rushed away. The colonel followed her.

Julie was next to leave, with me hard on her heels. I heard Morton call loudly after me. The thought entered my mind that now might be the time to kill him, in the midst of the chaos. I pulled up and turned, the gun in my hand. He read my intention quite clearly, I could see that, but there was no fear in him. He was shouting something at me, but against the clamour behind me I was unable to make out his words. After hesitating another couple of seconds I shoved the gun into my pocket. "Come and bloody help," I yelled. I don't suppose he could hear me, either.

In the hall a sweating Cesare yelled into a telephone, his free hand gesticulating wildly. I was cannoned into by a diminutive man carrying a fire extinguisher only slightly smaller than himself. Julie by this time having disappeared, I followed the fire extinguisher as it elbowed its way through a pair of doors, which swung back in my face.

Pushing past them, I found myself in the open air, gasping for breath as a bitterly cold head wind buffeted me full in the face. A lurid backcloth of flame lit the stable yard. Snow crunched beneath my feet; I felt the damp chill of it as it seeped yet again into my shoes and soaked my socks.

The air was thick with sparks and flying embers. The flames had not yet reached the loose-boxes but were annihilating the barns and outhouses immediately behind them. With the prevailing wind screaming in from that quarter, it would be only a matter of minutes before the wooden loose-boxes went up like tinder; smoke was already seeping through the timbers.

Grim-faced grooms and helpers moved around in disciplined manner, intent on getting the horses to safety. I caught sight of Julie wrestling with the bolts on one of the boxes and raced over to her. She waved me on with a yell. "I can manage. Give Gertrude a hand; she seems to be in trouble."

As she spoke, she shot back the bolts and flung open the doors. As a wild-eyed mare hurtled from the confines of the dark box, I caught sight of a dull lick of flame glimmering ominously at the rear of the stable. Time was running out.

I hurried on to the adjoining box, where Gertrude was fumbling with a recalcitrant bolt. "My hands won't work," she cried. "I just can't get it to budge. Please help. She'll roast in there. . . ."

Smoke billowed from the box. The rear wall, I knew, was already alight. Bundling her unceremoniously aside, I beat with both hands hard against the bolt. It loosened. Gertrude moved back, hitching irritably at the dark skirt of her long evening dress where it trailed in the churned-up slush. I swung back the doors. Hot black smoke gushed into our faces. Inside the box nothing moved. I peered into the darkness.

Against the far wall, rigid with fright, stood a pale grey mare, trembling, eyes starting from her head. Gertrude moved. I signed her away. "Try to cover her eyes," she called softly. "Your jacket, use your jacket."

Inside the box, the heat was lung-searing. Removing my jacket I approached the animal warily. In the uncertain light hysteria flickered in the wide eyes. Edging in alongside her and making what I hoped were soothing noises, I laid a calming hand on her quivering neck. The head jerked away, nostrils flaring. Reaching up I drew the jacket quickly over her head and eyes and immediately sensed a lessening of tension. I patted her neck gently. "Come on, old girl," I whispered. "Come on, it's all over now . . . one more effort and you're home. . . ."

Holding the jacket in position with one hand and gripping her nose with the other I turned her gingerly towards the open door. She had taken no more than a step when the wall behind us erupted in a sheet of flame; burning debris rained down on us, a blazing beam hurtled from the roof, disintegrating across the animal's quarters. She lunged forward with a snort, the jacket ripped from her eyes. I heard a shrill cry and peered wildly through the fire and smoke, half blinded with tears.

In the path of the crazed animal stood Gertrude, tugging at the skirt of her dress which, wet and heavy with snow, had wound itself about her ankles. Too late, she flung herself to one side. She was sprawling on her back, one hand clawing above her to protect herself when the hoof smashed into her skull. Blood spewed across the snow. . . .

My vision blurred. Waves of sound rolled and echoed in my ears. I was drowning in fire, fighting for breath. Someone was dragging at me bodily, hauling me to my feet, shouting something I couldn't hear above the wail of approaching sirens.

I must have blacked out momentarily. Next thing I remember, I was kneeling in the snow, retching violently, Julie beside me holding my head and murmuring the same sort of comforting noises I had used on the mare. Her hand was ice-cold on my forehead.

"I'm all right," I muttered, heaving myself on to one knee. "I'm okay." I wasn't at all. I was unable to stop shaking, for one thing. But I was well enough, with Julie's help, to scramble to my feet.

The sirens were deafening; the roar of engines, flashing blue lamps; flaring headlights blazed through the smoke; unhurried yet fast-moving figures of firemen were paying out hoses, clearing the ground, marshalling onlookers. One after another the sirens wailed and whined into silence.

Julie was saying something. I bent my head to her lips. "The horses are all accounted for. I'm going to look them over. They might be hurt."

Turning away, she hesitated for a second, then gripped my arm hard. I followed her gaze.

A dozen yards away, the colonel stood over the body of his wife. He was quite still, but his dark figure, silhouetted against the wall of fire beyond, seemed to tremble in the heat. He raised a hand to protect his face from the flames; otherwise he made no move. As I watched, I became aware of a group of dark shapes gathering slowly round him, six of them, ten, a dozen, closing about him in a circle, with a sinister, almost rehearsed, formality. Several, I noticed, wore uniforms.

A cordon of firemen approached, trying vainly to shepherd them away from the region of the fire.

The colonel stirred at last. Kneeling beside his dead wife, he took her and lifted her gently in his arms, cradling her against him like a sleeping child, her mangled head secure against his hard grey shoulder. Without a glance to right or left, he moved off in the direction of the house, the dark attendant figures closing about him like mourners at a funeral, their overcoats flapping like the black cloaks of operative conspirators.

"They've got him," whispered Julie unsteadily. "I feel almost sorry for him."

I felt nothing. No triumph, no satisfaction, nothing. I was later to recollect that not even the conspicuous absence of George Morton had occurred to me.

Julie said, "I must go."

I turned to take a last look at the blazing stables. The loose-boxes, now mercifully empty, were almost gone, but the flames were yielding reluctantly to the foam and water pumping into them from all sides.

A dark figure moved into the periphery of my vision. I turned my head.

The dying flames played upon the pale face. And I understood. The blood surged back painfully into my veins. I swore beneath my breath. Julie gave me a startled look. "What is it?"

"You go on," I muttered. "See to the horses."

Without waiting for a reply, I stumbled off in the direction of the gaunt figure.

Because he was intent on the flames, and the noise of the fire fighting was considerable, I was able to approach without his becoming aware of me. He was standing to one side, on a slight rise in the ground like a general surveying the state of battle.

I stood three paces behind him. "Mike."

He swung round. His eyes were glazed with tears, his lips drawn back from the small white teeth; the flames flickered eerily over his angular features. Only then did I notice the shotgun levelled at my stomach and held awkwardly in his bandaged hands. The bandages were torn and filthy; the front of his black jersey was rent and burnt.

I thought of the horses. "You bastard." I thought of Gertrude's terrible death. "You rotten, stinking bastard." I stepped in closer. "You did this, didn't you?" He began to retreat. I moved after him. "You're an old hand at fire raising, aren't you? You and the rest of that bloody mob of fanatics."

He stumbled slightly; the hand grasping the gun faltered. Before he could recover himself I closed with him, wrenching the weapon from him and flinging it into the darkness. He yelped with pain as the gun was torn from his hurt hands; I didn't care. I grabbed at the front of his jersey and jerked him towards me. His eyes were three inches from mine, the welling tears magnifying the sudden fear in them. The long hair whipped and flared about his sweating face. I could smell the stale smell of whisky on his breath. He struggled fiercely. "You can't prove anything," he shouted hoarsely.

"I know enough to prove you're out to get Hazlitt-Martin."

"He killed Barry."

"And you just killed his wife. Did you know that?" I spat the words into his face.

He was quite still for a moment, staring at me with wide, anguished eyes; then he writhed away from me, frantic in his efforts to free himself. I could feel the burnt threads of the jersey begin to part; he sensed it too; with both fists hard against my chest he shoved me from him. The jersey ripped open. I snatched at his streaming hair instead, catching it and winding it about my hand; but it slid wetly through my fingers and he was free, lurching through the snow towards the smoking buildings.

For a moment I hesitated, weary suddenly of my involvement with him. He was making a beeline for one of the still-blazing barns. A fireman barred his way, shouting, gesticulating. He raised an arm and lashed out viciously. The man went down, slithering backwards into a seething mess of foam and water.

Only then did I go after him. As he plunged headlong into the choking darkness of the building I was close behind him. I could hear him stumbling ahead, sliding and cursing among the wet and smouldering remains of baled hay; I also heard the ominous grinding of timbers above our heads.

A couple of firemen had followed us in, bawling at us to come back. The beams of their torches, rods of smoking steel, probed the darkness.

I ploughed on through the shambles, never once taking my eyes from the dark figure ahead. Then the torches found him, pinning him to the blackened wall which reared up in front of him. He battered at it wildly with clenched fists. A running stream of quicksilver flickered down the centre of it, bloomed into a blinding orange flare; as he flung himself backward, raising his arms to shield his face from the heat, the wall disintegrated and poured over him like a stream of molten lava.

Above the roar I heard him scream.

As I stumbled towards him, firemen in full cry behind me, the building trembled. Tears streamed from my eyes; the air was so hot I could hardly breathe. I retched and choked; the skin seemed to peel from my flesh. The smoke-laden darkness glittered with snapping sparks. Above and around me the entire structure was on the move.

I stood still and looked upward. Through the buckled and shifting beams I could make out the lighter darkness of the sky; I was watching a firework display; a shower of golden rain and multi-coloured sparks fanned out over me; something struck me violently on the shoulder. Here we go again, I thought. There came that familiar snapping sound, the sudden excruciating hurt. . . .

I think I smiled as I hit the ground and buried my face in the hot black ashes. A few glorious weeks, I thought, away from school, recovering in comfort, whilst the rest of the slobs sweated and toiled and kicked their inane football around. . . .

13

She was Chinese; dark, almond-shaped eyes and high, wide cheekbones; her starched white cap grew elegantly from the centre of her head like a lotus flower. She was surrounded by a soft golden aura.

I closed my eyes and thought about her for some time. When I opened them again, she was gone and I had a narrow clinical room to look at instead, which was less entertaining. I turned my head gingerly. Everything hurt. A bright orange-patterned curtain at the window was the only source of colour. Snow fell outside from a leaden sky. Here it was warm and comforting; I was glad someone had dug me out of that other place.

My eyelids were heavy and sticky. Various foreign bodies were stuck on my face like flags on a battle chart. My left arm was hooked across my chest, the hand wrapped up in gauze. I smelled of petrol. An electric clock clicked despondently in the silence.

Someone was looking at me through the small square of glass in the door. Her crisp uniform rustled starchily as she came in.

"Hello." She smiled. "You're back."

"Have I been away long?"

"Long enough."

Young, earnest, pretty, not Chinese. I squinted at the blue nameplate attached to the front of her white apron. Her name, it said, was R. Strauss.

"I've seen some of your operas," I told her.

She wedged a thermometer beneath my tongue without comment and went to stand at the window while it cooked; when it was done, the information it gave her clearly did little to raise her pulse beat. She replaced the thermometer in a small pot on the side table.

I nodded at the nameplate. "What's the 'R' stand for?"

"Richard," she said primly.

"And where am I?"

"Cardigan." She went out.

Some time later, she brought me a cup of hospital tea, weak, tepid and the colour of stewed tripe. I left it where it was.

Then a doctor came to look at me; tall, rangy, an untidy mop of greying hair and a droopy black Mexican moustache which didn't go with anything. "How does it feel?" he enquired.

"Like I've broken my collarbone."

He nodded sagely. "You've obviously done it all before. The collarbone's just a part of it. Don't worry about the burns: be right in no time. You're lucky. But you've been neglecting yourself. Who's been treating you, a horse doctor?"

I chortled inwardly but said nothing.

An hour later, the horse doctor herself arrived, wearing her Oxfam outfit and a long yellow woollen scarf, one end of which was tossed nonchalantly over her left shoulder.

"You look terrible," she informed me.

"Thank you." I told her what the doctor had said about her. Then, "How are the horses?"

She unwound her scarf and perched on the edge of the bed. "Three of them sustained injuries, nothing serious. But it'll be weeks before they settle down. Horses are like elephants, they find it difficult to forget."

"And Mike Davies? What happened to him?"

Her face clouded. "He died before they could get him to hospital."

I closed my eyes wearily, unable to speak for several moments. Then I told her what had passed between us. She nodded. "Apparently he said as much in the ambulance before he died." She was silent for a while. "Barry Newman cast a long shadow."

I gave a heartfelt sigh. "Didn't he just. Perhaps it's all just as well. Mike wasn't doing a lot to help himself, poor sod."

I watched her as she got up and divested herself of the mackintosh, flinging it untidily over the foot of the bed.

"Richard's going to love having that there."

"Richard?"

"The nurse. Her name's Richard Strauss."

She gave me a long level look and sat down again, leaning in to kiss me gingerly. "Poor old face. Everyone says you were lucky to get off so lightly." With her hand in mine she looked at me long and searchingly. "Will you always be doing silly things like that?"

"Like what?"

"Like walking into the fiery furnace."

The pain when I tried to shake my head made me think it was about to come off. "I can be a professional coward without actually having to prove it."

She stared down at our linked hands. I couldn't see the expression in her eyes, but I was willing to bet I would recognise it if she did it again.

I said, "Did anything happen at Wanhope last night?"

She raised her head. "Happen? Not as far as I know. Why? Should anything have happened?"

I felt depressed and, to prove it, uttered a heartfelt groan.

"What is it? Why so glum?"

"The bloody place should have gone up."

She was looking as mystified as I felt. "What are you talking about? Gone up where?"

"Wherever buildings go when they're wired up to a ton of explosives. Last night at midnight it should have gone there—to kingdom come."

Her eyes widened. "You didn't!"

I nodded smugly. "I did. With my own two hands. But I obviously buggered it up. Or that so-and-so Emrys Williams went back and dismantled it. Damn and blast him."

She grinned. "Perhaps you weren't meant to be a demolition expert. Not all of us are."

"I got it right. I'm sure I got it right. No, someone must have got at it, and it could only have been Emrys flaming Williams. And to think that I once thought he was on our side! You're the only one I know who's not in bloody George Morton's gang. Incidentally, what *about* our nasty fat friend? What happened to him? I didn't notice him putting any fires out."

"He just disappeared. I suppose when he saw the size of the opposition . . ."

". . . he crawled back into the woodwork. How could they have missed that fat rolling slob? Without him they've got nothing. He's Number One. I'll tell you something—when I get out of this flaming hospital I'm going to find him. Somewhere, somehow, I'll catch up with him."

God, how everything hurt suddenly. She must have understood, for she leaned in and closed my mouth with a kiss . . . and as she did so I caught a glimpse of that same expression—the one I'd known I'd recognise if she did it again. And this time I not only recognised the expression, I read the message that went with it.

I didn't have to wait until I got out of hospital.

When I opened my eyes after the quiet afternoon snooze, there he was, the hot, globular face hanging over me, breathing heavily.

I stared lengthily into the fox-red eyes tucked into their folded lids and felt nothing but hatred.

I tried to raise myself—to do what, I don't know—but he pushed me back on to the bed, nodded a couple of times in an avuncular sort of way, gave a parody of a wink and took himself off to the window, where he stood with his back to me and proceeded to turn over the loose change in his trouser pocket. His shoes squeaked too.

I closed my eyes painfully and waited, wondering if there was a weapon within reach and if so whether there was any way in which I could get up and use it.

"You did a good job," he grunted at last. And then, as if he was afraid his slip was showing, added. "A good job was done by all."

The clock ticked away the seconds with maddening rectitude. I drew a deep breath and sensed a turn of his head as if in expectation of some pronouncement on my part. He was disappointed. Or perhaps he thought the breath had been my last, for he squeaked over and stood between me and the light. I opened my eyes.

"How is it, then?" he enquired. I glared at him in silent loathing. "Or are we not communicating this afternoon?" What was he doing here, for God's sake, poncing about the hospital—free?

With a heavy sigh he reached into an inside pocket and produced a card. He held it steadily before my eyes, too close for me to read it; I wasn't that myopic. "That'll tell you who I am."

"I know who you are."

"You aren't reading it correctly."

"That's because you've got the fucking thing too close."

When he held it further away I refused to look at it. "Anyone can have a card."

He nodded. "True."

"You can pick up a dozen cards like that in the prop room of any film studio."

He snapped the card back into his pocket. "So what do I do to convince you?"

He stuck out his lower lip thoughtfully; then, reaching down into one of his gargantuan pockets, tossed something heavy on to the bed beside me. I blinked at it. It was a wad of ten-pound notes an inch thick, held together with a strip of brown paper. "How about that? Does that convince you? You did a job. There's the loot. Or is it glory you're after?"

"I need glory like a stag needs a hat rack."

He snorted with amusement. "I like that."

I glared at him, my mind in a sudden whirl. "Are you a general?"

He shook his head. "No."

"Is your name George Morton?"

"Sometimes."

"What's on that card?"

He pondered the question with exaggerated care. "Customs Investigation. Narcotics and all that. Will that do?"

I let out a long groan. "I don't believe it."

He nodded wisely. "You will if you stop being cross and start using your head."

I stared at him. "I've been working for Customs and Excise?"

"You've been working for me."

"You haven't told me who *you* are yet."

"Not going to, either. No need for you to know that—not unless we work together again." He was smooth and sweaty and I liked him no better as a customs officer than I had as a red-tabbed general.

"So who's the general, then?"

"The general is a gentleman whose shoes I've occupied, on and off, for the past eight months. I took over where he left off, as it were, when he suffered a small accident one slippery night on the way home from his club. So far as his intimate friends are concerned, he's in the Antipodes sussing out possibilities; his business associates wouldn't recognise him even if they came face to face with him; as in the case of wartime networks, the less personal contact the better; and I've taken great care to make no personal contact whatsoever with anyone until last night, when we stormed the colonel's castle." He wheezed merrily and I watched his face redden as the wheeze became a cough. Finally he went on, heaving for breath, "We got 'em all. Every single one of 'em. And not just here. A nationwide network of villains. Last night at precisely the same hour five swoops were made, two in Wales, two in Northern Ireland and one over a shoe shop in the Putney High Street. It took six long, gruelling months to mount that operation—eight for me, prancing about as the general. Your fire-raising friend nearly put paid to the whole thing of course, and the men who let him through are being shot at dawn. But luckily his zero hour coincided, pretty well, with ours."

He puckered up his eyes and looked at me for a long moment. "Any questions?"

"Yes." I listened again to that damned clock. "Why me? Why bloody me? Haven't you got enough loyal and dedicated workers on your books without going out soliciting?"

"No, frankly, we haven't," he said, suddenly quiet. "We never have enough. So I thought I'd lash out and have a go at you: put you through some paces."

"Aren't you supposed to ask first?"

"Oh, but I did ask. Didn't I? And you agreed—didn't you?"

Because he was standing between me and the light, I couldn't see his face distinctly. "Come round the other side. I can't see what you're thinking."

"I'm fine here." There was a moment's pause. "According to the Yellow Pages, you're for hire. According to Sam Birkett, a man for whom I have some regard, you're for hire. So I decided to hire you. Q.E.D. Money, Mr.

Savage, is the reason for your being here and there it is on the bed beside you, hard-gotten, cleverly stolen government money."

"Sam Birkett says he doesn't know you."

"I speak to him on the phone."

"He's never heard of George Morton."

"That's because he doesn't know me as George Morton."

"Oh, for Christ's sake." I closed my eyes wearily.

He was on the move again. I could hear him rustling his Gannex and shaking his pennies. "How did you know I knew Sam Birkett?" I asked.

"There's not a lot I don't know about you, Mr. Savage. I've had an eye on you for some time."

He was standing now at the foot of the bed. I asked, "It wasn't you tailing me on Monday, was it?"

He gave his wheezy laugh. "Not the right shape for that sort of thing any more. No, that was a minion."

"Minion or not, he was bloody good." I picked up the money with my good hand and flicked it through; it gave off a satisfactory fluttering sound and I wished I could have counted it without appearing greedy. "I owe you for two hundred cigarettes."

"We'll put it on the bill." He squinnied at me evilly; then, dragging up the only chair in the room, perched gingerly on its white plastic seat like a gnome on a toadstool, his back once again to the window. He spoke with slow emphasis. "I run a sort of . . . department. Unorthodox, virtually independent and therefore not popular upstairs. Occasionally we manage to come up with something to prove ourselves. Like now. Why you? I don't know. Instinct, p'raps. Fancied you, like a punter fancies a horse. Saw you a couple of times in the movies doing your bit of acting. Very revealing, watching an actor work. So when I read somewhere that you'd packed it in and taken up this lark, I filed it away and got myself interested. Been on your tail, off and on, for several months now. When this little lot threatened to break, it occurred to me that it might be the . . . testing ground I was looking for."

I stared at him. "For what? Testing ground for what? Now, look, if you have any ideas of recruiting me . . ."

He raised a hand. "Forget it. If you don't like the idea, forget it. I put a job in your way. You've done it and been paid for it. Finish. But, you know, in your humble way you performed an essential service. And very pretty it was, too. A week ago, Colonel Thing dropped out of sight. We lost him, utterly and completely. I was about to reach for the abort button—with zero hour coming up I was not prepared to go over the top and miss the chance of nabbing the commanding officer—but then I decided to set a cat among the pigeons: you. Your sudden appearance, your bumbling curiosity about Wanhope, followed by Mathews' killing, had the very desired effect; everyone went scurrying up the wall. Apart from Madam, there was no one to cope, and all she could think of doing was to reach for the phone and send out an alarm call for hubby to come quick and sort things out. Which he did. Very quick. On Tuesday. As a matter of fact, he was only in Fishguard interviewing a couple of likely lads from Ireland. That's the trouble with these one-man shows: take away the boss and everything goes to pot; no one else is capable of taking over. Not that he helped much even when he did get back. The rot you started had really set in. But you did the job, and a damned effective one it was, too, I'll give you that."

He breathed dispiritedly down his fat nose. "So go back to your divorce courts and your missing persons and good luck to you; no skin off my nose. But if and when you're looking for something more permanent, or a mite more rewarding, perhaps, without the bore of running that sleazy office of yours, come and work for me."

"For the last three days," I retorted rudely, "I've been cursing you uphill and down dale. I've even considered murdering you."

"Good, that's good," he wheezed, slapping his great thigh. "A little loathing is a splendiferous thing. I'm the one they love to hate. Unfortunately you're not likely to murder anyone—even under stress."

"For you I could make an exception." He thought that outrageously funny and chuckled like a demented gargoyle.

"Why didn't you bloody tell me anything?" I yelled, raising my voice to be heard above the cackles. "How were you to know that when I couldn't deliver that stupid box of cigarettes I wouldn't get into the car and drive straight back to London?"

"You didn't, though, did you?"

"You didn't know that."

"Didn't I?" He was wiping his eyes with the edge of a far from sanitary handkerchief. "Anyway, what the hell? I've backed many a wrong horse in my time. Mathews' death helped, of course. But you got intrigued and angry, which is what I hoped for and expected. Half of it was me and my cavalier ways and half sheer curiosity. True or false? If I'd told you what it was all about, you'd have blown it. You'd have been assuming things you couldn't possibly know about, because you're not trained in this particular field. So I left you to fall back on your own initiative, learn the hard way, which is the only way to learn; and you came out of it with pretty high marks, let me tell you. Everything I told the colonel about you back there last night was true. You split his security wide open without even knowing it. That's real initiative. However, it might interest you to know that you were never in any real danger."

My jaw dropped. "I just hope I never find out what real danger is."

He wagged a complacent head. "Someone was always around the corner keeping an eye on you."

"Like Emrys Williams, you mean? Then, where was he when I was being shot at, and then run off the road by that lunatic in the Volvo?" He wriggled uncomfortably. "All right," I said, "don't bother. I already know. He was on the phone ringing you."

He got up with a protesting creak and lumbered back to the window. Behind him, the sky was the colour of slate and darkening by the minute; the clock said it was three-thirty. I listened to him rattling his change again. "Williams is a good man. Lacks judgment, p'raps, when under pressure; he'd be the first to admit it. He's upgraded muscle, really, but good and solid to have around in a tight corner. Likes being on his own, has a certain amount of initiative and can fade into most landscapes. I sent him up here on a sort of fact-finding mission shortly after Newman's death and Operation Yashmak, which you might have read about in the papers. A big haul. But I was never convinced we had flushed 'em all out. A highly unpopular assumption in high places that, but—as it turned out—correct. What we'd unearthed was only the tip of the iceberg. Colonel What's-it had been operating in these parts for many long and profitable years."

"Before Newman was killed?"

"Oh, God, yes. He employed Newman, didn't he?" He burped genteelly and struck himself twice on the breast with a whispered *mea culpa, mea culpa.* "A busy boy, Newman, and bright. Too busy and too bright for his own good. Typical of what the big syndicates are always on the lookout for, young, footloose, ambitious, greedy, anarchic. . . . I don't know when they recruited him. As a courier he did a whole lot of travelling. His passport read like a gazeteer: Bogotá, Miami, Thailand, Hong Kong and all stations on the Mediterranean. Ostensibly he took his orders from the colonel, a not inconsiderable cog in a nationwide distribution network. Nationwide?" He echoed the word with derision. "Global would be nearer the mark. I only hope we've nailed the lot this time, but you never can tell. They hole up somewhere and reappear later in the most unlikely places. It's like painting the Forth bloody Bridge, never ending." There was a pause. "What else? Anything else?"

I chewed it over for a moment, then, "Mathews," I said, "how about Mathews? He had a little girl."

He squeaked over and lowered himself on to the bed; I levitated a good eight inches as he did so. "She'll be better off without him. So far as I can judge he wasn't all that good as a dad, even though I believe he was quite fond of her. He lived in a dreamworld and not a particularly savoury one at that. You know all about it, of course." I nodded. He chuckled. "Despite your protests to the contrary, there doesn't seem to be a lot you don't know. Emrys was on to it too—the pseudo-Nazi angle—and chanced his arm a bit by using the Nazi dreamworld as a basis for a spot of blackmail, worming information out of him regarding future dope shipments and the odd name and address—quite useful. That's how Mathews got on to you so soon. Williams overreached himself, I thought. I told him on the phone you were coming up, and to keep an eye on you. He leaked the information to Mathews as an extra turn of the screw. The story, apparently, was that you were a reporter on a Sunday rag, hot on his trail and bringing up photographs as evidence of his neo-Nazism and all that jazz. Load of rubbish, of course, but he fell for it." He shrugged. "Gullible, perhaps, but anyway, he was convinced to the point of ransacking your car in the hope of finding the nonexistent photographs."

"And got eaten by a dog, so it didn't do him any good."

"Put you on the alert, though, didn't it?" He yawned, leaning in towards me as he did so. I turned my head away; this time it was curry powder, not garlic. "Is that it, then?" he asked. "Can I go now?"

"What'll happen to the colonel?"

"A good many years inside, I reckon."

"What was he doing in the dope racket, a man like that?"

He gave me a despairing glance. "Money? Money's always in there somewhere. War games? Probably. He would have enjoyed running an underground network—Senior British Officer and all that rubbish. Must have loathed being retired. *The idle body and the idle brain is the shop of the devil.* That's what my old mother used to say."

"And Gertrude?"

"The brains, lad, the brains. I doubt if he had many of his own. A lot of senior army blokes aren't all that well-endowed up top, you know. And old Gertrude was a shrewd and clever manipulator. She was a tough old bird too."

"She was bloody rude to you last night, I'm happy to say."

He nodded sadly. "She was, wasn't she? Quite right, too. Not often I get spoken to like that nowadays."

I grinned lopsidedly. "That ought to surprise me. But what was it all about last night? Why the general bit and all that dinner charade stuff?"

"Best time to take somebody is when he's unsuspecting and relaxed. Middle of the night's excellent. Dinner's next best. Feet up, good wine and all that. I needed to know the truth about Newman's murder—and Pithy's. He told me. *They* told me. You and your bird were witnesses. Unfortunately Missus nearly blew the whole thing by walking out on us. Poor old bat. She didn't deserve to go like that."

"Nobody deserves to go like that."

"Oh, I don't know." He got up from the bed with an asthmatic hoot and I descended from my unnatural elevation. "I could name quite a few. Well, I'm off. Can't spend the rest of my life talking to you."

He buttoned himself noisily into his Gannex.

"Before you go . . ."

"Oh, Christ, now what?"

"What were you doing up on that ridge when I was being shot at?" I reached up, gritting my teeth against the pain, and switched on the lamp over my head. He was staring at me, his eyes blinking uncomfortably in the sudden glare. "Your hat was up there in the bushes among the spent shells. I found it."

He was very still for a moment. Then his hand dived into his pocket and for one fanciful beat of time I thought he was about to shoot me, but instead of a gun he produced that ghastly green tweed hat rolled up into a small ball. He smiled fatly. "Not mine, laddie." He unrolled it with the sort of tender care one would have associated with an archaeologist unearthing a priceless treasure. "You've been jumping to the wrong conclusions." He held it at arm's length so that I could feast my eyes upon it. "No wonder you wanted to murder me. Thought I was taking potshots at you." He clicked his tongue. "Never jump to conclusions: Rule Number One. Fact is, friend Deakin must share my taste in hats."

"Deakin doesn't wear a hat," I mumbled sulkily.

"Probably because he left it up there on the ridge and you bloody stole it. Anyway, not to worry. He won't be needing a hat where he's going. Champ and he are both in the cooler awaiting Her Majesty's pleasure." He stowed the hat away in his pocket.

"What about the cops?" I asked.

"What about them?"

"Are they going to turn nasty?"

"With you? Not unless you've been up to something I don't know about." He shook his head. "You're in the clear. You've got a blighty one. It's home for you. Get well, marry your vet and the Lord have mercy on your boredom. But I expect I'll be hearing from you some time.

He paused at the door. "Don't you want to know why they dumped Mathews' body in your car?"

I looked at him blandly. "Who wants a dead body?"

He pointed an approving finger at me. "You're even beginning to think like a pro." And with a gusty crow of laughter he departed, only to return a second later, his large round head poking in at the door. "By the way, should you be wondering why your bomb didn't go off, I have to tell you that, months ago, when nobody was looking, we replaced all that explosive stuff with genuine plasticine. Sorry about that. Good try, though."

The door gave a pneumatic and slightly derisive wheeze as it swung to behind him; its little square window ran through its repertoire of reflections, slowed down and came to a gentle standstill with a small, contented sigh. I listened to his footsteps as they stumped and squeaked away down the hollow corridor; his voice was raised once in a monosyllabic greeting to someone, the sonic waves taking the word and rolling it around the walls until I was ready to believe a swimming pool was out there; the dull thud of a slammed door, the echoes running on for a second or two before falling away into silence. . . .

It wasn't until I let out my breath that I realised I had been holding it. My eyes shifted to the wad of notes on the bed; I lifted it, weighed it, flicked it through and let it fall. I still didn't count it.

When Nurse Strauss arrived, shortly after, with four small triangles of wafer-thin, lightly buttered bread, a homemade fairy-cake and a pot of tea, she took up the money, placed it on the bedside table and had turned away before realising what it was she had been handling. She turned back slowly to take another look, then took it up again.

"This," she whispered with hoarse accusation, "shouldn't be lying about, you know."

I nodded. "You're quite right. Perhaps you would care to do something about it."

"I'll put it in the safe. How much is there?"

"I have no idea. Throw it away if you like. It's blood money." She looked genuinely shocked. "Licensed-to-kill money." She now held it gingerly between finger and thumb. "Take it away, there's a good girl, before it comes between us."

She said, stuffing the notes in her pocket. "I'll give you a receipt. Now eat your tea; you didn't touch your lunch." She then departed.

In transporting one of the bread triangles to my mouth I dropped it, butter side down, of course, on my naked chest, which maddened me so much that I didn't touch my tea either.

Sergeant Owen looked in later to tell me that the Triumph was awaiting collection at his police station and would I do that very thing at my earliest convenience. There was a severe frown in his voice.

"Perhaps you'd like to leave it at the Remington house; then you won't have it cluttering up your station," I suggested mildly.

"I have no authority to do that."

"I hereby give you authority."

That had him. Aware by this time that I was something of a government G-Man wheeling and dealing in the rarified circles of Whitehall and Scotland Yard, he conceded that he would see what could be done; when I pointed out that I should be unable to drive for at least three weeks, he said he would definitely see what could be done.

"Before you go," I said, "do you know what's happening about George Mathews' child, over in St. Dogmaels?"

His face crumpled unhappily. "Orphaned she is, poor mite. But it is thought that, all things being equal, her neighbour Mrs. Thomas would be quite happy to take care of her—adopt her, even, since she is already in many ways a part of her own family." He cheered up. "So not to worry."

And wishing me a solemn good evening, he took himself off, his helmet nestled against his arm in gentle and protective custody.

The telephone beside my bed rang. It was Mitch, coolly concerned for my welfare. I told her what had occurred, that I had been paid a vanload of money to stand in for James Bond and would be indisposed for several weeks, so if there was anything doing on the work front would she care to take over and attend to it with her usual efficiency.

"Shall I come and see you?"

"No, I look terrible."

"I know that, but shall I come anyway?"

"No."

"Are you all right?"

"I have a broken collarbone and have been ever so slightly grilled—like a raw steak; otherwise I'm fine."

"Will you keep in touch, then?"

"Of course, Mitch."

"Promise?"

"Promise."

She hung up and I had a fleeting image of her, poised over the telephone like a morose heron. Why did she make me feel guilty? I wondered.

When Julie arrived, later, I knew exactly why.

"Bruno's in the car, outside," she said, divesting herself of her mack and scarf. "They wouldn't let him in, but he sends his love and hopes you'll be better soon."

She perched on the bed and I told her about Morton's visit. Her eyes were quite rounded when I had finished. "If he'd told you what the job was," she asked, "would you have taken it?"

I thought for a moment in an effort to be honest. "I don't think I would. It's out of my league. It's like being asked to play Lear when all you've done is carry a spear." I hesitated. "However, that having been said . . ."

The unfinished sentence lay between us like a sword, and the silence went on for so long that I began to wonder whether we should survive it. At last, when I could bear it no longer, I held out my good hand. She took it tentatively.

I said, "It's the doubts, isn't it?"

"Doubts?"

"About us."

She smiled wanly. "They're there, yes. Life's going to be hell with you. I'll never stop worrying . . . like being married to a cop."

Her eyes suddenly brimmed with tears.

"Listen," I said. "It's not decision time for either of us. Let it ride for a bit. And if you want to come and talk, you know where I am. I shan't be going anywhere in the near future." I smiled at her. "It's all very silly, though, because I do love you, Julie Underwood."

That made her laugh. "Wrong typewriter."

"What's in a name?"

She snorted suddenly. "Oh, God, he's got the quotes again."

Then she became serious once more. "I think I may have to come and see you, though, fairly soon." She wiped her eyes impatiently with the back of her hand. "Like tomorrow."

Burrowing in the pocket of her jeans, she produced a handkerchief, wiped her eyes, sniffed, blew her nose and gave me a rueful smile. "There, that's over. Better now."

"Can I have a kiss, then, just to get me through 'til tomorrow? But choose your spot carefully."

We were in the middle of it when Nurse Strauss swanned in with yet another tray of unsolicited goodies. She didn't bat an eyelid.

"Your supper, Mr. Savage," she announced.

Julie said, "I must be going."

"You don't have to, you know," said Nurse Strauss.

"I must. My dog's waiting outside."

Unwillingly I let her go. She wrapped herself carefully in that beautiful ancient mack and wound the long yellow scarf securely about her throat.

I watched her with love. She blew me a kiss. "Was it still snowing when you came in?" I asked, needing to detain her a minute longer.

She shook her head. "No. It's frosty, with a huge moon." She smiled and was gone.

For some reason I couldn't hear her footsteps in the corridor. Desolation closed over me like a grey cloud.

I lifted the metal cover from my supper. "What is it?" I asked after a second or two.

"Shepherd's pie," said Nurse Strauss, identifying it knowledgeably. "You must eat, Mr. Savage, you really must."

I took up a fork.

"Richard," I said as she reached the door. "What became of that little Chinese nurse?"

"Chinese nurse?"

"The one who was here last night when I woke up."

She frowned. "You must have been dreaming. We don't have a Chinese nurse."

She went away. I eyed the mess on the plate before me. After several minutes of quiet meditation I carefully replaced the metal cover and laid the fork beside it.

When eventually I returned to base, Christmas was just around the corner. The shops were a-glitter and the snow six inches deep and still coming. British Rail had capitulated long ago and road transport was laughable. That one-time-evocative phrase White Christmas froze on chapped lips, and anyone with the temerity to say it aloud was liable to assault and battery. If you really wanted a white Christmas you could catch the movie on television.

I toiled up the seventy-eight steps to the office, shoes wet and socks soggy —would I ever again have dry feet? Outside the door, Mitch's yellow Wellingtons stood in a pool of slush like a couple of milk bottles awaiting collection. I pushed open the door.

She untangled herself from her creaking chair. "You've lost weight," she greeted.

"And you've lost height," I said. "What happened?"

"I'm wearing slippers. What's your excuse?"

"Hospital fare."

She took my raincoat and hung it up next to hers. "New coat."

"Yes."

"Nice."

I wandered through into the inner office and stared bleakly through the window at St. Paul's, elegant in its coat of sugar icing. One of the better things, I thought—along with buttered toast and Beethoven.

She came and stood at my elbow.

"Missed me?" I asked putting a brotherly arm about her bony shoulders.

"Yes."

"How have things been?"

She didn't answer for a moment. I looked at her. Her eyes were bright. "Lonely," she said. "How about some coffee?"

"Thought you'd never ask." I patted her arm as she went out. Then I sat at the desk leafing through the insignificant pile of mail.

"You must take up eating again," called Mitch above the singing of the kettle. "It's supposed to be good for you."

Nothing from Wales. Not that she had ever actually said she would write. But, then, Wales had practically been mislaid under a blanket of snow; her letter could be marooned in a mailbag on a snowed-up siding somewhere north of Cardiff.

I took the glossy pamphlet from my inside pocket, unfolded it and spread it open on the desk.

Mitch came in with the coffee. "What's that?"

"I've decided to give myself a Christmas present."

"A motorcycle?"

"Not just a motorcycle, Mitch. A Honda CB900 Supersport. In silver."

She eyed me in silence for a moment; then, handing me a steaming cup, she raised her own towards me. "Happy Christmas."

"To you, too," I replied and took a mouthful of the scalding coffee.

The telephone rang. She reached for it.

"Mark Savage."

Her eyes were on me as she listened for a second. "Hold on." She handed me the instrument and departed, closing the door discreetly behind her. Something in her manner stirred the hairs on the back of my neck.

I put the receiver to my ear and gave an appropriate grunt.

"Mark?" It was as if she was in the room.

"Julie? I don't believe it. Where are you?"

"Here. In London. Paddington, actually."

"The trains aren't running."

"This one was."

"Are you all right?"

"I just thought I wanted to see you."

"I'll pick you up. Just stay where you are."

"In a call box?"

"Under the clock."

"What clock? There isn't any clock."

"There must be a clock. There's always a clock. Go and stand under it. But don't talk to strangers." I paused for breath. "I still don't believe it. Are you sure it's you? It's been so long."

"All of four days."

"How shall I know you? I've forgotten what you look like."

"Well . . . I'm wearing a long yellow scarf, a yellow knitted hat, black rubber Wellingtons. . . ."

"And the longest, grubbiest, three-sizes-too-long riding mack."

She giggled suddenly. "You have it in one."

The phone began spitting pips at us. Her voice wailed through them in staccato bursts. "I've run out of change."

"I'll be with you in half an hour." I yelled.

The line cleared. "Hello, Mark Savage," she said quietly.

"Hello, Julie Remington."

Then the dialling tone took over and she was gone.

Two minutes later, having fallen over Mitch's boots, I had taken to the stairs and collided with a passing clergyman on his way into or out of the offices of the World Finance Corporation (a likely story).

On ground level and bursting through the open door, I skidded recklessly down the three ice-encrusted steps into the street and into the scarlet arms of a rotund Father Christmas who was drumming up business with the aid of a handbell. He fielded me adroitly, put me back on my feet, rang the bell in my ear and shook a slotted wooden box under my nose.

In the normal course of events he could have gone to hell. Today I gave him a pound.